If he hadn't decided to follow her out here...

Cait would be dead.

The knowledge slammed into Noah, a kick to the chest that felt as if *he'd* been shot.

But she was unharmed. Somehow she had escaped being shot at and having her car forced off the road.

When Cait started to struggle to her feet, he reached down to help her. She wasn't wearing heels, he saw; she had changed to athletic shoes before she headed out on this expedition. The rusty red dirt coated the gray-and-white leather and mesh.

Churning with emotions he had no ability to decipher, Noah couldn't help himself. He yanked her back into his arms, with no consideration for her fragile state. If she noticed, she didn't protest. She leaned as if she belonged right there, resting against him. Was that a very distant siren? He didn't care.

"Cait," he said hoarsely.

She looked up, her eyes dark, and the power of all that rage and helplessness and tenderness overcame him.

He kissed her.

Things are not as they seem in Angel Butte, Oregon. Read on to find out how Noah Chandler can protect Cait McAllister from the threats escalating against her in this second book of Janice Kay Johnson's latest series!

Dear Reader,

It's always been my opinion that women are more self-aware than men.

Of course I know some major exceptions to that rule (well, let's call it an observation), but still. My guess is that it's part and parcel of what makes women talk about experiences and emotions, even embarrassing ones, so much more readily than men do. In real life, a guy who never seems to quite get what he's feeling can be aggravating.

Writing fiction—I love men who blunder along, falling in love and even developing other kinds of relationships without exactly knowing what's going on, and who are genuinely flabbergasted when they discover they're in over their heads and haven't a clue how it happened. Noah Chandler is such a man. He's really smart, a successful businessman and politician, blunt and even ruthless, but convinced emotional crap is for other people. Leading him along gave me enormous pleasure, I have to tell you. Hmm. If only guys like that could be led along so easily in real life.... Come to think of it, there's a reason I write fiction!

Truthfully, one of the joys of writing romance is finding the two perfect characters who will both clash and mesh with each other.

Jayne Anne Krentz wrote, some years back, about how, on some level, the hero should also be the villain—i.e., a threat to the heroine. I think it works the other way around, too. Certainly, Cait McAllister is a major threat to the even tenor of Noah's life, and he is self-aware enough to know that from the very beginning. Meanwhile, he's the scariest kind of man to her... when he isn't making her feel safer than she ever has.

I hope you like these two people as much as I do. I've discovered some really great men live in Angel Butte, Oregon!

Janice Kay Johnson

PS—I enjoy hearing from readers! Please contact me on Facebook, or through my publisher, at Harlequin, 225 Duncan Mill Road, Don Mills, ON M3B 3K9 Canada.

JANICE KAY JOHNSON

—

Everywhere She Goes

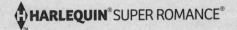

HARLEQUIN® SUPER ROMANCE®

Recycling programs
for this product may
not exist in your area.

ISBN-13: 978-0-373-60820-1

EVERYWHERE SHE GOES

Printed in U.S.A.

HARLEQUIN®
™ www.Harlequin.com

ABOUT THE AUTHOR

The author of more than eighty books for children and adults, Janice Kay Johnson is especially well-known for her Harlequin Superromance novels about love and family—about the way generations connect and the power our earliest experiences have on us throughout life. Her 2007 novel *Snowbound* won a RITA® Award from Romance Writers of America for Best Contemporary Series Romance. A former librarian, Janice raised two daughters in a small rural town north of Seattle, Washington. She loves to read and is an active volunteer and board member for Purrfect Pals, a no-kill cat shelter.

Books by Janice Kay Johnson

HARLEQUIN SUPERROMANCE

SIGNATURE SELECT SAGA

*The Russell Twins
**A Brother's Word
+The Mysteries of Angel Butte

Other titles by this author available in ebook format.

PROLOGUE

NOAH CHANDLER GLOWERED at the file that lay open on his desk. Failure was unacceptable. He still couldn't figure out how and why the bunch of fossilized, mule-headed, self-serving jackasses that constituted his city council had shot down his candidate for the job of police chief and chosen someone so ill-qualified—compelling *him* to make the offer.

By God, he was going to choke on it.

Noah had been trying to tamp down his anger since the vote after last night's meeting. When he had won the election in November and had taken over the mayor's office, he had known he would have to deal with a council composed primarily of good ol' boys incapable of objective, forward thinking. So far he'd succeeded in manipulating them into voting his way whatever their original inclination. What he couldn't figure out was why the rebellion had come now, and over something so critical.

Corruption ran deep in the Angel Butte Police Department, and this town needed someone fully competent to root it out, not a yeehaw cowboy who knew Southern California gangs and hookers but had next to no administrative experience and probably thought small towns were good only as a place to get off the interstate and fill up the gas tank. Had the city council members been thinking at *all?* Or were they interested only in thwarting him?

A third option had presented itself, and Noah liked it least of all. What if a couple of those fine citizens serving on the council, influential with their peers, had real personal motivations for ensuring the investigation into drug trafficking and illegal payoffs floundered?

Fuming, he picked up his phone and dialed.

Three rings and a brusque male voice answered, "Raynor."

Noah unclenched his jaw. "Lieutenant Raynor." His voice came out as a growl. "This is Mayor Noah Chandler in Angel Butte, Oregon. I'm calling to offer you the position of police chief. You were the final choice of our city council."

There was a moment of silence that lent him hope. The weather had been bitterly cold when Alec Raynor, a homicide lieutenant with the Los Angeles Police Department, had flown into Angel Butte for the interview. A blizzard had shut down the airport, delaying his departure for a day. Maybe in the past week he'd rethought the whole idea of accepting the job here. For all the line of bull he'd fed them during the interview, his motives for wanting the job were still a mystery to Noah.

"What about you?" Raynor asked unexpectedly. "Was I your choice?"

Noah swiveled in his desk chair to stare out the window at a partial view of Angel Butte, one of the small cinder cones that dotted this volcanic country in central Oregon. A nineteenth-century marble statue of an angel, imported all the way from Italy, crowned the crater rim. Back some years ago, before Noah's arrival in town, the angel had been given a granite pedestal to hoist her higher, maybe so she could keep a better eye on errant townsfolk.

"No," he said, blunt as always. "I was in favor of a candidate who had significant administrative experience. The job here doesn't have much in common with what you do down there in L.A. We don't have a lot of homicide cases to close. Our problems have to do with recruitment, staffing, training, scheduling, budget and morale." *Keeping our probably too-low-paid cops honest,* he thought but didn't say. "Politicking to bring in the money. Do you know how to do any of that, Lieutenant?"

"On a smaller scale, yes." There was a pause. "Did you have experience in city government when you won the election, Mayor?"

Noah rubbed the heel of his hand over his breastbone to settle the burning coal beneath it. "I'm a businessman. Running a city isn't all that different from running a business."

Raynor didn't have to say, *In other words, no.*

"This may not be what you want to hear, Mayor, but I accept your offer." The steel in Alec Raynor's voice sounded like a challenge to Noah. "As I indicated, I need to give notice here. Is your acting police chief willing to stay on for another month?"

That was the next call Noah had to make: the one to Colin McAllister, to let him know he wasn't being offered the permanent position. The news would not go over well. McAllister had every reason to think he had it in the bag.

"We'll work it out one way or another," Noah said. "Let us know your arrival date when you can."

"I will." Irony threaded the deep, crisp voice. "I'll look forward to working with you, Chandler."

Noah didn't have to manufacture any upbeat remarks; dead air told him the call was over. He grimaced. He'd liked Raynor better during this phone call than he had during the interviews. Noah preferred direct give-and-take, and that's what he'd gotten.

And, damn, he owed it to McAllister to tell him the decision in person, not over the phone. With a grunt, he pushed back his chair and rose. He'd walk. The route from the historic courthouse that now housed his office to the new public safety building would take him right past Chandler's Brew Pub. Wouldn't hurt to stop by, surprise his employees. Since going into politics, he had been forced to trust them more than made him comfortable. He might even have lunch there, he decided. Today was downright balmy for the beginning of March, which was still the dead of winter in central Oregon. He might as well enjoy the deceptively spring-like weather. He wouldn't even have to wear a coat.

Fifteen minutes later, he'd walked into the police chief's office and said his piece.

Colin McAllister's face had gone hard the minute Noah had started. He listened in silence, not rising from his chair behind the desk. "I deserve to know why I wasn't hired."

Only thirty-four years old, he'd been with the department since he'd started as a rookie right out of college. He had risen fast, making captain—only one rank below chief—two years ago. Noah understood him to be well liked by his officers, although he also had the reputation as a tough son of a bitch when being tough was called for. He was the one who'd uncovered the corruption in the Angel Butte P.D. and brought it to Noah. It was thanks to McAllister that Noah had been able to ask for the former chief's resignation. McAllister had handled the beginning stages of the investigation into the deeper layers of corruption well, as far as Noah could tell.

"I blocked your hiring," he said.

A man as tall as Noah if not quite as bulky, McAllister stood now, his hands flat on the desktop. Fury glittered in his steel-gray eyes. "Why?"

"I can't take the risk that you're part of whatever crap is infecting this police force," Noah said bluntly. He held up a hand to silence his acting police chief. "I have to ask myself how could you have worked here this long without seeing that something was wrong. You're young to make captain, even in a department this size. You've been rewarded with promotions a hell of a lot faster than is the norm. I'm making no accusations, but I also can't ignore the possibility that you got where you are by sharing information or worse. Even a willingness to turn a blind eye to illegal activities might have won you brownie points. I like you. I still had to make the best choice for this town."

"No accusations?" The gray of those eyes made Noah think of gun barrels now. "Sounds to me like you just made some. Tell me why, if I were dirty, I'd have been stupid enough to open this department to a top-to-bottom investigation."

"You might have thought you could get rid of Bystrom, step into his office and then block some turns of the investigation."

"If you'd asked, I would have shared my financials with you."

"You might be honest enough not to have accepted bribes, but not so honest you weren't willing to look away when fellow officers did."

The sound that came out of McAllister's mouth could have been a snarl. "You know you've opened yourself to a lawsuit."

Noah met that burning stare. "Tell me you

wouldn't have made the same decision if you were in my shoes."

"So now you want my resignation."

"No, I don't. My gut says you're clean. I want you to stay on as acting chief for the next month and to return to captain of investigative services after that."

Colin McAllister gave an incredulous laugh. "You're a son of a bitch. You know that, Chandler?"

Yeah. He could be. Today, a son of a bitch who felt like he was developing an ulcer. "Tell me you wouldn't have made the same decision," he repeated.

"I wouldn't have made the same decision." Muscles knotted in the other man's jaw. "Are we done here?"

"Think about what you want to do."

"Oh, yeah, I'll be thinking."

Noah nodded. "Then we're done."

He walked out, deciding he might have a beer with lunch, something he never did. He was also thinking he'd just made an enemy—and the new police chief and he weren't set up to be good friends, either.

Leaving the building and ignoring curious glances, it occurred to him that Colin McAllister and Alec Raynor were unlikely to have a real cordial relationship, either, not when one was taking over the job the other had wanted, and thought he'd earned.

Had earned, Noah admitted, if only to himself.

He paused on the sidewalk to let two lanky boys on skateboards shoot by before he turned back toward downtown.

Half the city council members despised and feared Noah, who despised them in turn and was plotting to get rid of them as soon as he could.

His mouth tilted up at the black humor. Yep, city government, as usual.

This called for two beers with the burger and fries he intended to have for lunch.

CHAPTER ONE

"GOOD WORKOUT," a woman called from down the row as Cait McAllister slammed her locker door closed and picked up her gym bag.

Smiling her agreement, Cait lifted a hand. "See you Thursday."

Today's class had combined step aerobics with what the instructor called "butt and gut," exercises aimed at core muscles. Cait was currently alternating this class with kickboxing. Conscious of a pleasant ache, she liked that she was getting stronger all the time.

She especially liked the feeling because Blake sneered at women wanting to be muscular.

Swiping her card to check out at the front desk of the health club, Cait grimaced. *Oh, sure, show how defiant you are* now.

The truth was, Blake hadn't liked much of anything that took her focus away from him. With every day, week and month since she'd broken up with him, she had realized how much she'd surrendered. Friends, activities, even time to herself. She still couldn't believe she'd let it happen.

Problem was, he thought their relationship had been perfect, with only the little flaw that she'd left him. Five months down the line, he still couldn't believe she had meant it when she'd said, "We're done." In fact, she paused now at the door, uneasy to be going out into the dark parking lot. In the glass she could see the reflection of the bright interior: herself, two guys leaving one of the racquetball rooms, laughing and wiping sweat from their faces, an employee behind the desk. Outside: nobody.

She could ask for an escort to her car.

Ridiculous. She'd moved a few weeks ago and was bunking with another grad student, so her name didn't appear on a lease anywhere. She was on a second new cell phone number. She'd changed health clubs again—this was only her third week coming here. She'd found yet another new favorite Thai restaurant, stopped at different coffee shops. Taken to varying her parking on campus when she needed to use the library at the university or talk to her adviser, rather than automatically heading for a certain lot. Shopped at a different grocery store each time. Tried to become unpredictable in as many ways as she could.

Blake actually *did* have a job. He couldn't possibly be stalking her 24/7. Plus, she really thought he'd freaked even himself out when they'd had that last fight in November and he had hurt her badly enough she'd had to be hospitalized overnight. So far, when he tracked her down, he'd been coaxing, not threatening.

Even so…it was April now, and he hadn't given up. To him, her "no" meant "I'm still mad at you, but I'll come around eventually." His frustration and anger had been thinly veiled the last time she'd seen him, when he'd suddenly fallen in behind her with his shopping cart in the cereal aisle at Whole Foods and stayed with her until she drove away. He had pulled out right behind her, too, and tailgated until she'd darted onto the freeway and then off, so last-minute she'd heard brakes squealing behind her and caught a glimpse of his furious face when he couldn't make the exit, too.

Cait squared her shoulders. He couldn't possibly know she was here. She refused to huddle at home every evening. Between her thirty-hour-a-week job and work on her dissertation, her days were full.

Nobody else seemed even to be close to ready to leave, so she pushed open the door and went out.

She was parked just around the corner of the building. There were pools of darkness, but really the lot was well lit. Lights of a passing car on the street washed over her, momentarily blinding her and leaving her trying to blink away dancing spots.

Even so, she was still a good ten or fifteen feet from her car when she saw that a man leaned against the hatchback. She stopped, and he straightened at the sight of her.

"Hey," Blake said, totally friendly. "I was passing and saw your car."

He *couldn't* have seen her car from the road. He'd either followed her or taken to prowling the parking lots of health clubs she might conceivably have joined.

Cait stayed where she was, wishing someone—*anyone*—else would come out. A couple of guys would be really good. Poised to run, she also eased her hand into her purse, groping for her phone and praying he couldn't see what she was doing.

"I've asked you to leave me alone, Blake." Thank God, her voice was calm and confident.

He took a step toward her. "I can't even say hello?" He sounded offended, as if she'd been rude.

Bad moment to be hit with how really skewed his perspective was. He was *not normal*. Of course, she'd already known that, but...

Later.

Refusing to retreat, she lifted her chin. Her fingers touched a smooth, flat surface. Her phone, thank God. Now, could she dial without being able to see what she was doing?

"No," she said. "I don't even want you to say hello. I *really* don't want you cornering me in dark parking lots."

"I didn't corner you—I waited for you!" Anger was making his voice more guttural. "How can I say I'm sorry if you won't listen to me?"

"You've said it."

"Yeah, and how many times do I have to? I'm sorry! Goddamn it, I'm sorry, okay?"

She licked dry lips. "Thank you for saying it. That's better than not saying it. But no. It's not okay."

"You love me. I know you do." He took a couple more steps toward her, his voice now low and persuasive. Warm, affectionate. "Jesus, Cait. I've gotten your message, loud and clear. I swear I won't do anything like that again. Why won't you believe me?"

"Maybe because you swore two other times that you wouldn't hit me again? And, oh gee, you did?" Making a decision, she yanked her phone out and dialed 911 really fast.

"You knew you were pissing me off!" The guttural, furious note was back. He seemed oblivious to the phone.

In the yellow light of the overhead lamps, she saw that his hands had knotted into fists. The sight made her pulse rocket. She slid one foot back, then the other. *Please, please, please, let somebody come outside. A car pull in.*

If she said no often enough, he'd eventually have to believe her, wouldn't he?

"I don't love you anymore. You killed what I felt for you. You need to accept that." Cait brandished the phone so he couldn't miss it. "If you don't leave right now, I'm calling the police. If I have to scream, a dozen people will come running out of the health club."

His face was ugly, transformed by shock and rage. She was shaking, and she *hated* knowing he could make her so afraid.

I should run.

He'd be on her before she could round the corner of the building.

She was still frozen with indecision when he snarled an invective and turned to her small car, then kicked the bumper until the car rocked.

"You bitch!" he yelled, and used his booted foot to crumple the fender. As she watched in shock, he circled the car, kicking, smashing, doing to it what he wanted to do to her.

Backing away, gasping for breath, she tore her gaze from him long enough to look down at the phone. Just as she reached the corner of the building, she pressed Send.

At that very moment, he went still and stared at her across the distance separating them. His voice floated to her, quiet compared to the invectives. "I will never accept that you're not mine."

Terrified now, Cait ran for the lighted front of the health club.

"TODAY'S MAIL," RUTH LANG announced and plopped a pile in front of Noah. Of course, she'd already slit each piece of mail open and paper-clipped the correspondence to the envelope.

He grimaced. "Thanks, Ruth."

His assistant's predecessor had retired when Mayor Linarelli lost the election. In the first week after he'd taken office, Noah had chosen Ruth, middle-aged, brisk and efficient, from internal applications. There'd never been a moment of regret. Choosing the right personnel was one of his strengths, although he was beginning to realize that hiring a bartender wasn't quite the same as hiring a city engineer or attorney. He'd been glad to have the chance to do both, but there were days he thought all he did was hire. Half the long-timers had decided to retire when they saw the way the wind blew with Linarelli gone.

Ruth smiled sympathetically. "That's what you get for advertising two jobs at once."

Yeah, it was. He wanted to get somebody competent in the job of city recorder, but his real interest was in filling the position of director of community development. Angel Butte had stagnated compared to comparable towns within a three-county area. The only significant move to alter that before his tenure had been the annexation that doubled the size of the city while leaving it struggling to provide expected services. Like too many city employees, the former head of planning had been an old crony, unimaginative and more interested in hanging on to the way things had always been done than he was in new trends in the field. Noah had been hoping that, at sixty-two, he was starting to think retirement. What happened instead was a heart attack. The guy had survived, but he'd admitted to Noah that his wife had put her foot down and refused to hear about him returning to work.

Noah had hoped for more applications than he'd received so far. He supposed Angel Butte seemed isolated to most potential applicants, a backwater with a lousy climate. But the area was booming economically thanks to tourism. It was beautiful, and there had to be *some* people in the field who loved to ski or hike or fish. Or, hell, just wanted to breathe air that wasn't yellow with smog, or commute five minutes to work instead of spending two hours a day crawling in heavy traffic on the freeway.

He'd already received three online applications that morning. Now, he flipped through the day's mail, which included several more résumés for people interested in the city recorder job and five for the community development one. Two of those he tossed in the recycling bin after barely a skim. Two were possibles, but not exciting. The fifth… He couldn't quite decide. In one way, she was overqualified, apparently only months from receiving an interdisciplinary PhD in urban design and planning. Actual work experience was somewhat scantier—after getting her master's degree in urban planning from the University of Washington, she'd worked as a planner in community development in Kitsap County, on the other side of

Puget Sound from Seattle. From there she'd gone to Spokane, where she'd spent a year completing a special position as parks project manager, preparing an updated plan for the city's parks and open spaces. She'd included excellent letters of recommendation, as well as one from her dissertation adviser at the UW. Noah had advertised for someone with a minimum of four years' experience in a position of comparable seniority to the one in Angel Butte. This woman didn't quite have that—although close if he added in her various internships—but she shone if he wanted someone with cutting-edge knowledge of the field.

He glanced again at her name. Caitlyn McAllister. As it registered, a frown gathered on his forehead. The last name had to be coincidence. Didn't it? He went back to the first page of the résumé to see when she'd received her degrees. BA in political science from Whitman College... The date of graduation likely put her in her late twenties now. Thirty at most, if she'd been a slow bloomer.

He had no idea whether police captain Colin McAllister had a sister. If this Cait was related to him, that might explain why someone of her education was interested in a town so off the beaten path. On the other hand—as pissed as McAllister was, as undecided as he was about his future in Angel Butte—surely his sister wouldn't have applied to work closely with his sworn enemy, the man who had in his eyes betrayed him.

Damn it, if she was related to McAllister, did he even want to consider hiring her?

Noah read her qualifications again and, impressed, thought, *Why not?* By the time they reached the interview stage, he might have half a dozen other strong candidates. So far, though, she was the cream of the crop.

He reached for his telephone.

CAIT'S EYE CAUGHT the blue-and-white roadside sign. Entering the City of Angel Butte, Population 38,312.

Oh, boy. She hadn't expected to be so nervous. She didn't even know why she was. Some of her memories of the years before her mother had taken her away weren't so good, but she also had happy ones. So it wasn't the town, per se.

Seeing her brother, maybe? The farther she'd gotten down the road, the more she wished she'd called to let him know she was coming. It was just that she didn't know how he'd feel about her moving back here, and really their relationship was so stiff and distant, she wouldn't blame him if he was less than thrilled.

My fault.

Yes, it was. He had tried. She knew he would have liked to be closer to her. Her feelings had been so complicated, her memories so muddled, she was the one to keep him at arm's length. At the same time... Well, she remembered him walking her to school, holding her hand. With seemingly endless patience, Colin had taught her to ride a bike, not Dad or Mom. When she'd started playing soccer, he'd kicked the ball with her by the hour. He'd teased her, and put up with her trailing him around like a hopeful puppy even though he was six years older than her. He'd been sixteen when Mom had hurriedly packed her own and Cait's things one day, loaded her in the car and driven away. By then Colin was a man, with a stubbly jaw come evening and a man's muscles, capable of such terrifying anger and violence.

The tumble of images and memories running like YouTube videos were so vivid and frightening, she put on her turn signal and pulled to the shoulder of the two-lane highway leading into town. Stopped, she clutched the steering wheel, closed her eyes and breathed deeply.

Her father had hurt her mother. Hurt Cait, sometimes. Colin and Dad had fought viciously, even sometimes punching holes in walls or breaking furniture. How, growing up in that kind of environment, had she let herself get sucked into an abusive relationship? Shame rose in her, making it hard to breathe.

Why? she cried inwardly, and had no answer.

There was no way she could ever tell Mom. Cait didn't know if she could bring herself to tell Colin, either. Except…if there was any chance at all that Blake were to follow her to Angel Butte, she'd have to, wouldn't she? Wasn't she there to interview for this job *because* of Colin? Because he was a cop, and she knew he'd protect her? Because he'd persisted in saying, "I'm your brother"?

Yes. But…she could wait to see if Blake appeared, couldn't she?

Why did she care what Colin thought of her?

Because. Because he was her brother. Because he loved her, and she knew it.

The last time she had seen him, this past November when he'd come to Seattle for some kind of law enforcement conference, she had wanted to really talk to him, maybe even tell him she was in trouble. But Blake, of course, had insisted on going with her when she had dinner with her brother, so she'd found herself being stiff as always, struggling for anything to say, letting Blake dominate the conversation.

There it was again, a burst of the shame. She didn't understand herself at all. She was a professional, for heaven's sake, smart, assertive on the job and in the classroom, well educated. Likable, with lots of friends—until she quit having time for them, because her boyfriend wanted all her time.

Was achieving understanding of her own horrible choices too much to ask?

Her breathing had grown calmer and her grip on the wheel more relaxed. She put on her turn signal, looked in the rearview mirror and pulled back out on the highway when there was an opening.

She'd printed out directions to her brother's house from the internet. Since it was only midafternoon and she assumed he wouldn't be home, she took the time to drive first through the urban sprawl on the outskirts of the old town, then through downtown and marvel at the changes. A multiplex movie theater? Really? And Target and Staples and Home Depot and just about every fast-food chain restaurant in existence? In Angel Butte?

On the main street, she spotted the old theater, where the whole family had occasionally seen movies, and where Colin had more often taken her. At least it still existed, although it looked as though it was a playhouse now. Which, come to think of it, was probably how it had started, so maybe that was fitting. Cait couldn't believe the number of coffee shops and bistros, art galleries and boutiques. This was like a mini-Aspen or Leavenworth without the schmaltz. In early May, ski season was past, but that didn't mean there weren't still plenty of obvious tourists window-shopping and going in and out of restaurants.

Cait's stomach growled, and it occurred to her that she couldn't exactly drop in at her brother's at dinnertime and announce, *Guess what! I came for a visit.* Especially since he'd gotten married only two months ago. Cait had read about his new wife, Madeline Noelle Dubeau, although the wedding invitation had made it plain that she went by Nell. Even in far-off Seattle, it had been impossible *not* to read about Maddie Dubeau, miraculously found after she'd disappeared when she was fifteen. Cait even remembered Maddie. She kind of thought they were in a class together. Third grade? Fourth, maybe? She was a skinny, shy girl, but really smart. Cait and she were in the top reading *and* math groups together. It was Colin who had brought Maddie home to Angel Butte and protected her when someone tried to kill her. Cait found herself really hoping that Maddie—no, Nell—truly loved Colin.

The whole idea of showing up out of the blue was a horrible one. What had she been thinking?

Ahead she spotted an obviously new, redbrick public safety building that, according to the sign, housed both police station and jail. Colin was likely in there right this minute.

Cait grabbed the first open curbside parking spot, then took out her phone. Scrolling to Colin's cell phone number took only a few seconds. Working up the courage to actually call him—that was harder.

FILLED WITH CONFLICTING emotions, Colin turned into his driveway. He stopped long enough to hop out and grab the mail and newspaper, but he didn't even glance at the headlines.

Cait was here. In Angel Butte. Dazed, he shook his head. Damn, better than that, she was really *here,* meeting him at home. Potentially, home to stay.

He only wished he understood why. The familiar reserve had been in her voice when she'd called, and he couldn't get a good read on her, but she had admitted that she hadn't made hotel reservations and, when he'd asked her to stay with him and Nell, she'd accepted. Not until they set a time and ended the call had it hit him what job she had undoubtedly applied for.

Director of community development, working right under that slimy bastard Noah Chandler. Of course, since Colin and Cait hadn't talked since she'd called with an excuse for not attending his wedding, she didn't yet know what kind of man Chandler was. And might not care what Colin thought, he realized; why would she, given the barely-there state of their relationship?

A strange car sat in front of his garage. A peanut like Nell's, this hatchback differed in being shiny and new-looking. He pulled in next to it, and his sister got out of the driver's side.

He met her near their rear bumpers. "You look good," were the first words out of his mouth.

She smiled, and suddenly that smile was wobbling and there were tears in her eyes. "Colin."

He took a couple of steps, she took a couple and then they had their arms wrapped around each other, and he laid his cheek against her hair.

"Damn, Cait," he murmured. "I can't believe you're here."

She gave a choked laugh. "I'm not sure I can believe it, either."

They separated slowly, reluctantly on his part. He couldn't be sure how she felt, although something was different about her from the last time he'd seen her. Her face was more open. She was looking him over as frankly as he studied her, her gray eyes a match for his.

One thing that had changed was her hair. Lighter than his, almost blond, it had flowed damn near to her waist the last time he'd seen her. Now it was pixie-short, highlighting the delicacy of her features. He'd kind of known his sister was beautiful, but he hadn't been hit with it like this before. She was also thinner than she'd been in November, he thought, but not in an unhealthy way. She looked leggy and athletic.

"How's the married state?" she asked.

He grinned. "I recommend it."

Her eyes seemed to darken, as if a cloud had momentarily covered the sun, but all she did was nod. "I'm glad for your sake."

"You haven't taken the plunge without telling me, have you?"

"You mean get married?" Her laugh held no hint of real amusement. "No. In fact…" Momentarily she pressed her lips together. "I've broken up with Blake. Um…you remember him, right?"

"I remember him." Colin hadn't much liked the guy, although he hadn't been able to put his finger on why and suspected he had a mental block when it came to liking anyone who shared his little sister's bed.

She nodded, her gaze sliding away from his. "Thing's didn't end that well, so..." The sentence drifted into the ether.

Colin's eyes narrowed. Had the bastard ditched Cait? The way she was wringing her hands together, "not well" had to have been pretty damn hurtful.

"How long ago?" he asked.

"As it happens, only a few days after we had dinner with you."

So November. Six months hadn't been long enough for her to start healing? That sent up a flare. *But she's here,* he reminded himself. They had time to relax with each other, talk. Pushing too soon would be a mistake.

"Hey," he said. "Come on inside. Do you have a bag I can carry?"

"Oh. Sure." She grabbed her purse from the car, then went around to the back and unlocked it. His surprise at seeing two enormous suitcases, as well as a smaller one, must have showed, because she explained, "I was staying with a friend whose boyfriend is suddenly moving in. So, well, I packed everything." She shrugged.

"You must have furniture, kitchen stuff..." He floundered.

"In storage. I've been sort of on the move a lot lately."

Since she and Blake had split up, he diagnosed. But that sounded as if she'd moved a couple of times or more since then. More flares shot into the sky. *Still too soon,* he told himself.

"I only need the small one," she said. "I can get it—"

"Don't be silly."

As he gave her the tour of his home, she seemed genuinely impressed with the house, its open spaces, river rock fireplace and vast windows, which let in a flood of light and a view of the surrounding ponderosa and lodgepole pine forest, as well as some raw outcroppings of lava.

Colin carried her suitcase to the spare bedroom, pointed out the bathroom and left her to settle in while he went to put on coffee. Cait joined him only a minute or two later, perching on one of the tall stools at the breakfast bar as if she'd been there a thousand times. Colin leaned back against the cabinet, hands braced on the countertop edge to each side. Again they studied each other.

"You finish your dissertation?" he finally asked.

"Mostly." Cait wrinkled her nose. "I'm at the cross-checking and polishing stage. I can do that long-distance as well as I could in Seattle."

"Why this job?" He made sure his voice was quiet, nonthreatening.

"Why not?" his sister challenged him.

"You've never expressed any interest in coming home before."

"I don't think of Angel Butte as home. Why would I? I haven't so much as set foot in town in eighteen years."

"So why now?" he persisted.

"The job's really perfect—"

He didn't let her finish. "I thought you were aiming for a career in academia. Isn't that why you went back for the PhD?"

Her shrug was jerky. "I'm not so sure anymore. No matter what, I want more real-life experience before I consider going into teaching. And, like I said, getting out of Seattle seemed like a good idea right now."

"Do you want to tell me about it?" he asked gently.

Her eyes met his. Hers were bright with...something. Anguish? Fear? Nothing he liked. But she only shook her head. "Not right now, okay?"

His fingers tightened on the tiled edge of the countertop, but he tried to hide his reaction from her. "You know I'm here for you."

Her head bobbed. Her "yes" came out as a whisper. "I suppose...that's why I came. Because you always said that." She tried to smile. "I'm hoping you aren't dismayed to have me take you up on your offer."

"Never," he told her, making sure she heard how serious he was. "You're my family."

After a moment, she nodded again, then cleared her throat. "So, what can you tell me about the mayor and city council and everyone else I'd be working with if I take this job?"

His grunt wasn't quite a laugh. "That'll take me all evening. But let's start with the mayor."

CHAPTER TWO

RUTH KNOCKED LIGHTLY and stuck her head around the door. "Ms. McAllister is here, Mayor."

Noah looked up from Cait's résumé, which he'd been reviewing. "Good. Send her in."

He hoped she wasn't a disappointment. He'd interviewed two candidates so far and been underwhelmed by both. Her, he had a good feeling about—unless she was Colin McAllister's sister, a relationship bound to taint their association.

He rose from behind his desk just as she walked in. Tall, slim and beautiful. Stunned, he probably gaped. Hair cut short to lay in feathery wisps around her face was darker than honey and sunstreaked. She wore heels, black trousers and a formfitting, short royal blue blazer over a simple white camisole. Gold hoops in her ears. Her stride was lithe, her smile pleasant and luminous gray eyes wary.

And—*hell*—he knew those eyes, color and shape.

"You have to be related to Captain McAllister," he said.

Her smile didn't falter. "That's right. He's my brother."

"Ah." He held out his hand anyway.

She studied it for a moment that stretched a little too long before allowing him to envelop her much more slender hand. It was unexpectedly chilly to the touch. Resisting the temptation to hold on, maybe take her other hand and warm both, Noah let her go and nodded toward the grouping of chairs around a low circular bird's-eye maple table that gave him a comfortable place to hold long conversations.

"Coffee?" he asked. "Or tea or water or...?"

"I'm good, thank you."

He waited until she chose a chair and sat before doing the same himself. They looked at each other for a long minute. He wondered how she saw him. He wasn't a handsome man. The face he saw in the mirror every morning was downright ugly, in his opinion. Maybe unfortunately, it suited his aggressive, straight-to-his-goal, probably brusque personality. On the other hand, he'd never had any trouble getting women. This one had to have heard an earful from her brother, though.

Yeah, so? he asked himself, irritated. This was a job interview, not a date. If he didn't hire her, she wouldn't stay in town. If he did, he'd be her direct supervisor. Coming on to her wasn't an option.

Ignoring the inconvenient attraction, he started with the usual chitchat. She had lived in Angel

Butte only until she was ten, she explained, at which point her parents had divorced and she had moved away with her mother. Yes, she had to admit that her brother's residence here had something to do with her interest in the advertised position.

Noah hesitated, but he decided to get this out of the way before either of them wasted any more time. "Are you aware that your brother and I have our differences?"

"Yes."

That was all. *Yes.* Even her expression didn't alter.

He pushed a little harder. "Is that going to be a problem?"

One sculpted eyebrow quirked slightly higher than the other. "It won't be unless I take the position and you fail to back me up when I need your support." The emphasis on "me" was there, but subtle enough he couldn't call her on it.

Annoyed for a different reason now, he met her challenging stare. He'd have had no trouble labeling her as an ice princess, except that her eyes were the furthest thing from cold. There was one hell of a lot going on in her, but she was repressing it. Only those big, shimmering gray eyes gave her away.

He didn't see what he could do but nod although he felt his jaw muscles spasm. "All right. Let's talk about your background."

They dived right in. Her dissertation had to do with the cultural assumptions that led, and sometimes misled, urban planning. She had the academic stuff down pat—she talked about natural resources, engineering, public decisions, leadership and the conflicts inherent in those elements.

Insofar as he understood what the position entailed, he aimed his questions at finding out how practical her knowledge was versus ivory-tower theory and idealism. She got right down to the nitty-gritty, talking about planning, sure, but also code compliance, her ability to evaluate complex data, read and interpret plans, specifications, maps and engineering drawings. They ended with a heavy focus on the people-management component. She would be directly supervising an assistant director, chief of building inspectors, administrative services manager and others. She claimed understanding the real needs of citizens was her first priority, followed by balancing the goals she set with the reality of dealing with politicians, developers, landowners, protesters. They talked about the frequent presentations she'd be giving to city council committees, civic groups and more.

She asked about those committees, and he tried to give her a sense of city council personalities and how they related to the Infrastructure Advisory Board, the Arts, Beautification and Culture Committee and Economic Development Committee, all of which would demand her involvement.

Cait McAllister remained poised, articulate and knowledgeable. She never faltered. She was so damn cool, he tried to shake her, jumping topics from zoning to budgets, EPA requirements, water reclamation, citizens versus tourists. Nothing. She jumped with him.

She'd driven around town this morning, she told him, and already had some observations.

"I admit," she commented, "that I was dismayed by the, er, shopping strip that was my first impression of Angel Butte."

"All that was county until an extensive annexation took place a year ago."

"I imagine that was good for the tax base."

"Yes and no." He ran a hand over his jaw, feeling the scrape of whiskers. "The campaign for the annexation was intelligently run. Unfortunately, nobody did any planning to speak of for handling the newly annexed areas. Your brother may have talked to you about the challenge it provided the police department. Our former mayor and a good part of the city council were opposed to expanding the number of officers in the department. Instead, they were spread so thin, in no time problems arose. I imagine it goes without saying that we've had plenty of other similar issues."

Her eyes had widened. "I can imagine. Sewer, water, fire department... I'll bet there's a huge backlog in approving building permits."

Noah smiled grimly. "Two city council members are major local developers. You'd think they'd have foreseen the problems, but apparently not. Now they're unhappy."

A flash of humor on her face almost took his breath away. "I have yet to meet a happy developer," she murmured.

He chuckled, a rusty sound. "Now that you mention it…"

Her smile lit her face. He stared for too long; the smile died and her gaze became wary.

"What do you see as priorities for new projects?" he asked gruffly to cut short the moment.

"I can only address the obvious," Cait pointed out. "There may be urgent need for storm-water projects or the like. I see Bend is expanding their water reclamation facility, for example."

He nodded. "We have some of the same issues. I've been looking at possible sites for a new sewer treatment facility. But go with the obvious. What jumps out at you?"

"Some visual mitigation of the less than appealing approach to town," she said bluntly. "Broader streets, landscaping, at the least. It's great to have those kinds of businesses, both for the convenience of citizens and visitors alike and from a tax standpoint. But it's ugly. Not an appealing first impression of what proves to be a charming town. We might even consider a bypass route."

He nodded. That was on his list, too.

"Second, if Angel Butte is to continue to draw tourists in the numbers I saw this morning, I'd recommend major infrastructure work aimed at improving bicycle and pedestrian traffic. Right now, parking downtown is an exercise in frustration. You've got people jaywalking everywhere, and I'd be scared to ride a bike on most of the existing roads. You don't want people staying at local resorts and inns to have to get into a car to go out for dinner, for example. They may end up irritated, and they may even decide to drive up to Sunriver to eat instead. Looking to the future, I'd argue that this would be an economically intelligent direction." A wry smile flickered. "You might prevent some traffic fatalities besides."

"I came close to taking out a tourist myself the other day," he admitted. "And as it happens, I own Chandler's Brew Pub on the main street. Parking is grossly inadequate. That's part of why receipts lag behind my locations in Sisters and Bend."

He saw no surprise on her face, which meant she'd done her research on him in advance. He had expected no less.

"You must have questions."

She did. Some he'd anticipated, some not. All of them gave him a good idea of how smart she was.

When she seemed satisfied, he considered her for a minute. She withstood his scrutiny with no more than a slightly raised chin. He was amused to see that her chin was on the square side. When she jutted it out, the effect was pugnacious.

"Would you take the position if I offer it?" he asked abruptly.

Even that didn't shake her composure. "Assuming compensation is adequate, I believe I would."

"When would you be able to start?"

A ghost of some emotion showed in her eyes. He wished he had some idea what she was thinking. Not knowing worried him.

"Immediately," she said after a moment. "I plan to stay with Colin for a few days, at least. I can continue work on my dissertation without being in Seattle. I'll need to make a few trips back, of course, but…I find myself at loose ends right now. This job would suit me very well."

Right now? "I'm looking for someone who will be making a long-term commitment, not taking the job as a brief fill-in."

"I didn't mean to suggest I was thinking short-term."

Noah nodded. "I'll need to follow up on your references. I can promise to get back to you within a matter of days."

She rose gracefully to her feet. "Thank you for your time. You have my phone number."

He stood, too, aware that he physically intimidated many people but also sure that, for some reason, she wasn't among them. "I do," he agreed.

They shook hands again. Hers was a little warmer this time. He squeezed gently and let her go sooner than he would have liked. He walked her to the outer office and watched as she strode away toward the elevator or stairs, the swing of her hips subtle but sexy as hell.

Not until he turned did he realize that his PA had been watching him. He saw curiosity in her eyes.

"How did the interview go?" she asked, just as she had after all the previous ones.

He grunted. "Good. If her references pan out, I think she's the one."

She cleared her throat. "You do know—"

"That her brother is Captain McAllister? I know." He frowned. "How do *you* know?"

Ruth smiled. "We chatted."

"Did you chat about anything else I ought to know?"

She tilted her head while she thought. "No, I don't think so," she said after a moment. "She seems like a lovely young woman."

Lovely was definitely one word for Cait McAllister, Noah reflected as he returned to his office. *Sexy* was another. The fact that he was thinking that way about her had the potential to be a huge problem. Did he really want to hire a woman likely to distract him the way she had today?

Muttering under his breath, he went to the window and stared out. Not, he told himself, because he might be able to see her walk out to her car— although there she was, and he couldn't have taken his eyes off her if the most aggravating of city councilmen was tapping on his shoulder.

Looking toward the cinder cone usually clarified his thinking.

Somehow that didn't happen with him focused on Cait McAllister's long-legged stride, the sway of her hips, the gleam of spring sunlight on her hair.

Not until she got into a little blue car that, a moment later, joined the traffic on the road and passed out of his limited line of sight could he look away.

"Damn," he said aloud, but quietly.

There were other words he could use as descriptors for the woman who had just left his office. *Brilliant,* he suspected, was one. Definitely *highly qualified.*

Which made him blessed that, for whatever reason, she wanted a job in Angel Butte, Oregon.

What he'd really like to know was why she was willing to take it. His gut said she was desperate for a change. He wondered if her brother would know what she was trying to leave behind.

Maybe the bigger question was whether he could quit noticing how lovely and, yes, goddamn it, sexy she was and see her as a professional.

If not…

Noah sank heavily into his desk chair and gazed, unseeing, at one of the paintings that hung on his office wall.

Who was he kidding? Of course he was going to hire her. And, no, he wasn't going to be able to turn off his libido. He'd have to aim for reining in his response. If he was really lucky, her personality would begin to grate on him and he'd quit caring what she looked like.

"I KNOW COLIN is estranged from your mother." Nell poured balsamic dressing from the little plastic cup over her salad. "He seems to think you're still close to her?"

Cait and her new sister-in-law had spent the morning browsing shops and were now eating at a café owned by a friend of Nell's, who had come out when they arrived to say hi and inspect Cait with obvious curiosity.

So far, Cait really liked Colin's wife. If Nell was being nosy...well, who could blame her? She was, after all, married to a man with major family issues. Who knew better than Cait, who had issues, too, if different ones from her brother's.

What's more, Nell wasn't a casual acquaintance. Strange as the realization was, they were family.

"Not so much," Cait admitted, answering the question about her relationship with her mother. "Once I hit my teenage years and rebelled, things went downhill. We've never quite recovered."

Nell nodded. "Does she know you're here in Angel Butte?"

Cait winced. "No. If I get the job, I'll have to tell her eventually."

Nell didn't say anything. Tiny lines on her forehead suggested she hadn't raised the subject only in a casual, get-acquainted way. *Good lord,* Cait thought; *Mom is her mother-in-law.* Cait knew Colin hadn't invited their mother to his wedding.

"I suppose Colin's told you that…our father was abusive," she said carefully.

"Yes."

"He and Colin fought a lot."

"He told me that, too." Nell still hadn't reached for her fork. "He thought he'd probably scared you and your mom both toward the end. He was trying to draw your father's anger away from the two of you, but he admits he was filled with a lot of rage, too."

"That last couple of years were really horrible. I remember getting off the school bus and dragging my feet because I dreaded going home." Cait tried to smile. "Anyway, if Mom was ever happy here in Angel Butte, she's long since forgotten. I think she feels guilty about Colin, too."

"She should," Nell said sharply, after which she made an apologetic moue. "That was tactless, wasn't it? I won't take it back, though. I don't mean to offend you, but the truth is, she abandoned him. Having his own mother leave him behind with the father he hated… He has scars."

"He seems so…together," Cait said hesitantly. "Except…I guess I could always tell that he wanted more from me than I knew how to give." Her laugh was sad. "Family life at its finest."

Nell's laugh held a similar note. "My family is

no better—I assure you. One of these days, I'll tell you more about *our* soap opera."

"I'd actually like that." Cait smiled. "Misery loves company."

"Absolutely."

They both chuckled and, as they began to eat, turned the subject in other directions. They were talking about a women's self-defense class Nell had taken over the winter when Cait's phone rang. Of course it had sunk to the bottom of her too-roomy bag, but she snagged it by the fourth ring. The number was local, and not Colin's, unless he was using a landline at the police station.

"I'd better take this," she murmured to Nell, and answered.

"Ms. McAllister." The gravelly voice was unmistakable. "Noah Chandler."

Her heart raced. Truth time. "Mayor."

"Why don't we progress to Noah and Caitlyn? I'm calling to offer you the position."

The relief was out of proportion, especially considering her mixed feelings about her return to Angel Butte. *A journey back in time,* she thought flippantly. "I go by Cait," she said, sounding completely collected and mildly pleased. She impressed herself sometimes.

"Cait it is. Do you have a minute to talk?"

She grimaced apologetically at Nell, who waved her understanding and eavesdropped with interest.

A minute was all the conversation took. Mayor

Chandler did not believe in beating around the bush. He laid out compensation, medical and dental benefits, retirement and vacation package with a take-it-or-leave-it curtness. She told him, equally briefly, that his offer was acceptable. He asked when she could start. Cait took a deep breath. "How about tomorrow morning?"

The momentary silence suggested she'd surprised him. But when he said, "Good. Let's meet in my office at nine," his voice didn't confirm that impression.

Cait felt more than a little dazed as she dropped her phone back in her handbag. "Wow. The job's mine."

Working with *him*.

She didn't let herself linger on that vague sense of apprehension. Only that wasn't quite right.

She didn't have time to, anyway, since Nell jumped to her feet and hurried around the table to give her a quick hug. "I'm glad. Having you close will really make Colin happy, and I think you and I are going to be friends."

"I think so, too," Cait agreed. From their first meeting, she'd had the feeling she and Nell already *were* friends. Maybe that was because her face was so disconcertingly familiar—Nell/Maddie hadn't changed as much as most people did from when she was a child. With that pointy chin, sharp cheekbones and disarmingly high forehead, she looked thoroughly adult and yet still like the little girl Cait remembered, scattering of freckles, big brown eyes and all. She had claimed to vaguely remember Cait, too, but sounded more uncertain. Cait knew her own face was nowhere near as distinctive.

It wasn't only familiarity that made Cait feel comfortable with this new sister-in-law, though. Nell had an air of reserve that reminded Cait of her own. Even after several months together, Nell seemed surprised by Colin's smiles, touches and the intimate way they sometimes looked at each other. Or maybe, Cait reflected, Nell was surprised by her own response to him. Cait knew enough from what she'd read about Nell's ordeal to be sure she understood self-doubt—and why trust could be hard.

Cait insisted on paying for lunch, which Nell finally accepted. They were walking out when Nell asked if she'd mind stopping to grocery shop on the way home.

"Of course not—" Head turned, she walked smack into someone. A man who asked if she was all right at the same moment she exclaimed, "I'm so sorry!"

And then she really looked at him. Shock seemed to squeeze her throat. "You," she whispered.

Echoing shock showed on his fleshy but still handsome face. He was middle-aged, the auburn of his short hair muted from what she remembered by a substantial sprinkling of gray. He'd softened some around the middle, too, but…she did know him.

Oh, why hadn't it occurred to her that he might still live here?

"Cait," he said, sounding rueful. "I'm surprised you recognized me. What were you? Nine, ten, when you moved away?"

"Ten." Her voice was a little too high. "Jerry, that's right, isn't it?"

"Jerry Hegland." His gaze flicked to Nell, who was watching the odd encounter. "Aren't you—?"

"Nell McAllister."

He looked momentarily confused.

"My sister-in-law," Cait contributed.

"That's right." He was apparently putting the pieces together and realizing Cait's companion was Maddie Dubeau. "I heard you'd married the police officer who found you. Ah, I knew Cait and Colin's mother," he explained. His gaze traveled back to her. "We were getting to be good friends, weren't we, Cait?"

She managed a nod, her usual social skills having totally deserted her. This man had been her mother's lover. Of course, she hadn't known the truth until years later. Back then, she'd thought he was a nice man who Mommy and she happened to run into really often. He'd bought them lunch several times.

"I'll bet you remember me best for the handprints I left in your concrete slab," she blurted.

He stared at her. "What?"

"You didn't know it was me?"

"I don't know what you're talking about." Suddenly he was as brusque as Mayor Noah Chandler at his most impatient. He looked over her shoulder. "If you'll excuse me, I'm meeting someone."

"Of course." She wouldn't lie and say, *Great to see you.* It wasn't, even if she wasn't being fair. After all, Mom was the one who'd been married.

Unless he had been, too?

She didn't care.

I am angry at her. Had been, still was. She had been only sixteen—and an already confused sixteen, at that—when she'd found out her mother had had an affair.

An affair? Who knew? Maybe she'd been screwing around on Dad for years. Cait wanted to think the betrayal explained his rage.

She didn't look back as Nell pushed open the door and the two of them exited.

DINNER STARTED WITH them all clinking wineglasses in a toast to her new job. Cait was still feeling the glow, if also a whole lot of trepidation, when Nell glanced at her.

"So, who was that guy we ran into at the restaurant?" She transferred her gaze from Cait to her husband. "Please pass the butter."

He did so automatically, but he was looking at Cait. "I didn't think you'd remember anyone from that long ago."

Here was where she could say, *He wasn't any-*

one important. But Colin likely knew him, she realized. Her brother had been enough older than her to be aware of relationships and undercurrents to which she'd been oblivious. In fact, she'd nursed some anger at him, too, for leaving her in ignorance even though, all grown-up now, she could see why he hadn't said anything to his little sister.

"Jerry Hegland."

He frowned. "Who?"

She set her fork down. "You don't know him?"

"The name is vaguely familiar." He seemed to be searching his memory. "Wait. Something to do with the airport?"

"I don't actually know." But, yes, once Mom and she had gone out there to watch planes take off and land. Angel Butte Regional Airport wasn't all that exciting, of course; at least in those days, aside from privately owned small planes, traffic had consisted of no more than a couple of flights a day to Portland and Seattle using turboprop commuter planes that carried something like fifteen or twenty passengers. Still, she remembered standing beside the runway as one of those planes tore by, gaining momentum and then lifting into the air. *She* had been amazed. Her family had never flown anywhere.

That had been one of the occasions when the nice man bought lunch for her and Mom, at the café in the airport terminal.

"Then how do you know him?" Colin asked.

"Mom." She sounded like a crow. Harsh. "He and Mom…"

Her brother's expression gradually changed with dawning horror. "He and Mom *what?*" he asked in a hard voice.

Cait was distantly aware that Nell's mouth hung open. She'd had no idea what she was starting.

"They had an affair. Didn't you know?" she begged.

"Hell, no!" He gave his head a shake. "I can't believe— How did *you* know?"

"I always assumed… Wow."

"Cait."

"Don't snap at me!"

Now they were glaring at each other.

Well, what difference did it make? she reasoned. Colin and Mom never talked anyway.

"I had no idea back then. I thought he was a friend of Mom's. But when I was sixteen, I was rooting in her closet looking for something." She'd been snotty, and Mom had taken away her cell phone in punishment. The minute Mom left for work the next day, Cait in a fury had dug through all of her mother's dresser drawers, looked inside coat pockets in her closet, then taken down every box on the closet shelf. In the second one, she'd found a couple of photo albums and letters and been distracted from her search. She remembered sitting on the bed turning pages in the albums. Already her memories of her dad and her brother were fading. But here were Colin's and her school photos, as well as lots of family snapshots. Mostly those weren't all that great—people were squinting against the sun or looked posed and uncomfortable. There were first-day-of-school pictures, when Colin or she were stiff in their new clothes. And some of Dad laughing with his arm around one of them. She'd felt strange, seeing those.

She hadn't paid much attention to the letters, beyond dumping them out on the bed so she could look at the loose photos. There had been a bundle tied in ribbon with handwriting she'd recognized as Nanna's. But then she saw that a picture of a man she had recognized was bundled with a few notes that weren't in envelopes.

"I found some notes he'd written Mom," she said. "They were...um, kind of explicit. And then in one he was pleading with her to leave Dad. He said he'd take us, too. In the last one, he said, 'Why won't you call me? You're wrong, whatever you think.'" She remembered it word for word. "It freaked me out. I guess Mom slept with him, but then she ditched him when he got serious about her. Which made me wonder if there hadn't been other men, too."

Colin hadn't moved. "Mom?" he finally said in a low, dark voice.

Cait bobbed her head. "I always thought..."

His eyes focused on her.

"That you must know. I mean, you were older—"

"No. I had no idea. What does he look like?"

She did her best to describe the Jerry she remembered from back then and the one she'd encountered today.

"That son of a bitch," he muttered.

"Maybe," she said. "But it's still mostly Mom I stumble over. I mean, she was married. She had *us* to think about."

"You mean, she had *you* to think about," he said, with less emotion than she suspected he really felt about being deserted by his own mother. But then his eyes narrowed. "Why would she have introduced you to him?"

"I guess sometimes they wanted to get together and she didn't have any place to leave me. Or maybe they were playing family. I don't know. I was a kid. I thought we ran into him by accident." She told him about having lunch with the man, and the treat of getting to go practically out onto the runway to watch planes take off and land. "One time we had a picnic. I don't remember where. We swam. I remember the water being really cold, but it was fun." She shrugged. "All innocent, until I found out it wasn't."

"Goddamn it," her brother said bitterly.

"Do you think Dad knew?"

Colin's face was transformed by anger, his eyes the color of storm clouds. "I have no idea. I tried not to listen when they were screaming at each other."

She nodded her understanding; sometimes she'd run to her room and pulled her pillow over her head. The yelling so often ended in crashes and grunts and sobbing. She hadn't wanted to be anywhere near her parents then.

Right now, she was feeling something of the same choking sense of anxiety.

A muscle ticked beneath Colin's eye. "I may have to meet this Hegland."

She seemed to have quit breathing. "You look like Dad right now."

"I don't look anything like him," he said in a low growl. But he did. He did. Dad's face had always been so flushed when he lost his temper, worse when he'd had too much to drink, of course. Right now, dark color suffused Colin's face and tendons stood out in his forearms. His hand had fisted around his bread knife.

Just like Daddy's.

"Yes, you do." She bent her head so she didn't have to see him. *Oh, God.* This was what she'd felt every time Blake started to get mad.

"Colin, you're scaring her," Nell said softly. When Cait sneaked a worried peek, she saw that her sister-in-law had laid a hand on Colin's arm. He'd turned his head and was looking at her.

After a minute, during which Cait didn't dare move, he said, "Cait." His voice was gruff but also somehow gentle. "I know what you saw back then, but I'm not like Dad. I've never wanted to be anything like him. I fought with him to keep you and Mom safe, but I'm not a violent man."

She looked up to find him regarding her ruefully.

"Seeing you look scared of me," he said, "that's one of the worst things you could do to me." He made a rough sound in his throat. "I would never hurt you."

She gave a quick little nod, and, after a moment, he answered it with one of his own.

"All right," he said.

Embarrassed at her over-the-top reaction—could she call it a past life regression?—she told him she was sorry. Colin insisted she had nothing to be sorry for.

Nell interceded by getting them talking about something else, and later, when they were alone in the kitchen, she apologized to Cait for mentioning Jerry.

"No, it's all right. I just had this sort of flashback." Cait even managed a small laugh. "The perils of coming home."

"Which I fully understand." Nell bumped her shoulder against Cait's. "You should go figure out what you're going to wear tomorrow."

"Oh, boy." New anxiety instead of anticipation, and Cait didn't even know why. Because this was Angel Butte? Because, in running away from Blake, she'd made a sharp right turn in her life? Or because she would be seeing Noah Chandler at 9:00 a.m. tomorrow, and had no idea why he made her feel so edgy?

CHAPTER THREE

WHEN NOAH AND Cait walked into Chandler's Brew Pub, a host rushed to greet them, and what other employees Cait could see were suddenly very busy. Cait would have been more amused if *she* didn't now work for him, too.

He'd been nothing but agreeable all morning, from the minute he had walked her to her new office. After barely giving her a chance to glance around, he'd hustled her back out so he could introduce her to half the people who worked for the city. Within an hour, names were running together in her head. Perhaps seeing that her smile was growing strained, he had decided to drive her around in his truly enormous SUV so she could see ongoing projects.

"I'd like to take you to lunch," he had then declared.

She felt a flutter in her chest at the idea of having to look at him over a table for an hour and make conversation. She found herself wishing he was married, maybe had a couple of kids she could ask about. Knowing he was single was part of what had her on edge.

Noah Chandler was an incredibly sexy man despite the fact that he was the next thing to homely. Or maybe that wasn't it, she'd found herself thinking as she stole glances at him while he drove. Colin had said he was an ugly bastard, but Cait couldn't imagine any woman agreeing with that assessment. No, he only surprised her because, except for the very sharp blue eyes, he looked like a laborer, not a politician. He ought to be operating a forklift or heaving heavy loads in and out of trucks or railroad cars, not wearing a beautifully cut suit and running a city. She wondered how he kept that powerful physique. Certainly not by scowling at his computer monitor and hammering the keyboard, the way he'd been when she had stepped into his office that morning.

He wasn't a physical type that had ever attracted her, for which Cait gave thanks. Surely she'd become inured to the intensity that seemed to be as much a part of him as his raspy voice and tendency to be abrupt when he forgot he was trying to give the impression he was an easygoing man.

They had barely been seated by the eager host when a pretty blonde waitress magically appeared with menus. She wore a tight little black skirt and a crisp white shirt that strained over generous breasts.

"Mr. Chandler," she purred.

He glanced at her with scant interest and nodded. "Jess."

Looking disappointed, Jess retreated with their drink orders, walking more like a model prowling a catwalk than a busy waitress.

Cait was mildly surprised that her new boss had asked for iced tea rather than a beer.

"You said you have three locations," she said.

He hadn't even opened his menu. "This was the first." He looked around, as if appraising the place. "The one in Bend is the busiest. We have live bands playing three or four nights a week. Comedians do better than music in Sisters, for some reason. Here?" He shrugged. "The Friday- and Saturday-night crowd like entertainment. Otherwise, food and drinks seem to be the appeal."

Curious despite herself, she had to ask, "You were so bored, you decided instead of expanding your business or finding a new hobby, you'd run for mayor?"

His grin gave her a few palpitations she should definitely ignore. Cait was a long way from even *thinking* about getting involved with a guy again, and if and when she ever did, she was looking for gentle, funny, intellectual. The reasons she'd always been drawn to domineering men were not subtle. Now that she'd faced them head-on, she would make better choices. All she had to do was remember her father. The terrifying fights he and Colin had had.

Blake.

Never again.

And even if she had been attracted to Noah Chandler, she now worked for him. Would, in fact, be working closely with him. *So knock it off.*

All that intensity was being trained on her right now, though, which made it hard. His eyes were a startling blue, especially considering his hair was dark.

"What's good to eat?" she asked, hiding behind the menu.

He laughed. "Now, what do you expect me to say to that? Everything, of course. I usually have a burger or one of the potpies, but I'm thinking pizza today."

They agreed to share one called "The Farm Kitchen" that had a delicious-sounding combination of roasted red peppers, black olives, artichoke hearts and more with a roasted garlic tomato sauce. Jess took their order of pizza and salads and again retreated, with a last, sulky glance over her shoulder.

"I think your waitress has a crush on you," Cait observed.

His eyebrows climbed in surprise. "I can't imagine. What is she, nineteen, twenty?"

"And you're such an old man?" Oh, teasing him wasn't smart. *Professional,* she reminded herself. *Keep it professional.*

"Thirty-five. Not quite old enough to be her father, but close enough." Those vivid eyes stayed on her face. "Now that I've hired you, am I legally safe to ask how old you are?"

"Twenty-nine. The same age as Colin's wife. Have you met her?"

"In passing. I've read plenty about her."

Cait nodded. "It's funny, because I remember her from third or fourth grade. Or maybe both. Do you think I'd recognize a single other kid from that long ago?"

His rough chuckle felt like a touch. "No? But I understand why you did. The paper printed plenty of pictures from when she was a kid and then when she appeared last year. Not much change."

Cait laughed. "She claims to remember me, too, but I think she's making it up."

"What about you? How much have you changed?"

Something about the question froze her in place. She wanted to believe…oh, that she was nothing like that timid ten-year-old. But everything that happened with Blake had made her realize that she couldn't shake her past.

"I was a beanpole," she told him, keeping her voice light. "Taller than all the boys at that age, and ridiculously skinny. I had white-blond hair then, too. You wouldn't have recognized me, I promise you."

"I'm not so sure," he said, sounding thoughtful. "Why did you look so unhappy when I asked you that?"

Her eyes widened. "What?"

He shook his head, impatience on his face. "Never mind. None of my business."

Silence enveloped their table. Cait looked down at her place setting to avoid his too-keen gaze. *Oh, why not?* she asked herself. Blake was the only secret she had.

"We weren't a happy family," she said, probably startling him.

He'd been scowling toward the cluster of employees who hovered near the check-in at the front entrance, but his head turned sharply when she spoke. Without looking at them, she knew they had to be sagging in relief. She would have been.

When he said nothing, she gave a one-shouldered shrug. "In those days, I mostly tried to disappear into the woodwork. I was safest if no one noticed me, you see."

"Safest?" He sounded out the word. "Were you abused?"

"Our father was violent." Now her voice sounded small and tight. "Mostly when he was drunk. Unfortunately, he owned a bar and, by the time he got home, he was almost always drunk."

"I had no idea."

"Why would you? You and Colin aren't exactly friends, and I doubt he talks about it anyway."

"No." Noah sounded disturbed. "No, I don't suppose he would."

"Men don't like to, do they?" What made her say that? she wondered, appalled. Was she hinting *he* tell *her* his background?

If so, he didn't take her up on it. Their salads

arrived, saving them from awkwardness. Noah asked how much seemed familiar here in town, and she was able to reminisce about the much smaller town from her childhood.

"I was remembering going to the movie theater." She smiled at memories that were good. "Colin took me sometimes when Mom or Dad wouldn't. He's five years older, you know. I hate to imagine the kinds of movies he sat through for my sake! And just think if one of his friends had seen him."

Noah's mouth curled up on one side. "Death to a guy's reputation," he agreed. "Just think, now you can choose from half a dozen movies or more any Friday night."

He admitted, when she asked, to attending the community theater's productions on a regular basis. He had even acted in high school. "I was always the villain, of course."

"Of course?" she echoed in surprise, then flushed when again his eyebrows rose.

"Not even my mother would call me handsome," he said drily. "I did a hell of a job with Iago, though, if I do say so myself."

What could she do but laugh?

The pizza, when it came, proved to be fabulous. Prompted by her questions, Noah was willing to talk about opening his first brew pub. "I still okay every menu item," he admitted, "but I was never a cook. I have a recurring nightmare about drowning in beer, though. Kegs breaking open, and I'm trying to get them stacked but meantime the beer is pouring down on me, into my nose and mouth."

She chuckled but had a feeling this was black humor for him. She wanted to ask if he liked his product as well as her father had his, but she refrained.

"Lucky I'm a workaholic," he said finally.

Cait could have guessed that. "What made you run for mayor?"

He eyed her, and she suspected he was trying to decide how honest to be. "Frustration," he finally said. "That's probably what drives most businessmen to get involved. You discover too many factors are out of your control." He tipped his glass of iced tea to her. "Traffic. Zoning, taxes, the adequacy or otherwise of local law enforcement. In my case, once I started expanding, I had a chance to compare how three different cities operated. I'd lived here too long to want to pull up roots, so I decided to remake Angel Butte instead."

That really made her laugh. Answering amusement in his eyes told her he at least recognized his hubris.

"Colin said you moved here about ten years ago?"

"Nearly eleven, now." He hesitated. "I learned that my father was here. Hadn't seen him since I was a kid, but for some reason I decided to look him up."

She wondered if he really didn't know why he'd

felt the need to track down his father. Studying that rough-hewn face and the intelligence in his eyes, she thought, no, of course he knew.

"So you found him and stayed."

Noah shook his head. "I never did find him. He'd disappeared." His expression closed. "I guess he'd moved on."

Cait didn't believe in his outward indifference, but clearly he was done sharing confidences. She could take a hint.

They kept chatting, but more like the employer and employee they were. He asked that she attend the city council meeting the following Tuesday, told her about his second hire of the week, the new city recorder who'd be starting in June.

He paid, and as they walked out, wanted to know if she'd yet found a place to live.

Cait shook her head. "I haven't even started to look. If you'll recall, it was only yesterday you offered me the job."

He gave her an odd glance. "I guess it was."

It was a little silly that they had to get back in his big SUV for a whole two-block drive, but earlier he hadn't suggested parking at the city hall/courthouse complex and walking back.

She looked straight ahead as he maneuvered out of the slot. "Did you have any suggestions? I mean, about where to live. I'll have to rent for now."

"I suppose you don't want to stay at your brother's."

"No-o." She drew that out. "He actually has an apartment above his garage. So I might stay there." She liked the idea of having Colin close if Blake showed up in town. On the other hand... "I'm not sure I want to be accountable to him for my comings and goings."

"It would be a little like moving back in with Mom and Dad," Noah mused.

Cait rolled her eyes. "It might be worse."

"Your brother the cop." He was highly amused; she could tell. "I guess it might be."

"Well." She shook herself. "No hurry to decide."

"There are some new town houses available for rent in a nice location," he said after a minute. "I hear they're decent."

When she asked why he sounded grudging, he admitted they had been built by Earl Greig, who sat on the city council.

"One of the not-so-happy ones."

"That would be him." Noah's tone was sardonic.

"Not-so-happy means they're more likely to support you in making changes, doesn't it?"

"In theory." He made an indecipherable sound. "*You* should be welcome, at least."

This was really out of line, but... "Earl doesn't like you?"

"Earl can't bring himself to forget that I used to wear my hair in a ponytail."

Cait choked.

He flashed her a grin that was so devastating, he might as well have kissed her.

"Yeah, stubby little thing." He reached up to his nape as if fingering hair that wasn't there anymore. "Shocking, I know."

Smiles like that—*they* were shocking. And, dear God help her, she had to pretend they had no effect on her at all.

"Lucky Earl doesn't live in the big city," she said.

"Earl is daily torn between his greed and disapproval of all newcomers as well as tourists. Makes his votes kind of chancy."

He pulled into the parking slot reserved for the mayor, set the emergency brake and turned off the engine. Cait scrambled out, not wanting to take a chance he'd turn his head and gaze at her with that thoughtful look that made her wonder whether he saw straight through her.

She felt him glancing at her as they walked through the garage, but he didn't say anything until they were on the elevator and it was rising, floor numbers pinging.

"I'll let you have the afternoon to yourself," he said, his tone distant as if he'd almost put her out of his mind already.

"Thank you for taking so much time for me," she said formally when they reached her floor and the door slid open.

He dipped his head, a frown making his features

harsher. Whether he looked after her as she exited, Cait had no idea. She didn't dare glance back.

NOAH TRIED LIKE hell to stay away from his new director of community development for the rest of her first week of work. That didn't mean he didn't hear constant reports about her and have to field a couple dozen phone calls asking about her. It also didn't mean he didn't catch glimpses of her entirely too often. There was one day he swore he couldn't step out of his office without seeing her hurrying down the hall or engaged in conversation in a doorway or walking out to her car.

Earl wasn't real happy that a woman had been hired instead of a man, a hidebound attitude that didn't surprise Noah at all. Noah listed her qualifications for possibly his most contentious city council member, who grumbled but went away. Beverly Buhl, chair of the Arts, Beautification and Culture Committee, called to burble her delight about how "forward-thinking" Ms. McAllister was.

"And charming," she enthused, to which he growled agreement; something about his voice momentarily silenced her.

Taking Ms. Cait McAllister out to lunch had been his mistake, he concluded. He'd done fine up until then. Lunch might have been fine, too, if they'd stuck to business. Instead, they'd sounded each other out about their pasts, their likes and dislikes as if they were on a first date.

Damn it, she'd made him laugh!

He wanted to be grumpy because she didn't dress professionally enough, but the truth was, she did. She went so far as to wear a suit the second day. Unfortunately, she never seemed to wear the kind of colors that would have allowed her to blend in. The suit was lemon-yellow, the skirt reached only midthigh and the jacket was short and fit snugly over very nice breasts and a slender torso. She even wore high heels in a matching shade of yellow. When he spotted her down the hall in that one, he was blitzed by the thought that she looked like a sexy ray of sunshine. Furious at himself, he blundered into the men's room, stared at himself in the mirror with incredulity and took a piss when he'd rather have whacked his head against the wall.

Day three of her tenure, he almost walked into her as he was heading out midafternoon. Today she wore linen slacks and a thin sweater set the color of the ocean off Belize. He nodded; she offered a single, distracted smile and returned to conversation with her assistant director.

His mood darker, Noah stalked the several blocks to the public safety building for a meeting with Alec Raynor. As he was ready to go into the building, Cait's brother happened to be coming out.

McAllister stopped, his eyes narrowed on Noah.

Since the one hostile scene back in March when Noah had admitted he had chosen not to hire McAllister for the head job, they had managed to hold semicivilized conversations; they had to, once McAllister made the decision to stay on as acting police chief and then captain of investigative services. Enmity was never far below the surface, though.

Today, McAllister stepped aside rather than continuing on his way.

Seeing no choice, Noah did likewise. If he were prone to regrets, he'd be sorry about the tension between them. But he did what he thought was best, and he didn't allow himself second thoughts.

"Before the rumors hit," McAllister said tersely, "I thought I'd tell you I'm running for county sheriff."

Noah digested the announcement. The current sheriff was on a par with Mayor Linarelli, as far as Noah was concerned. In other words, lazy and very possibly crooked. "Interesting," he mused. "Are you asking for my support?"

McAllister snorted. "That did not cross my mind."

"It should have." Noah was given to making decisions fast—as he'd done where his police captain's sister was concerned. "You have it," he said.

The other man stared at him. "Why?" he finally asked.

"We both know you're good at your job. I think you have what it takes to clean up the sheriff's department."

"Just not Angel Butte P.D."

"You know why I didn't want to take a chance."

McAllister gave a half laugh, shaking his head. "Do you have any idea how badly I want to tell you where to shove your support?"

An involuntary grin twitched at Noah's mouth. "I can guess."

"Unfortunately, I'm too ambitious to actually do that."

Noah thrust his hands in the pockets of his slacks. He waited while a cluster of women came out of the building, their heads turning at the sight of the mayor talking to Captain McAllister. To his credit, the guy had kept his animosity quiet, but there had to be talk anyway.

When they were out of earshot, Noah asked, "You and Raynor getting along okay?"

His expression veiled, McAllister shrugged. "Why wouldn't we?"

Noah nodded, even though that was no answer. "Let me know when you want a statement from me." He pushed his way inside and continued up to Alec Raynor's office.

The new chief's PA waved him in. "He's expecting you."

In fact, the door stood partially open. Talking on his phone, Raynor half sat on his desk, a foot braced on the floor. He glanced at Noah and lifted one finger. Noah nodded and wandered over to study a new painting on the wall.

It was disturbing, he decided, not the usual government-office pretty. Even he had gone for pretty in decorating his own office, figuring his role was to be a booster for the city and area in general. He'd bought local artists and photographers. This—he couldn't imagine a local had done it.

From a distance he'd seen that it was some kind of street melee. Closer up, components broke into shards and you didn't see the overall scene. Faces stood out, though they were far from realistic. No matter how simply these faces were constructed, though, anger and despair jumped out.

"The artist is a friend of mine," Raynor said behind him.

"I was thinking that most of us go for decorative."

Raynor's laugh sounded like rusted gears grinding. A little like Noah's own, he reflected. They had that in common.

Not looks, though. His new police chief was whipcord-lean and not much above average height. Five foot ten, maybe. He had dark hair and eyes as dark a brown as Noah had ever seen. By this time of day, he already needed a shave. During the interview in February, Noah had thought he looked Italian. Now, with the Southern California tan fading, the effect was diminished. Unless the guy took up skiing this coming year, he was going to turn pasty white like the rest of them who didn't have the time or inclination for winter sports.

Raynor circled his desk and sank down in the

big black leather chair. He looked weary. "I fired two officers today," he said bluntly. "A sergeant on the patrol side and a detective who was one of our representatives to CODE." CODE was the coalition of police agencies, including the DEA and FBI, that fought drug trafficking.

"Damn." Noah lowered himself into a chair facing the desk. He'd known this was coming but hated to have his assumptions confirmed anyway. "Tip-offs to drug dealers?"

"That's what it looks like. No question they took bribes. Maybe even offered guard service. Hard to be sure. We're still working on who the money came from." His eyes met Noah's. "We've traced one payment for sure to the same source that paid off Bystrom."

Gary Bystrom was the former police chief whose corruption had been uncovered almost by accident in McAllister's investigation of a murder that had taken place in the city park the same night his now-wife, Maddie Dubeau, had been abducted when she was a teenager. Found along with the boy's bones was a backpack that contained, among other things, a snapshot of the police chief shaking hands with a known drug dealer and a bank deposit slip for a hefty sum into his account. The Drug Enforcement Agency had mostly taken over digging into the source of those bribes, a real challenge. Raynor was stubbornly refusing to let go entirely of the investigation, with the result that the DEA agent in charge was kindly deigning to keep them informed. Noah and, he suspected, Colin McAllister in particular were getting damn frustrated by the snail's pace of inquiries that left Bystrom free as a bird. Probably putting away his winter clothes right now and getting out his fly-fishing gear. The only consolation Noah could find was that, at the very least, the feds had him for tax evasion.

What they'd known all along was that he had to be getting tip-offs from officers in the department about police raids. McAllister had found the first two; these were the next to fall.

"It's still only the beginning, I suspect."

Noah grunted. He wanted to see some trials and prison cell doors clanging shut.

The dark eyes were direct. "You know most of the work on this was done by McAllister."

"You're asking why he isn't sitting in your chair?" Noah rolled his shoulders and then told him.

"I think you misjudged him." Raynor's smile was razor-sharp and came and went swiftly. "To my benefit, of course."

"Is it? I still don't know why you wanted this job."

Still eyeing him, his police chief ran a hand over his darkly shadowed jaw, maybe to give himself a moment. "I was looking for a peaceful town. Not for me." He hesitated. "My brother was special forces, killed in Afghanistan. I've been stepping in to help his widow with their kids. The boy's thirteen, gotten to a rebellious stage. L.A. wasn't the place for him."

"I didn't know you'd brought family with you."

"They're not here yet. Took a while for Julia to sell her house." He shrugged. "Now she's waiting out the rest of the school year. They're moving up here as soon as the kids are out the end of June."

Noah was unexpectedly relieved to have the answer to the questions he'd asked himself. It was even one he could understand, although this was a big change of direction for a man to make for his sister-in-law and her kids.

"Are we as peaceful as you thought we'd be?" he asked.

Raynor gave a bark of laughter. "Sure. There's only been one murder since I arrived, you know." That had been a domestic. "Now, honesty, that's another story."

Noah laughed. "Okay," he said, pushing himself to his feet. "Keep me informed."

Raynor stood, too, presumably from courtesy. "Will do."

Noah left, thinking that the past hour had been exceptionally informative. Now all he asked was that he make it back to his office without so much as another glimpse of his new director of community development.

COLIN SET ASIDE the newspaper when he saw Cait come out of the guest bedroom. "You going out this evening?" he asked with deceptive casualness.

"City council meeting," Cait reminded him.

"Oh, right."

She grinned at his tone. "Isn't there such a thing as a county council?"

"Don't remind me."

She gave him a saucy look. "You could come keep me company."

"A fate worse than death."

Chuckling, she twirled in a circle, arms outstretched. "Do I look all right? I want to dazzle 'em." She didn't mention who in particular she wanted to dazzle. The suit was one of her favorites, a deep rose she'd worn over a yellow shell. These were about her highest heels, too, saved for occasions like this when she wouldn't be on her feet for eight hours.

Her brother did relax enough to smile. "Can't fail," he assured her.

"Good. Don't wait up, I don't know how late I'll be."

He frowned, rose to his feet and followed her to the door. "Why don't you park right by the front porch when you get in instead of off to the side of the garage?"

"You let Nell park in the garage even though she has to scamper all the way across the yard when *she* gets in at night." This was one of those evenings when Nell was working at the library in Sunriver until nine, which meant she didn't get home until close to ten. Cait knew her brother didn't like these evenings but had resigned himself.

"I listen for her," he said simply.

Cait sighed. She liked his protective streak. She did. She just wasn't sure she could live with it. Maybe cops were always like that with their own families, given what they saw on the job. She admired how patient Nell was with him, although, come to think of it, in her case it was only a few months ago that someone *had* tried to kill her.

Cait had a flash of memory: Blake smashing his booted foot into the fenders and doors of her small car, the screech of metal giving. His last, quiet words before he melted into the night.

I will never *accept that you're not mine.*

She was careful to hide her shiver from Colin. She should hope he decided to wait up for her, too, so she didn't have to be afraid when she let herself into the dark house tonight.

She hadn't been in Angel Butte that long. How would Blake find out where she'd gone?

But she didn't kid herself. Short of assuming a new identity, disappearing wasn't possible in the modern world. Within the next few days, the city website would be updated with her name and bio. Blake might not even have had to wait for that. He'd met Colin; he knew where he lived.

He could show up anytime.

So, for now, she would be grateful for her brother's watchful eye, Cait promised herself. She kissed his cheek and said, "I'll park so close to the front steps you won't be able to squeeze by in the morning yourself," and hurried out the door to the sound of his chuckle.

The council had their own chamber in the city hall wing off the historic courthouse, she had discovered her first day during the whirlwind tour Noah conducted. She'd seen the agenda for tonight and knew there were no very exciting decisions facing them, so she wasn't surprised to find the audience thin. Noah had a place at the raised semicircular table along with the nine council members. He wasn't sitting yet, although he stood behind the table talking to a balding, potbellied man and a woman who looked to be in her forties and wearing a fire-engine-red suit Cait admired.

Either he was keeping an eye on all arrivals or watching for her, because his gaze flicked to her the minute she walked in. He'd been in the middle of saying something but stopped midsentence, seeming momentarily paralyzed by the sight of her.

Feeling unwarranted satisfaction at the idea that she'd dazzled him, Cait gave herself a stern talking-to. *Repeat to self—I do not want a man, especially a man as overbearing as this one. Who so happens to be my* boss.

Without looking at him again, she strolled up to the curved table and held out a hand to the city councilman at the end.

"Hi, I'm Cait McAllister, new in the Office of Community Development."

Two hours later, she was struggling to hold on to her expression of eager, or even polite, interest. She had been introduced at the beginning and received with reasonable cordiality. From that point on, much of the discussion concerned possible alterations to the noise ordinance. The citizens who did appear mostly wanted to hog the microphone as they vented about a neighbor's barking dog or teenagers who were apparently free to party until all hours almost nightly. Nobody showed up to say, "Screw the ordinance! I have a constitutional right to make all the racket I want!" A police captain named Brian Cooper droned on with statistics relating to noise violations and possible repercussions should the projected change be voted through. Cait couldn't decide if he was really that boring or whether he was trying to put everyone to sleep. *To prevent a vote?* she wondered, momentarily amused. She'd have to ask Colin about him.

Cait found herself surreptitiously watching Mayor Chandler. Patience was not one of his virtues, it appeared. Expressions flowed across his face—disbelief and exasperation alternated with the expected boredom. He eventually started either making notes or doodling. Cait leaned toward the doodling explanation.

Once he lifted his head unexpectedly, and his eyes met hers. They stared at each other for long enough to excite comment if anyone had been paying attention. There was an openness in his eyes and, she was afraid, in hers, as if they hadn't had time to shield themselves. Even so, she wasn't quite sure what he was thinking. She discovered, when he suddenly turned his head, that she must have quit breathing. She hoped the gasp wasn't obvious when she sucked in air.

She probably should have lingered when the meeting ended, but she couldn't make herself.

Oh, God. I shouldn't have taken this job, she realized as she fled. She couldn't keep dodging Noah. She either had to get inured to him, or...she didn't know.

Joining a cluster of five people who got on the elevator together, she pushed the button for the parking garage and watched as someone else did for the lobby. There was no conversation; everyone stared politely straight ahead.

She stood aside when the doors opened at the lobby. To her dismay, everyone but her got off. As the doors shut, she weighed the possibility of going back up and hovering until the next group was ready to depart. Nothing but the city council meeting had been happening tonight. The lot would be deserted.

But the doors were already opening, and she saw that the space was well lit. With relatively few cars left, there weren't a lot of places for anyone to hide. Nonetheless, she reached in her purse for both her car keys and her pepper spray.

She walked confidently, heels striking on the cement floor. She had the passing thought that four-inch heels were *not* a good choice for a woman alone this late in the evening. Unless, of course, she took one off and used it as a weapon.

Picturing herself brandishing a pink high heel in self-defense almost made her smile.

No dark figures stepped out from between parked cars. She reached her Mazda unscathed and was dropping the pepper spray back into her purse when she saw the rear window. A lopsided heart speared by a huge arrow had been drawn on it in some kind of greasy red paint.

Shocked, she stopped, her gaze involuntarily surveying first her surroundings again, then the rest of her car. Dear God, what was that on the windshield? A crack? Or…?

She backed up, peeked around her car to be sure no one hid there, then took one slow step at a time until she could see what had happened to the windshield.

The same smeary red paint had been used to write in foot-tall letters:

MISS ME YET?

"Is something wrong?" a man asked from behind her.

CHAPTER FOUR

HAVING EXPECTED CAIT to hang around to talk to council members, Noah was taken aback when he realized she was gone. *He* had nothing to say to anyone—what a waste of an evening this had been—so, nodding to Brian Cooper, he left the council chamber.

The elevator doors were just closing. Behind him, voices spilled out of the room. He shot a hunted look behind him. Damn it, if he waited for the next elevator, he'd get stuck making conversation, the last thing he had the patience for tonight. Reversing direction, he escaped into the stairwell in the nick of time.

Noah emerged into the parking garage to echoing silence. He could see only one person—a slim woman in a deep rose suit that revealed mile-long legs enhanced by heels that had to add four inches to her height. Cait McAllister wasn't a woman who worried about deferring to men, he figured, or she wouldn't wear shoes that made her taller than most of them.

He was halfway across the bare concrete space

before he started wondering what she was doing, just standing there staring at her car. No—her head turned, almost surreptitiously, and then she ducked around to the passenger side. Hiding from someone he couldn't see? Damn it, from *him?*

But she reemerged from the space between a concrete pillar and her little hatchback and kept staring at her car. Had she locked her keys in it or left the lights on and killed the battery?

"Is something wrong?" he asked.

She gasped and whirled, one shaking hand holding out some little gizmo. Mace, Noah realized belatedly, or pepper spray. He also took in the shock that dilated her eyes. And then his gaze went past her.

"What the hell…?" he murmured.

She seemed to sag. "It's…the windshield, too."

He walked around her car and saw.

MISS ME YET? in enormous capital letters. The writing reminded him of the Just Married he'd sometimes seen in the back windows of cars also festooned with dangling cans or streamers.

"Never given a woman a valentine before," he remarked, "so maybe I'm not an expert, but I can't say this one strikes me as very romantic."

Cait's laugh sounded semi-hysterical. "No," she agreed. "*Romantic* is the last word I'd use."

He looked at her. "Do you know who did this?"

She closed her eyes. After a moment, she gave a stiff little nod.

She was not only shocked, but scared, Noah diagnosed. "No sign of him?" he asked.

"No, but I didn't exactly mount a search."

"I'm glad to hear you had the sense not to poke around all by yourself in a deserted parking garage for the asshole who'd do this," he said grimly. "Stay put."

He didn't consider her a meek woman, but she nodded in acquiescence.

It didn't take him long to determine that they were alone down there. Had been alone. As he walked back toward her, the elevator disgorged five people, two of whom separated from the pack, going straight for their vehicles, while the other three stood talking.

"Oh, God." Cait sounded frantic. "I don't want them to see this."

"No." He took an experimental swipe over the heart and discovered the color didn't come off on his finger. "You can't drive the car like this."

"No. I'll call Colin."

"Don't be ridiculous. I'll take you home." He frowned. "I've got a tarp. I can toss it over your car."

She thanked him.

He wasn't parked far away. It took him only a minute to unlock the rear of his Suburban and grab the heavy canvas tarp he'd been using to keep the cargo space clean when he hauled construction materials. Returning, he found her staring at that damn pierced heart as if she couldn't tear her eyes away. Noah pulled the tarp over her car, glad to hide it from her gaze.

"I thought you were new in town."

Her mouth twisted as her eyes met his. "I am."

Seeing how frail she suddenly looked, he shook his head. "Come on."

He circled around in case she needed a hand getting in with those damn heels. Or maybe so he could catch a glimpse of an extra few inches of thigh as she hiked herself up.

Once in, he started the engine but didn't release the emergency brake. "All right, what's the deal?" he asked.

Her glance was swift. "Does it matter?"

"Yeah, I think it does. Was this meant to be fun? Some kind of prank? Or should we notify the police and have your car fingerprinted?"

Staring straight ahead, she chewed on her lower lip. Finally she let out a long breath. "I'll tell Colin and see what he thinks. I hoped…"

Noah waited.

She still didn't seem to want to look at him. "An ex-boyfriend has been stalking me. It's one of the reasons I didn't want to stay in Seattle to finish my dissertation."

Anger balled in his gut. "Define *stalking*."

"Mostly following me. Popping up everywhere I went. I changed health clubs. He'd show up at my new one. Trail me through the grocery store. That kind of thing."

Mostly following? The tension in her voice told him there was substantially more.

She turned her head, her eyes still dark with unhappiness. "I could tell he was getting mad. The last time I was coming out of my health club after an evening class and he was waiting at my car."

"Tell me you hadn't gone out alone." His voice sounded like the crunch of gravel.

"Well, I did," she said with a spark of defiance. "Until then, he really was just a nuisance."

He gripped the steering wheel hard. "Until then."

Her eyes shied from his. "When I said no again, that I didn't love him and he needed to accept that, he, well, sort of threw a temper tantrum." She paused. "*Did* throw a temper tantrum. He was wearing heavy boots, and he kicked my car, over and over. He did a lot of damage to the body."

Goddamn. The thought of those boots slamming into her little car had Noah's whole body rigid with the need to do battle. Useless, but he couldn't seem to help himself. He didn't have to be a psychologist to know the ex-boyfriend had wanted to hurt *her,* not the car.

"And while he was doing this?"

"I dialed 911, of course! What do you think, I'm stupid?"

"Was he arrested?"

"Some people were coming out of the health

club, and he took off. The police did charge him later and he did some kind of plea deal. But, um, the last thing he said was that he'd never accept losing me."

"And that's when you decided coming home to your cop brother was a good idea."

"Well...yes."

"Does Colin know about this creep?"

She visibly winced. "Um...no. I really did hope Blake wouldn't follow me. He has a job. I can't imagine what he's thinking!"

"How long had this been going on?"

"Like...six months?"

He swore under his breath and reached for the gearshift. Having backed out, he then punched in the code to open the iron grill of the gate, closed at night. Within moments, he was driving through downtown, which had gone pretty well dead except for a few places like Chandler's that stayed open until eleven on weeknights.

Cait was quiet for close to five minutes. Then, "Do you know where Colin lives?"

"Someone pointed his place out to me."

Another couple of minutes passed. "Will you say something?" she burst out.

"Better if I don't."

"Why not?"

"Because I'd give you hell for not taking precautions!" Despite his best intentions, his voice had risen. "What were you thinking, going down to your car all by yourself tonight?"

"I was thinking he was in Seattle!" she yelled back. "And…and I did look around the garage before I got out of the elevator." That part came out more subdued. "I'm not stupid," she said again but softly, as if she was trying to convince herself.

Feeling like he had grit in his chest that scraped when he breathed, Noah grasped her fine-boned hand in his. Cait gave a little jerk, as if he'd startled her, but after a very still moment, she squeezed back. *Holding on,* he thought.

"Your hand is cold," he said quietly.

"My hands are always cold." It was a poor excuse for a laugh, but Noah admired the effort. "My feet, too. Lousy circulation, I guess."

He was betrayed into imagining himself sandwiching her cold feet between his shins at night, warming them.

No. Don't go there.

Neither of them said another word until he had to take his hand back to steer into the dark driveway leading through a tall stand of pines to her brother's house. He was glad to see that the front porch lights were on. A floodlight over the detached garage lit up, too, presumably motion-sensitive. He drove as close as he could get to the front steps and then braked.

"Thank you for the lift," she said, already releasing her seat belt and reaching for her purse. "And for listening."

"I'm coming in with you."

Door halfway open, she swiveled back to look at him. "What?"

"You heard me."

By the time he turned off the engine and walked around, her brother stood on the porch looking down at them. "Cait." His eyes narrowed. "Chandler."

"You really don't have to..." she tried.

Noah gripped her elbow and started her up the porch steps.

"Your car break down?" Colin asked.

At the top of the steps, she shook free of Noah's hold and glared at him. "No. I'm going to have to get someone to clean it in the morning. It suffered from...I guess you could call it graffiti."

"Shall I tell him about it?" Noah asked.

She'd gotten over being scared and was mad. "This is none of your business!"

"It happened in the city hall parking garage. While you were attending a city council meeting." He put some extra weight on the word *city*. "You work for me. That makes it my business."

Her brother's narrow-eyed gaze moved back to his sister. "Cait?"

"Oh, fine." She stomped past him into the house.

Colin glanced back. "You coming in?"

Surprised at the invitation, he said a firm, "Yes."

He was damned if he'd leave her alone to make light of the whole story to her brother.

Only a single lamp was on in the living room. A newspaper lay open on the hassock. He'd been waiting up for her, Noah guessed. Or for his wife?

"Is Nell home?" Cait asked.

"She's taking a shower and getting ready for bed." Although she'd perched on the sofa, Colin still stood, arms crossed. "Quit procrastinating."

Her mutinous expression amused Noah despite his dark mood.

She sniffed. "You remember Blake."

"We already established that I did," her brother said slowly.

"Well, he's been stalking me." She told the story briskly, not minimizing but not revealing the fear Noah had seen. He didn't comment, however.

Colin, he suspected, wasn't deceived.

"And you didn't tell me about this.... Why?"

She had a pretty mouth, but Noah wouldn't have called it sultry until now, when her lower lip protruded. "I really didn't think Blake would follow me."

"That son of a bitch. If he thinks he's going to terrorize you here in *my* town—"

"He's convinced that he can talk me into going back to him," she tried to explain.

"Is there a chance in hell of that happening?" Colin asked, the timbre of his voice roughening.

She scowled at both men. "Of course not!"

"All right," Colin said. "He's got to be staying somewhere local. We'll look for him in the morning. I want to see your car."

Cait nodded unhappily. "You'll have to drive me to work anyway."

"For now, it might be better if I drive you and pick you up every day."

Noah approved.

"You're overreacting. He painted a heart on my back windshield. It wasn't a threat."

"Yeah, it was." Noah had been content to allow her brother to grill her until now, but her intransigence was beginning to annoy him. "He's letting you know he's in town and watching you. Given his history, that's a threat."

"Do you have a restraining order?" Colin asked.

"I didn't think I needed one."

Noah stared incredulously at her, and realized Colin was doing the same. Cait's expression grew mutinous.

"We'll get a restraining order first thing in the morning," Colin said.

"Good," Noah agreed.

Colin cast him a not-so-happy look. "Say goodnight to Mayor Chandler," he said. The momentary accord had apparently dissolved. "He's leaving now."

She rose and thanked him politely again, talking to their backs as Noah found himself being hustled out by Colin. On the porch, Noah balked.

"Your sister is trying to play down any threat. Don't let her."

The police captain's jaw tightened, but to his credit, he also nodded. "I noticed. I can't believe she didn't tell me."

"It's ugly." More urgency than Noah wanted to feel infused his voice. "The arrow is way bigger than the heart. It's not piercing it—it's stabbing. She's more frightened than she's letting on."

Unblinking, shadowed gray eyes held his. "I notice everything about my sister."

That almost sounded like a threat to Noah, who began to wonder if he'd get tossed off the porch if he stood his ground. *Let him try. Immature,* he decided.

Nodding, he retrieved his keys from his pocket and started down the steps. He was circling his SUV when the quiet voice carried to him.

"Thank you." It was grudging as hell but genuine.

He stopped briefly. "I like your sister."

No answer to that, but he hadn't expected one.

APPARENTLY, THE RIGHT kind of cleaning solution took any kind of paint right off glass. As if her car was a serious crime scene, Colin had pictures taken from every angle but hovering above in a helicopter. He did concede that fingerprinting was useless, given that she'd lived with Blake for two years and he'd been in her car countless times. His fingerprints shouldn't be on the exterior since she'd had the bodywork done and the car was returned to her with the paint job gleaming, but it was still conceivable.

Colin had her talk to a female attorney who was starting the process of requesting the restraining order. It was midmorning Wednesday before Cait had a chance to escape to her office.

She was struggling to concentrate on a preliminary design done some months back for a pipeline replacement project when Noah appeared in her doorway. With the breadth of his shoulders, he completely filled it.

"You okay?" he asked gruffly.

"I'm fine." Same thing she'd told Colin when he'd let her off in front of work that morning.

She had a bad feeling Noah's sharp blue gaze saw the dark circles under her eyes she'd tried to hide with makeup that morning.

"You heard from your brother?"

"He called a few minutes ago. My car is clean and ready to go. He can't get away soon enough to follow me home today, but assumes I'll use my head and have an escort when I go down to the garage."

Noah's grin flickered at the sarcasm she let edge into the direct quote.

"Officers have as yet failed to locate Blake," she added, drolly using cop-speak.

The grin vanished. "Why the hell can't they put their hands on him?"

"This can't possibly be the highest priority for the entire Angel Butte P.D.," she protested.

"You want to bet?"

He actually sounded serious. Cait didn't know whether to be flattered, grateful—or to scream.

One overprotective man was enough.

"There's no saying Blake is staying in town," she pointed out, the voice of reason. "He could be all the way back in Seattle by now. He could have a room in Bend or Prineville. There are places he could pay cash. Heck, he could conceivably be at a campground or even just camped in the woods somewhere."

Deepening lines made Noah's brow heavier. "It's still damn cold at night." The month of May in country caught between the foothills of the Cascade Mountains and the high desert wasn't like May in the milder climates of Portland or Seattle. "Is he an outdoorsman?"

"He and I did some backpacking. He has a two-man tent."

"Did you tell Colin that?"

"They've only been looking for a few hours."

Noah grunted. "What are you doing for lunch?"

"I'm eating at my desk."

"I'll walk you down when you're ready to leave. Call me."

He was gone before she could get a word out.

Cait was beginning to think there was an excellent reason he and Colin clashed: they were too much alike. She had a vision of the two of them charging at each other like two elk in rutting season. She restrained a snort. She doubted either of them actually cared about the female elk, who had probably wandered away to graze.

She, of course, wasn't the female elk; they had entrenched their dislike of each other long before she'd arrived. Their dispute, she suspected, was territorial. *My town,* Colin had said. Cait was pretty sure Noah would claim Angel Butte as his.

With a small laugh, she wondered what the angel would think of all this.

NOAH CALLED AT five minutes to five. "You ready to knock off?"

"Actually, I'm planning to have dinner with Beverly Buhl and someone she wants me to meet. Um." She hunted on a cluttered desk for her notepad. "Michael Kalitovic? Did I get that right?"

"His hobbyhorse is affordable housing."

"Oh. That's not really my bailiwick."

"No, but he's got his fingers in a lot of pies. You should get to know him."

"Anyway, it appears I don't need an escort."

He wasn't listening. "Maybe I'll join you," he said, sounding thoughtful.

"Were you invited?"

"You don't think I'd be welcome?" To her exasperation, he sounded amused.

"They might be trying to get my ear when you're *not* around, you know."

"They might. All the more reason for me to stick close."

Cait sighed. "Noah, really…"

"What time? Where are we eating?"

She couldn't shake him, with the result that forty-five minutes later, she was once more ensconced in the passenger seat of his black Suburban as he drove the quarter of a mile to the Newberry Inn. Beverly had insisted that, if Cait didn't remember the inn, she would enjoy the chance to eat there.

"It's one of our finest historic buildings," she had enthused.

Cait remembered it, but she had never been inside. Her parents wouldn't have been able to afford to dine there. In fact, her family had hardly ever eaten out at all, which was probably why she remembered those lunches Jerry Hegland had bought for her and her mother so well. A burger and fries at the Icicle Drive-Thru had been a huge treat in her eyes.

"You just want to come so you can assess your competition," she accused Noah as he parked.

"I don't consider the inn a competitor. We're in different weight classes."

"What's that mean?"

"I go for a younger crowd. This is where the matrons lunch." He shrugged. "Sure, some of the tourists try it because of the historic designation, but the next night they want something more casual." A smile lurked in his eyes as he took the keys from the ignition. "The food's better at my place, too."

He was right. It was. More imaginative, too. This menu ran to steaks, a few chicken dishes, a nod to vegetarians and a variety of salads. Cait went with one of them and found the dressing to be bland and the romaine damp.

Noah sawed unenthusiastically at his filet mignon. Michael Kalitovic was too busy expounding on his passion to seem to notice what he was putting in his mouth, and Beverly seemed to be occupied trying to figure out why Noah had accompanied Cait. She did wax rhapsodic to the idea of a bypass route into town. Next thing they knew, she'd whipped out her smartphone and pulled up a local map, which to her frustration repeatedly whisked out of sight as she tried to draw new lines.

"I do believe in affordable housing," Cait kept having to say to Michael. "But you'll have to interest a developer in a project."

By the time Noah announced brusquely that he and Cait had to leave, she was so grateful she didn't object to his high-handedness.

"You weren't kidding about his hobbyhorse," she muttered as they cut through the dark parking lot.

She loved his low, rough laugh. "No, I wasn't.

I've been known to hide in a janitor's closet when I see him coming."

Cait giggled. "Beverly is almost as bad. Nice, but I'm kind of sorry I threw out the bypass idea. I may have created a monster."

He unlocked his SUV. "Yeah, until now Beverly was thinking in terms of a ten-foot-high hedge of yew to hide Target and Home Depot from passing traffic."

The image of the highway into town tunneling through high walls of greenery made her laugh again. "Well, making the approach slightly more appealing is still an alternative, and a less costly one."

Noah's craggy face was a lot more attractive when he was smiling, like now. "Too late to suggest it without crushing Beverly."

Back at city hall, he pulled in right behind her small car, set the brake and got out with her. Somehow she wasn't at all surprised when he circled to examine her little Mazda, even ducking down once to peer beneath.

She crossed her arms and watched. "Looking for a bomb?"

He didn't appear amused. "I'll follow you home."

"You really don't have to."

"It's not far out of my way."

That got her wondering where he *did* live and what his home was like. Was he a condo kind of guy? She tried to picture him mowing a lawn on

Saturday morning, but that seemed too domestic.
Not that he was the slick kind—it wasn't hard to
imagine him, say, building a house single-handedly.
He could be sweaty and physical.

"Fine," she said with a sigh, and got into her car.

His headlights stayed in her rearview mirror the
entire way; he went so far as to pull into the driveway behind her, reversing to leave only when he
saw that Colin had stepped out onto the porch to
see her safely into the house.

"Chandler?" her brother asked with a scowl.

"Yes."

"I thought you were having dinner with that Buhl
woman."

"I was." She watched as he locked the door once
they were inside. "Her and a Michael Kalitovic—
do you know him?—and Noah."

"I know Kalitovic. He has a teenage son who is
a little wild."

She blinked, picturing the earnest guy with the
receding hairline, which he tried to disguise by
shaving his head. "Really."

"Oh, yeah. Dad and son both have become familiar faces at the station." His mouth twitched.
"That's small-town life, you know. No secrets."

"That could be good," she said doubtfully.

"And bad," he agreed. "You get used to it."

Angel Butte, Cait reflected after she'd said good-
night to him and was getting ready for bed, had

been even smaller when she'd lived here as a child. Her mother had had a secret. *Had* she somehow kept it? And if not, who had known?

CHAPTER FIVE

A RAP ON his half-open door brought Colin's head up from the equipment request he'd been considering when he wasn't brooding about the fact that Cait had had dinner with Chandler last night. Sure, with two other people also, but what if the bastard had his eye on her?

"Captain?" It was Jane Vahalik, the detective he'd promoted to lieutenant last fall after he'd had to shoot and kill her predecessor, who in turn had been trying to kill Nell. Vahalik was young for the job of supervising the detective unit, but, despite a few missteps, he thought she was going to be up to it.

Jane was thirty-four, average height, no beauty but with an interesting face, an unruly mass of dark chestnut hair she usually wore in a ponytail and hazel eyes. He knew she was a swimmer, which kept her more fit than three-quarters of the other officers in the Angel Butte force.

He waved her in. "What's up?"

"Thought you'd want to know we have a murder."

He raised his eyebrows. Their murder rate was

low for a town this size. The statistic was one he took pride in. "A visitor or a local?"

"Local." She sat without waiting for an invitation. "He still had his wallet, or we might be floundering for an ID. He's not the kind of guy who's likely to have prints in the system."

"Anybody I'd know?" His patience was wearing thin.

"Maybe. He's the airport manager. We're pretty sure he is," she corrected herself. "He's not married, so we've asked a maintenance supervisor out at the airport to give a positive ID."

What the hell? "Not Jerry Hegland?" he asked.

"You do know him."

He shook his head. "I know of him. Not sure I've ever come face-to-face with him." That was true enough, as far as it went.

What were the odds, he had to ask himself, that Cait would mention him in such a context and the man would turn up dead ten days later? Chance, of course, but one that unsettled him.

"Tell me about it," he ordered.

The body had been found on the shoulder of a rural road. A home owner on her way to work early that morning had spotted it. She'd assumed the man to have been the victim of a hit-and-run. The medical examiner had immediately determined that the victim had been shot.

"Two shots, back of the head. Classic execution.

Only one exit wound, though, so we ought to be able to recover a bullet in the autopsy."

"Jesus. Is his face recognizable?"

"Yeah, from one side." She grimaced. "He's a mess."

"Killed there?"

"Sanchez says no. There wasn't much blood. He likely hadn't been dead long when he was dumped, though. Best guess so far, he was killed something like eight to ten hours before the body was found."

"All right. Keep me informed."

She nodded and left. Somewhat reluctantly, he went down the hall to Raynor's office.

The office that should have been his.

"Your boss in?" he asked the assistant.

"He just got off the phone. Go on in."

Having to knock rankled, as did the sight of another man behind that desk. He tried not to hold getting screwed out of the job against Raynor, but he couldn't always help himself.

He shared the details he knew, shook his head when Raynor asked if he'd known the victim and left as soon as possible. As he strode back down the hall to his own office, he was thinking about Cait. He'd have to tell her before she heard from someone else.

"JERRY HEGLAND WAS found dead today."

Cait was dishing up asparagus when Colin's

words sank in. She carefully set the serving spoon back in the bowl and looked at him.

"Dead?"

He had set down his own fork. Nell, across the table from Cait, looked from one of them to the other.

"He was murdered, Cait."

"But..." Her brain was foundering. "I just saw him."

A nerve ticked beneath one of his eyes. "I know."

She could not tell what he was thinking. Her own brother.

"How?" she asked, her voice high and breathless.

"Shot. He was dumped next to a road out past Thunder Creek."

"You didn't go talk to him, did you?" she blurted.

His expression changed. "What are you suggesting?"

"Nothing." She shouldn't have said that. But remembering Colin's rage when she'd told him about their mother's affair, she couldn't help *thinking* it. "I just wondered—"

"Whether I killed him." He said it slowly. "You're asking me if I killed a man because I don't like that he slept with my mother damn near twenty years ago."

"No." She still didn't sound like herself. "Of course I didn't mean that. Only that...maybe you'd talked to him. Know more about him than you did."

He pushed away from the table although his plate was still full. "What kind of man do you think I am?"

"I don't know!" she cried. "I don't know you very well."

Nell seemed to be frozen in place, only her eyes vividly alive as she watched the scene unfold.

Colin rose, looked at Cait for a long moment and walked away. The bedroom door closed quietly.

At last, Nell shot to her feet. "He's a good man. For you to imply—" She shook her head and hurried after her husband.

Cait looked down at her plate, not seeing the food she'd dished up. Instead, her head was filled with a kaleidoscope of memories: the brother she had loved so much pitching a softball to her and laughing when she swung hard and missed entirely. Lifting the bike from her after she had fallen, insisting she'd done great; she'd get it. Kicking the coffee table over and launching himself at their father, his face suffused with red. She was screaming and she thought her mother was, too. Both shrank into a corner. Snarled obscenities as the two men's bodies crashed against the sofa and then the wall. Fists flying.

I don't *know him.*

But she'd run to him for safety.

Feeling sick, she scraped her untouched food back into serving dishes, then did the same for her brother's and sister-in-law's plates. Carried them to the kitchen, covered them with plastic and put them away in the refrigerator. Rinsed dishes, filled the dishwasher, started it running, all the while wondering, shell-shocked, what she had just done.

He wasn't a murderer. She didn't believe that. She didn't.

But...she remembered how furious he'd been when she had told him about Jerry Hegland. And now, so soon, their mother's lover had been found dead. How could she help but wonder?

Was there anything more horrible she could have said to her brother?

She stole down the hall to the guest bedroom, hearing the murmur of voices through the door to Colin and Nell's room. Cait didn't want to think about what they were saying.

I can't stay here.

She pressed her fingers to her mouth on a broken laugh. All she had to do was close her eyes and see the way he looked at her. The way *Nell* had looked at her. It was safe to say she'd worn out her welcome.

But she wouldn't flee into the night. Colin deserved an apology. Tomorrow morning, she'd go look at the town houses Noah had recommended and any other rentals she could find online. She might even be able to move tomorrow.

No, she couldn't stay here under Colin's protection, not even in the apartment over the garage, not after what she'd said. Implied.

She huddled in bed, not sleeping, shriveling from the memory of Colin's shock. Remembering Jerry Hegland's face when he recognized her, remembering his kindness to her when she was a little girl, imagining that face drained of life.

And then she thought, *Oh, God, should I tell Mom?* Who still didn't know that her daughter had moved to Angel Butte, the town from which they'd fled with little more than their clothes?

She might have slept finally, although she saw gray dawn creeping around the slats of the blinds. Cait got up when she heard somebody come out of the bedroom across the hall.

She found Colin in the kitchen, adding water to the coffeemaker. He glanced at her, then back to what he was doing. He looked as if he'd aged ten years overnight. Cait had a bad feeling she did, too.

"I'm sorry," she said. "I had a flash of remembering how angry you looked. I opened my mouth too soon and said something stupid. That's all it was."

He nodded.

She bit her lip so hard she tasted blood. "I'll leave today."

"Now you are being stupid." His voice was completely devoid of emotion. "Of course you're not going anywhere. Not when that creep's after you."

She only shook her head. She couldn't stay. She didn't deserve his protection. "I have to get dressed."

"When you're ready, I'll follow you into work." He still sounded like a stranger.

Deep breath. "Thank you" was all she could manage.

She didn't cry until she stood in the shower, hot water washing away her tears.

WAITING FOR THE elevator Friday morning, Noah glanced over his shoulder when he heard the squeal of a vehicle turning sharply. Every sound was magnified down there. He tensed when he saw the blue of Cait's car. The elevator doors opened, and he was torn between escaping and waiting. While he hesitated, the elevator lost patience with him, closed and went on its way.

She walked hurriedly from her car, although there was a hitch in her step when she saw him. "Noah."

Today's garb was more subdued than her usual—black slacks and a three-quarter-sleeve V-neck camel-colored sweater. Stood to reason not everything in her wardrobe was bright and cheerful. But, seeing her face, he suspected her clothes reflected her mood.

Then she got closer, and his eyes narrowed. She looked like hell.

"Cait," he greeted her.

"Caught coming to work late." She might have been trying to make light of it, but her voice was subdued, too. "I was looking at rentals. I know I should have waited until tomorrow, but I'll make up the time."

"You're not on the clock," he said impatiently. "I know you have to find a place to live. I thought you'd stay at your brother's for now, though."

"No, I—" She gave an awkward shrug, bumping a heavy messenger bag against her hip. "Actually, I put down first and last month's on one of the town houses you told me about. I can move in today."

"But they're not furnished." What was going on?

"No, I'll send for my furniture from Seattle. But I needed a new bed anyway. That was my second stop this morning, at Larson's."

Fred Larson, who owned the furniture store, was one of the local businessmen who'd served on the city council for far too long, in Noah's opinion.

"I picked out a bed and a couch. Oh, and stools the right height for the breakfast bar. The manager promised they'd deliver at five, so I'll need to cut out a little early, too."

"You know that's not a problem." Her living for a week or more in a two-bedroom, two-bath town house furnished only with a bed, sofa and bar stools, *that* was a problem. He still hadn't punched the button to summon the elevator, and he didn't now. "Cait, what's going on? You know you shouldn't be alone until this Ralston guy gets picked up."

Noah had looked up Blake Ralston online, and although he wasn't 100 percent sure he'd found the right guy, he thought he had. The one he'd found was some kind of water system engineer, which made sense—Cait would have reason to meet him in the course of her work. He'd been displeased to see that her ex-boyfriend—if this was him—was model-handsome in a dark-eyed, intense way. Given the education and qualifications the company website listed, he seemed an unlikely stalker, but Noah had long since learned that crazy came in all shapes and sizes.

"It's been three days. The police haven't been able to locate him, and I haven't heard a peep from him. You know he's probably back in Seattle. His flying visit was a...a jab." She was trying to sound like she believed herself. Failing, of course. "That's all," she concluded.

"Bullshit," he said bluntly, earning a shocked stare. "How did he find you in his 'flying visit'? Tell me that."

"Remember he's met Colin. All he'd have to do was stake out Colin's house and follow me."

"You wouldn't have noticed a car on the side of the road?"

"It was dusk. Besides, he could have been half a mile away!" She was getting mad that he wasn't buying her little fantasy. "Using binoculars."

It was possible, Noah could concede. But he didn't believe for a minute that someone as obsessed as this guy would be satisfied with one nasty little trick.

"Did Colin check to find out if Ralston has been at work?"

Her eyes fell away from Noah's. "He's taking some vacation. Um." She looked past him at the elevator. "Shouldn't we…?"

"Not until you tell me what's wrong."

"What makes you think anything's wrong?" she fired back, that square chin thrust out. "Colin and Nell are still newlyweds. They don't need a never-ending guest. It was time for me to find a place to live. I did."

He shook his head. "That's not it." He touched his forefinger to the puffy, bruised skin beneath one of her eyes, ignoring her flinch. "Did you sleep at all last night?"

"I can do my job!"

"I'm not worried about your job. I'm worried about you."

Suddenly there was a sheen of tears in her eyes. Cait turned her face away from him. Bothered at his own powerful reaction, he let her take a minute to recover her dignity.

When she looked at him again, the tears had been vanquished, although a few droplets clung to lashes. "It's not that big a deal. Colin and I had… I guess you could call it a fight. He told me I didn't have to go, but I can't—" Her voice broke. She squared her shoulders. "Sometimes I don't know when to keep my mouth shut. It's better this way."

He wanted in the worst way to take her in his arms, but he was her boss, not her lover, not even her friend. What disturbed him was realizing he felt like both. He didn't like knowing she had nobody here in Angel Butte.

"Was it over Ralston?" That he could understand. But she shook her head.

He sighed. "I'll go with you to meet the delivery guys." He held up a hand when she started to speak. "I don't want you opening your door when you don't know who is on the other side of it. Then we'll have a housewarming." He smiled slightly. "Order a pizza."

She looked, suddenly, absurdly young. Bewildered. "I don't understand."

"You don't have to understand." *Oh, damn*—he didn't sound like a boss. He cleared his throat. "It's in my interests to see that you settle happily into Angel Butte." *That was stuffy enough,* he congratulated himself.

She continued to study him for an unnerving length of time, those dove-gray eyes soft but also more perceptive than he was comfortable with. At last she bit her lip and nodded. "If you really have time."

"I have time." He turned and punched the button. They both stared at the elevator doors as if they were the Rosetta stone. Same color but less absorbing. He heard faint dings from the elevator shaft. "You haven't said anything you shouldn't to me," he heard himself say.

Her laugh was almost sad. "I will. Blake says—"

He almost heard the tires skidding as she stopped.

"What does Blake say?"

Cait shook her head. "He was easy to annoy."

With a louder ding, the elevator doors opened. They both stepped into it. He pushed buttons.

"He in water systems?"

Her glance was startled and then wary. "How did you know?"

"I looked him up." He shrugged. "Call me nosy."

"Yes," she said after a moment. "He's really good at his job."

"Is that damning with faint praise?"

He heard a little sound and realized she was trying to repress a giggle. But her lips were curved as she stepped out at her floor.

"Maybe," was the last thing she said.

NOAH WAS AS good as his word, which didn't surprise her. At four-thirty, he appeared in her office doorway.

"We should be going."

Cait shut down her computer, collected her bag and let him escort her to her car. She was very conscious of the interest they were garnering by leaving together, but Noah seemed oblivious. He once again minutely inspected her car before letting her get in and promising to follow her.

She'd liked the town house right away. It seemed to be well built and had luxurious touches she appreciated. The entry and living room boasted gleaming wood floors, the bathrooms Corian countertops and molded sinks and the kitchen a granite-topped island and a copper backsplash behind the stove. Kitchen appliances, including refrigerator, were included, to her relief. She'd never owned a washer or dryer and would have to buy those, but otherwise she was set.

Noah had followed her into the alley, where she felt lucky to have a single-car detached garage. Cait took pleasure in using the remote control and watching the door rise. She'd never had her own garage before, either.

He pulled into the single parking space beside it and was waiting inside the fenced yard when she came out the garage's side door with one of her big suitcases. "Do you have more?"

He ended up pulling the other large one and carrying the small case. As they crossed the yard, his gaze took in the deck with built-in benches and landscaping.

"I wish you didn't have the distance to get in the house."

Colin cloned. The thought of her brother hurt. It took an effort to make a clownish face at Noah. "Don't rain on my parade. This is a nice place."

A grunt was her only answer.

He did concede after a brief tour that, as rentals went, this one seemed fine. She teased him that he just didn't want to admit how nice it was because Earl had built it.

The glint of humor in his eyes was the closest she got to an admission from him.

The front doorbell rang, and she stood back as two hefty men carried in the new sofa. When they asked where she wanted it, she made a hasty decision and they set it down, then went out for first the bar stools, then the mattress and springs. They put together the simple metal frame way faster than she could have, heaved the springs and mattress into place and departed as briskly as they'd come.

Aware of Noah watching from the bedroom doorway, Cait said, "There. Halfway to furnished."

"Do you have a pillow? Linens? Towels?"

"I plan to go out this evening for the basics."

He frowned. "I thought I was going to leave you safely tucked away for the night."

The idea of going out again held no appeal, but sheets weren't the only necessity she lacked. "I suppose I should have taken another hour this morning."

"You don't have groceries."

"I'll do that tomorrow. I can pick up a couple of cheap bowls, paper plates…" She shrugged. "I'll survive until my stuff gets here."

"You could have borrowed from your brother."

"I…didn't think to."

Colin had clearly been stunned when he'd seen her suitcase that morning. His gaze had traveled slowly from it up to her face.

"What the hell do you think you're doing?"

"I told you. I can't stay," she had repeated. She'd known she was hurting him again but was unable to imagine what it would be like if she did stay.

His face had closed—*bang*—until it was hard and almost unrecognizable. She supposed it was his cop face, one she'd never seen. He didn't say another word, only followed her back in, grabbed the larger of the two remaining suitcases and hoisted all of them into the back of her small car.

"Where are you going?" he'd asked.

"I'll let you know."

He nodded and went back in the house, leaving her to depart unescorted for the first time since Tuesday night.

Thinking about Colin now made her chest constrict painfully. She couldn't imagine anything she could say that would undo the damage. The awful thing was, a small part of her still wondered. Hadn't she read that no one in law enforcement believed in coincidences? In the moment when she'd told him about Hegland and their mother, she'd seen hate in his eyes for a man who, barely a week later, was murdered.

Not Colin.

But that sick fear lingered.

Not something she could tell Noah.

The doorbell rang again. "Pizza," he said briefly and disappeared.

It turned out he'd ordered from Chandler's,

which did not as a rule deliver but, of course, did for the boss.

The cheerful kid had also brought thick stoneware plates, napkins and a liter of cola, as well as several glasses with "Chandler's" in gilt on the sides.

It felt a little odd to open the box on the narrow breakfast bar and sit so close to Noah that his shoulder bumped hers. When she looked down, she couldn't help seeing the way his dark trousers pulled taut over powerful muscles.

"How do you stay in shape?" she asked before she could think—and, gee, what was new in her opening her mouth too quick?—and felt her cheeks warm.

He lifted an eyebrow at her. "I run and lift weights both. Plus, I'm remodeling an old house in my spare time." His tone was dry. "Helps keep me active."

"What I was really wondering was about health clubs." *Sure you were.*

"Don't use one. I have my own equipment at home. I hear good things about Newberry Square Athletic Club, though."

"I enjoy classes," she explained. "I think I need other people's enthusiasm to motivate me. Plus, well, I was really enjoying kickboxing, and I'd feel silly doing it by myself."

"Have you taken self-defense?"

"Of course I have! And the kickboxing isn't because—" She abandoned a hopeless cause. "I'll check them out."

"You look like a runner."

"I expect I'll do more of that here. In Seattle, you either run on a treadmill, risk life and limb and the longevity of your knees running on sidewalks and cross too many city streets or you drive to a park. I might take up cross-country skiing, too. Since I don't suppose running outside is an option in the winter here."

"Some days." He chuckled. "I run to the top of Angel Butte three or four mornings a week. You're welcome to join me."

She snorted. "Get real."

His laugh deepened. "It's a good workout. Great view when you get to the top. Then the easy part is going home."

They both grabbed second slices of pizza.

She ate a few bites, washed them down with soda, then decided to tell him something that had happened at work.

"I think someone tried to bribe me the other day."

"What?" Noah set down his pizza and turned those startlingly keen blue eyes on her.

"You heard me. It was…oh so smoothly done I'm not positive that's what he was doing, but I think so."

"Good God." He shook his head.

"I take it you didn't, well, suspect things like that were going on with my predecessor?"

He huffed out a breath. "Maybe. I wouldn't be shocked. There was definitely an old boy's club going on in Angel Butte. Rooting out the remnants of it isn't making me real popular."

"You mean with the old boys. There have to be a lot of newcomers who'd be outraged to know if things like that have been the norm."

She found she could interpret his grunts, which expressed anything from indifference to, in this case, "maybe."

"You going to tell me who?" he asked after a minute.

"Phil Barbieri."

"Now that doesn't surprise me."

She knew what he meant. From what she'd heard, Phil was one of the most successful contractors in the county, surpassing even Earl in the number and breadth of projects he had going at a time. Unlike Earl, he went for government contracts as well as residential projects. He looked the part of a long-time member of that old boy's club, too—a hefty, powerful body thickening at the waist, a broad, bluff face, weather-beaten and, she suspected, showing signs of too-frequent alcohol consumption. His complexion was red, his noise showing purplish veins.

"It's the damn septic facility, isn't it?" Noah said in resignation.

"Bingo. Phil does *not* want it placed out on Bond

Road. I gather he has a lot of money already sunk into a projected development there."

"Yeah, Phil has expressed himself to me." One side of Noah's mouth turned up. "Probably a lot more crudely than he did to you."

"He wasn't crude," she conceded. "In fact, he was so delicate, I can't absolutely swear I understood what he was saying. It was something to the effect that the builders liked having a good relationship with the planning department, and they knew how to take care of their friends in government. What's good for me is good for them, and vice versa." She wrinkled her nose. "I think that was the gist of it. *Good* is his favorite word, apparently."

"He didn't say, 'You scratch our backs, we'll scratch yours'?" Noah asked sardonically.

She laughed. "No, no, he was much too subtle for that."

"What are you going to do about it?"

For all his amusement, she didn't kid herself that the question wasn't dead serious.

"Nothing," she told him. "Nothing at all."

After a minute, that too-sexy mouth curved again. "Good."

"Can we label my tactics something else?" she begged. "Smart, maybe?"

Now he did laugh, stretching at the same moment. She heard a few bones crack and saw an impressive flexing of muscles.

"More?" she said hurriedly, poking the pizza box toward him.

"Nah, thanks. I'll leave you some leftovers." He frowned. "Are you serious about heading out this evening?"

"I really need sheets and a towel, if nothing else. I won't worry about groceries until tomorrow. Thank goodness for the weekend."

"Where are you going?"

"Walmart or Target. All I need is one set of everything, plus some basics like a can opener and a coffeemaker. I'll eat out a lot until my stuff shows up."

"All right," he said reluctantly. "I'll follow you over there."

Indignant, she stared at him. "What? No. You're not going shopping with me."

"Wasn't offering. I'll just make sure you're not being followed."

She argued; his face looked like one of the Easter Island statues. Once he made up his mind, he was not a flexible man. *What a surprise,* Cait thought in irritation.

But also, she had to admit as she made the drive in the dark, there was a tiny bit of gratitude mixed in. She had no doubt that if Blake had been lurking down the street and was following her, Noah would have noticed. At least she could feel pretty confident Blake wouldn't appear tonight in the bedding aisle at Target.

Noah, though, scared her a little, with his combination of unexpected charm, sense of humor and outright kindness, all coupled with the personality of a bulldozer. A big one, not one of the wimpy little machines gentlemen farmers bought as toys to push earth around their five acres. Noah was the leveling-forests kind.

So far, she hadn't demonstrated any ability to stand up to men who wanted to push her around. Wrinkling her nose, she thought she'd probably still be okay if she weren't attracted to him.

Unfortunately, that was a big "if." Exasperated with herself, she found a parking spot only steps from the doors leading into Target.

As she locked her car and hurried in, it struck her that she was in trouble in more ways than one.

CHAPTER SIX

NOAH DID HIS damnedest not to think about Cait
over the weekend, and he dodged her for most of
the following workweek. Every time he saw her
coming his way, he summoned his new mantra:
Use Your Head. Usually followed by: For God's
Sake. Add an exclamation point.

There were a lot of reasons why any kind of personal relationship with her wasn't smart, starting
with the fact that, yes, she worked for him. Women
employed at Chandler's were off-limits, too.

It wasn't only that, though. Cait McAllister had
wounds that he could almost see, like the fading
yellow of bruises. She was not up for casual sex,
and that was all that interested him. The emotional
crap wasn't his style, and God knows he had never
imagined a wife and family. He had neither the
experience nor the skill set to make a success of
either. He barely remembered the father who'd appeared and disappeared from his life until that last
fishing trip when Noah was something like eight
or nine. Mom had remarried about then, and his
stepfather had been disgusted with the baggage she

brought. He was never abusive, just tried to pretend Noah didn't exist. Kind of like a man who'd reluctantly allowed the kids to get a dog but didn't want anything to do with it and threw a fit if it tripped him or dug a hole in the lawn. Noah thought he'd been eleven or twelve—huge for his age and, predictably, clumsy—when one day he overheard him and Mom talking in their bedroom, the door not quite closed.

"Your ex must've been an even uglier son of a bitch than he looks in pictures, if the kid is anything to go by."

Noah should have kept going, not waited to hear what his mother replied.

She clicked her tongue in that way she had. "You shouldn't say that, Dennis!"

He remembered relaxing slightly, forming the intention of walking on.

Too late. Because she continued. "It does bother me that he looks so much like his dad, though. I wish he took more after my side of the family. There isn't a single good thing he could have inherited from his father. *Nothing,*" she finished with vehemence, and even hate, which slid between his ribs like a switchblade.

Sometime that night, lying in bed unable to sleep, filled with an adolescent's oversize hurt and anger, was when he formed the intention of finding his father someday.

Over the years, he didn't quite forget how often

his father had disappointed him, but he dwelled more on the few times Dad had taken him to see the Trail Blazers play at the Rose Garden, the summer afternoons getting stuffed on hot dogs while they watched a minor-league baseball team play their hearts out. His father had taken him camping, too. He sent a very occasional child support check for the next few years, the last from Angel Butte. By the time Noah set out on his futile quest to track the man down to an obscure town in central Oregon, he had grown up enough to know better than to expect much. Maybe all he'd wanted was to say, *I needed you. Where were you?*

He still regretted not getting the chance.

Noah knew what he was good for and what he wasn't. He was a ruthless workaholic who didn't have time for a serious relationship, never mind a family even if he'd wanted one. He had enough of a conscience to go out of his way to avoid hurting the women he used for sex.

One who bore her hurt so visibly was off-limits, all other issues aside.

This driving need to protect her—well, she was his, in a sense, just like the town was. That's all it could be.

So he kept his distance when he could.

What he didn't like was knowing she had nobody to follow her when she left work each day. He was aware that she attended a couple of evening meetings that week, too, which meant she'd be driving home alone at night and having to cross her dark yard to the safety of the town house. If it was safe, given that it had no security system and could easily be breached by a man determined to terrorize her—or to claim her, once and for all.

A few times, he found himself driving by her place, just casually glancing to see if her lights were on, not sure what that told him or what he'd do if they weren't.

One night at the library, they sat two chairs away from each other in a brief meeting about the pipeline replacement project. Walking out, he asked if the moving truck had showed up yet.

She shook her head and said in a low voice, "I'm getting by."

He had clenched his teeth on the impulse to ask if she'd had dinner. She'd murmured a vague goodbye, her eyes not quite meeting his, and veered off to talk to someone else.

Good, Noah told himself, but he felt irritated instead of relieved.

The murder of a respectable and longtime local citizen was causing a lot of talk and worry, but the investigation had apparently stalled. Jerry Hegland had often stayed late in his office at the airport. Nobody had seen him leave the night before his body was found. Investigators were confident he'd made it home, though, and eaten a typical bachelor's meal of a couple of microwave-heated burritos and a beer. All that went in the dishwasher was a dirty fork, which meant he'd eaten out of the tray the food came in. One beer can, crushed by hand, reposed in the otherwise empty recycling container. His Jeep was in the garage. It seemed likely his killer had come to his house, but the absence of blood said he wasn't murdered there. Unfortunately, the neighbors either hadn't been home or had pulled the blinds and been engrossed in television shows or their own doings. Nobody saw a thing.

The latest came from Cait's brother, whose path crossed Noah's in front of the courthouse that Friday. Both men hesitated, then met under a cherry tree in full bloom.

"I haven't heard an announcement yet," Noah commented.

"Next week or two." Colin squeezed the back of his neck as if it hurt. "You're following the Hegland murder?"

"Yes." He was getting a little pissed because most of what he knew came via gossip, listening to the police band or overheard conversations rather than directly from his police chief the way he expected.

"Lieutenant Vahalik let me know this morning that it's looking like he's been taking payoffs for years."

Noah muttered an obscenity.

Colin made a noise suggesting agreement. "This thing is spreading far and wide."

"But why would they have knocked him off?"

All he got was a head shake.

"The appointment of his replacement will be mine," Noah said, frowning. "I'll be damn careful. Traffickers have lost the airport."

"Maybe they don't need it anymore. There are half a dozen private runways in the area now."

"You mean he'd become redundant."

Colin lifted a shoulder. "It's possible. If they wanted to cut off payments, and he threatened to talk…"

What else was there to say? Speculation didn't get them anywhere.

"What happened with you and your sister?" Noah asked.

"None of your business." There might be a dark shadow of pain in those gray eyes, but no give in the hard voice.

Noah moved his shoulders in what he meant for a shrug, but it felt more like an attempt to lessen tension. He couldn't claim her family problems *were* his business. Hadn't he been trying to make sure they weren't?

"I take it you haven't located the boyfriend?"

Looking no happier than he felt, McAllister shook his head. "It's been a week and a half now. She might be right that he didn't hang around."

"Do you believe that?"

"Goddamn it, no, I don't!" Her brother glared at Noah. "Tell me what I can do that I'm not."

He felt violent and had to hide it. "You could

have avoided getting into it with Cait, so she doesn't have to go home to an empty house every night."

McAllister closed his eyes. "*Shit*. You think *I* like it?"

"No." Noah didn't have to admit it, but he wasn't being fair. Cait wasn't a pushover. In fact, given her feisty personality, he could see her being at fault.

"I've hung on to the memory of my kid sister," said Colin in a strange voice. "She hit me with how little I really know her." After a brusque nod, he strode away.

As he watched the police captain go, Noah had an uncomfortable realization. He'd taken to thinking of him by his first name. As if... He didn't know. Didn't want to know.

Mumbling under his breath, he went the opposite direction.

THANK GOD THE moving truck was supposed to arrive tomorrow. Of course, the company had first promised to deliver on Saturday. The cause of the delays meaning they wouldn't arrive until Tuesday had been unspecified.

Cait was especially irked because, once again, she'd have to take time off work, but she didn't care. She wanted her television, her big squishy chair, a dresser with real drawers, so she could put her clothes away. Pans, a mixer, cookbooks and her box of recipes. And her books—she missed her books.

She turned into the alley behind the row of town

houses, and her headlights picked out garbage cans behind a lot of the other units. That meant tomorrow morning was pickup. Not really cooking, she hadn't generated that much trash yet, but she had some. She might as well put her brand-new can out.

The garage door rose as she approached and she turned neatly into it, leaving the door open so she could pull the can out.

Not for worlds would she have admitted to anyone—specifically Noah or Colin—that she dreaded that quick dash across the small yard to let herself into the back door when she got in at night like this. But it would be two weeks tomorrow since Blake's last stunt, and she was starting to cautiously believe he really *wasn't* in town.

Even so, after letting herself out into the yard, she peeked cautiously around, then hurried. She should have left a back porch light on. No, better— she'd get a motion-activated floodlight installed, like Colin had over his garage.

The yard wasn't totally dark, because neighbors on each side had outside lights on and second-story windows were lit, too. Even so, she was almost to the back door when she saw that the siding looked funny. Like…something was smeared on it?

Heart pounding, she unlocked and flipped the switch that turned on lights both over this door and on each side of the French doors that led from the dining room onto the deck. They were enough to illuminate the entire tiny enclosed backyard. She was alone out there.

Still cautious—someone could have hoisted himself to watch over the fence—she took only a couple of steps out so she could see.

Words seemed to be scrawled in dark paint all over the lower rear of her town house. They started small at the far corner, getting bigger and bolder as they got closer.

"Sorry Sorry Sorry." Over and over and over.

Dear God.

Gasping, Cait scurried back inside and locked the door, leaning against it until she could catch her breath.

911? Colin?

Noah.

Her hands shook as she pulled her phone from her bag and scrolled for his last call, then pushed Send.

"Please, please, please," she whispered.

"Cait?" he said.

"Blake has been back," she said, and her voice shook, too.

Noah DROVE so quickly he should have gotten a ticket. He'd have been glad to pick up a cop on the way.

"It's not an emergency," she had assured him and then sounded embarrassed. "I shouldn't have called you. I'm sorry. I guess I just need to report this and then..." She'd lapsed into silence.

And then what? he thought savagely as he rocketed around a corner. She'd go to bed and get a good night's rest?

He slammed to a stop in front of her town house, lit from top to bottom, and ran up on the porch. He was reaching for the doorbell when the door opened. Cait had been watching for him.

He hated seeing how finely drawn her features were, how pale her face was. Even so, she gave a brave attempt at a smile.

"I *really* shouldn't have called you. I'm sorry, Noah. I panicked."

He stepped over the threshold, shouldered the door closed and took her in his arms. For a moment she stayed stiff, vibrating like high-tension wires, but then as if someone had pulled the plug on the power, she sagged against him. Her arms came around him, and he felt her grab handfuls of his dress shirt as if afraid he'd push her away.

She wasn't crying, but fine tremors shook her body. In the heels, she was tall enough to bury her face against his neck, where he had unbuttoned his shirt earlier after ripping off the tie the minute he'd walked in the door at home.

"Of course you should have called me," he murmured. He kept on, probably repeating the same thing half a dozen times before progressing to, "I'd have been pissed if you didn't. I'm sorry. Damn it, I'm sorry."

Her shoulders shook, and for a moment he thought she finally had broken down, but then he realized she was laughing.

Whatever had struck her as funny gave her the strength to pull back. Noah reluctantly let her go, realizing the laughter had the shrillness of hysteria.

"What do *you* have to be sorry for?" she asked.

"That we haven't been able to stop this son of a bitch." He frowned, realizing what he was most sorry about. "I don't like you having to come home alone at night," he said more slowly.

"None of it's your fault."

"It's because you're working for me that you have so damn many evening meetings."

"This kind of job always does," Cait pointed out, steadier now. "I considered applying for a couple of jobs in California. Would it be better if this was happening in Santa Rosa or Escondido? Where I don't know *anybody?*"

"You know that's not what I meant. Have you called your brother?"

"Yes. Right after you." She cocked her head. "That's probably him now."

It was. He opened the front door to see Colin moving as fast across the pocket-size front yard as he had earlier. Noah would have sworn McAllister's dark SUV was still rocking.

Her brother's gaze went to her face first, assessing, worried. Then it hardened when he looked at Noah.

"What are you doing here?" he asked, irritation plain.

"I called him," Cait said.

Bristling, he entered the town house. His gaze swept the front room, bare but for the lonely sofa, pausing on the fireplace, moving on to the entirely empty dining area and the French doors covered by drawn vertical blinds.

"All right," he said. "Show me."

She nodded, tension tightening her face again, and led the way to the kitchen and the back door with the glass pane inset.

Colin said what Noah was thinking. "This place would be damn easy to break into."

She rolled her eyes. "It would be so cozy without windows."

Despite the snappy comeback, her hesitation was more obvious than Noah suspected she'd want it to be before she opened the door. She peered outside like a turtle sticking her head out of her shell, then led the way.

Colin had brought an enormous black flashlight, which he switched on to supplement the porch lights. They all stared at the spray-painted writing, which got larger, more ragged, angrier, as it went. The lettering was scrawled across the French doors, windows, kitchen door.

"Sorry Sorry Sorry Sorry."

Colin growled something profane as the beam of his light moved steadily across the back of her rental. It stopped at the end, where "Sorry" changed to "Is that enough?"

Both men looked at her.

Her arms wrapped herself tightly and she pressed her lips together. Nobody moved.

"The last time I saw him," she said in a taut, reluctant voice, "he kept saying he was sorry and he asked how many times he had to say it."

"Sorry for *what?*" her brother asked suspiciously.

She didn't want to tell them; that was obvious. Her gaze darted from Colin's face to Noah's and back again, her eyes widening at the implacable expressions she saw.

"What difference does it make?" she cried.

Noah let Colin handle this. He didn't trust himself to open his mouth.

"Did that piece of shit hurt you?"

Brother and sister stared at each other for a long moment. Then she straightened. "I will not discuss my relationships with you. Or what ended this one. It really doesn't matter. I told him apologies were irrelevant. He's refusing to accept that I'm done with him. I have no idea why he won't let go of the idea that saying 'I'm sorry, I love you, come back to me' is all he has to do."

Noah wanted to get his hands on that scumbag. Ralston might have lost his temper and hurt her; he might have cheated on her. Either way, Noah could understand her not wanting to talk about it. But, by God, he wanted to know which it was.

"All right," Colin said with a sigh. "We'll get pictures in the morning. The usual. I want you to pack a bag and come home with me."

"You don't really think he'll be back tonight."

He frowned. "No, I don't, but I can't be sure. What if he shows up on your doorstep to find out whether you *are* satisfied by his apologies?"

"I won't answer the door. I'll call 911."

A predictable argument ensued. Noah stayed silent, although he'd have been happier if she'd agreed to go home with her brother. He wished he understood whether she was just being stubborn because that was her nature, or whether this had to do with the argument the two of them had had.

Finally Colin snapped, "On your head be it," and stomped back into the house. The front door closed a moment later.

"Let's go back in," Noah said, gripping her arm above the elbow.

He locked the door, thinking how useless it was to install a dead bolt when all a would-be intruder had to do was tap the glass to break it, then reach in. Still, the glass breaking would give Cait some warning.

He started opening cupboard doors. "Do you have tea? Something warm and sweet would be good."

Her eyes were a little glassy. "Oh. Yes. To the left of the refrigerator."

At least she *had* done some serious grocery shopping. He put water on to boil in the one and only saucepan she had, then chose a decaf orange-spice tea. She had only one mug, too, which meant he was probably the only visitor she'd entertained here yet.

"If you want something—" she began.

He shook his head and found a ten-pound bag of sugar in another cabinet beside bags of white flour, whole wheat flour, rolled oats and other staples. Tearing open the sugar, he put two spoonfuls into the mug.

She still stood in the middle of the kitchen, her arms wrapped around herself. It was all he could do to lean a hip against the counter and keep his distance.

"Why don't you pull up a stool?" he suggested as gently as his rough voice allowed.

Cait nodded with unexpected docility and obeyed. He was able to pour boiling water into her mug and carry it over to her, staying on the kitchen side of the breakfast bar.

"You want to talk about this?" he asked.

Her eyes met his, then shied away. She shook her head.

"What do you think he'll do next?"

She used the spoon he'd left in the mug to stir, her head bent. "I don't know."

"You have any reason to think he's done this kind

of thing before with other women?" Noah asked. Surely Colin had looked for a police record.

"I… If he has, I didn't know. Neither of us were seeing anyone else when we met. At the time, he seemed smart, funny, kind of intense but in a flattering way." She stole a look up at him. "How could I have had a clue?"

Noah shook his head. "You couldn't," he said flatly. "Short of doing a background investigation on every guy you date."

"And even then…"

"He may never have been this obsessed before."

She screwed her face up in an unhappy expression. "Wow. I hope that's not true. I don't want to think there's something about me—"

"Don't be ridiculous." He found he was scowling. "This isn't your fault in any way, shape or form. Got it?"

Her lips quivered into a near smile. "Understood, sir."

Okay, Mr. Sensitive he wasn't.

"Here." He pulled the plastic trash container out from beneath the sink. "Let me have that tea bag."

She squished it with the spoon and deposited it in the container, watching as he put it away again. "It was nice of you to come, Noah, but I'm okay now."

"Trying to chase me out?"

"As soon as I finish this—" she lifted the mug "—I need to shower and get to bed."

His entire being revolted at the idea of saying

good-night and leaving her there alone, but he really didn't see the scumbag making another appearance tonight. And anyway—what was he doing there?

Say it again. I am not her boyfriend. I'm not even a friend. There was a whole lot of awkwardness attendant on him doing something as stupid as offering to spend the night on her sofa.

"All right," he said with deep reluctance. "You'll keep your phone close." It wasn't a question.

"Of course I will." She finally took a sip of the tea and grimaced. "How much sugar did you put in here?"

"Drink it. You've got to be in mild shock."

She heaved a sigh and slipped off the stool. "I'll walk you to the front door."

What could he do but let her escort him out? He told her to call him if anything happened, said good-night, then hovered on the porch until he heard the dead bolt strike home.

Then, every bit as unhappy as her brother had been, Noah left, knowing damn well Cait was unlikely to get any sleep at all.

CAIT CAREFULLY SET the iced tea and sandwich on the table in Subway and let her heavy bag slide from her shoulder onto the seat beside her. She had maybe ten minutes to eat, which meant gobbling. Sitting so she faced the back wall was her best tactic for going unrecognized, so she might actually *have* a chance to gobble without interruption.

"Mind if I join you?" said a cool voice.

Oh, God. Nell.

In the act of unwrapping her sandwich, Cait looked up. "Of course not, but I have to tell you, I'm in a huge hurry."

"That's okay, I don't plan to eat." Her sister-in-law slid into the booth across from her.

"How did you find me?"

"I just finished grocery shopping at Safeway and saw your car when I was leaving."

Cait swallowed. Funny, she'd believed herself more anonymous here than she'd have been in a deli near city hall. "I'm assuming you want to chew me out."

A girl-next-door face like Nell McAllister's—freckles across a small nose, pointy chin, childishly high forehead—shouldn't be able to project icy disdain. Maybe she'd been taking lessons from Colin.

"Tell me you don't really think Colin would have killed some guy in cold blood because he dared to screw around with your mother twenty years ago."

"I told him I was sorry, that I didn't mean what… what I guess it sounded like."

"*Sounded* like?" Nell echoed, her incredulity plain. "I saw your expression. I heard you. You devastated him."

Cait bent her head. She was having weird symptoms, her body flashing hot one second and cold the next. "It was…it was only for a minute. You weren't there—"

"I was!"

"I mean back when I was a kid." She made herself look at Nell. "He was already taller than our dad. And so filled with hate. He was scary. You don't know what it was like."

"What I know is that he was trying to draw your father's fists so he didn't use them on you or your mom."

Heat blossomed on her cheeks. "I do know that," she said in a small, tight voice.

"Because he loved you."

"I know that, too."

"He built that apartment above the garage for you. That's the only reason. In case you ever needed him. Until me, he said you were his only family. Having you come home was this huge gift to Colin, and now it's like it's blown up in his hands." Nell slid out from behind the table and stood. "You are so wrong. In hurting him this way, you've lost something precious." She shook her head as she looked down at Cait. Then she walked out.

With her back turned, Cait couldn't watch her go. She sat, not moving, feeling sick. She couldn't eat now.

After a minute, she wrapped up the sandwich, a drippy thing she didn't dare stow in her messenger bag. When she felt confident she could stand, she dropped drink and all in a trash can and went straight to her car, parked only a few slots from the door.

Having you come home was this huge gift to Colin.

She'd known that. She'd known for a long time how hungry he was to reclaim her as his sister. His family. And as long as she'd known, she had resisted, as if…

That was the part she didn't know. The only two people she'd ever really trusted were her mother and Colin. Even though what Mom had done with Jerry had nothing to do with Cait, it still had felt like a huge betrayal. *My mother had an affair.* In Cait's youthful world, her father had been the monster, her mother the…the good queen who had saved the princess by taking her away even though Mom didn't have the skills to make an adequate living at first. Cait hadn't told Colin that she and Mom lived in shelters off and on that first year. The battered wife who had fled with her young daughter. After finding out what else there was to the story, Cait wondered if she'd been a prop. She did know that Mom never mentioned the son she'd left behind to counselors or welfare workers. She also never said, *I was having an affair and that might be what enraged my husband.*

And maybe that wasn't true at all. Cait's father might never have known about Jerry Hegland, or other men if there were any. But…he might have, too.

Cait *didn't* think Colin would have killed Jerry. Why would he have? It all happened so many years ago. He'd been mad when she'd told him, but probably only because she'd turned a part of his history inside out and it felt as if it were happening *now* to him, just as it had for her when she had found out. All she had to do was remember the way she'd gone off like a rocket, screaming at her mother the minute she'd walked in the door. *And* clung to her disillusionment all these years, as if…it was a form of protection?

She shied away from the thought, which didn't really make sense anyway. And, gee, what great timing to be psychoanalyzing herself. She'd already been in a hurry to get back to the office. Sitting there brooding was accomplishing exactly nothing.

Her hands mostly steady, Cait finally started her car, put it in gear and looked over her shoulder for the next opening in traffic.

CHAPTER SEVEN

CALL HER OLD-FASHIONED, but Cait liked maps. Real ones printed in color on paper. Laminated was okay. She even liked folding and unfolding them. She'd left the one of Angel Butte and environs spread out on her passenger seat even though once she'd scanned it she knew where she was going.

She had yet to find a map updated since the annexation. Bond Road, the object of so much interest recently, meandered out of town, following Allen Creek and ending at a small lake. Most of the length of it would have been outside the city limits two years ago. She was surprised at how completely she'd left town. The road traversed stretches of the dry forest typical of the area interspersed with a few small ranches. A faded sign in front of one advertised trail rides with horses to suit all ability levels.

Cait speculated on why the line had been drawn to encompass an area with so little growth. Had Phil and other developers already owned land out here and wanted to latch on to city services? It might be interesting to find out whether the two developers who sat on the council also contemplated projects west of town.

She had decided to take an hour or so to check out both the site being considered for a septic treatment plant and the acreage Phil owned. Having already stopped and looked at the uninteresting plat that was Noah's current favorite for the city-owned facility, she was now keeping her eye on the rolling mileage counter on her dashboard, unsure whether Phil had marked his acreage. Of course, he'd have been glad to give her a tour if she'd asked, but a little of Phil Barbieri went a long way.

Cait had passed only a couple of cars going toward town, and they looked like they belonged to visitors. Maybe there was a campground or rustic resort on tiny Lupine Lake, where Bond Road ended.

Once she reached the mileage marker she'd been told to watch for, Cait slowed. Supposedly an access road had been bulldozed in for a quarter of a mile or so. Spotting it almost right away, she glanced in her rearview mirror and saw an SUV or pickup closing in on her. She promptly put on her turn signal and eyed the dirt track, which plunged at a steep decline for the first fifty feet or so. Her small hatchback did *not* have four-wheel drive. At best, this little outing would result in a detour through the car wash.

Resigned, she turned anyway, aware of the SUV starting to pass. She forgot it when she heard a popping sound and the steering wheel spun out of her control for a frightening instant. Grimly, she grabbed it and hung on. Flat tire. She knew that feeling. Thank God she'd already slowed down, she thought, pulse racing, still battling for control on the sharp hill with only loose dirt for traction.

When the ground leveled out again, she was able to brake to a stop. Shaken, she didn't move for a minute.

Well. She had a jack and a spare tire, albeit one of those shrimpy ones that looked like they'd been made for a motorcycle. Or—better option—she'd call for a tow truck. Given that she'd worn a favorite linen suit, she thought it would be worth paying someone else to change the blasted tire.

Decision made, she grabbed her phone, then got out to see which tire had gone. To her surprise, she caught a glimpse of the silver SUV backing up. The driver must have seen what happened and was being nice enough to stop. Maybe some chivalrous guy would offer to change the tire for the helpless little lady and save her a boring wait *and* some bucks.

On the other hand… It occurred to her how very alone she was out there. That silver color was really common for rentals. If the driver had hung back, he could have been following her without her noticing. This scenario was made to order for someone like, say, Blake. *He* could be chivalrous and say things like, *A woman alone can get in trouble, you know,* and she'd have to be nice as if she were glad to see him.

Driving out here all by herself might have been a dumb thing to do.

No. She had to do her job.

The vehicle didn't pull into the access road. Instead, it hovered, blocking the turnoff. Uncertainly she stood there beside her open car door, noticing the passenger-side window of the SUV was down even though no one sat in that seat. With the sun bright behind the strange vehicle, she couldn't make out the driver. Was he going to get out? The silence was absolute but for the sound of the idling engine. She was weirdly aware of everything: the sharp scent of volcanic dirt and ponderosa pine, her skin, the rasp of every breath, her own heartbeat, the smooth texture of the phone she clutched.

And then there was movement and she thought, oh, he's leaning down to say something, only what she saw made her think—

Pop. Cait dropped to her hands and knees as the window inches above her exploded into shards. *Pop.* She scrambled behind the door then around to the front of the small car. *Pop.* Her Mazda shuddered. She turned her head frantically. All he had to do was get out and walk down there. Could she make it to the closest trees? But the trunks were scrawny, and there was virtually no undergrowth to hide behind.

911. Call 911. But when she tried to dial, her hand

shook so badly she dropped the phone. It landed in a small puff of dust below the bumper. She scrabbled for it even as she strained her ears for the sound of a door opening or closing. Or, please God, another approaching vehicle.

Nothing. She felt like an animal hiding from a predator but knowing it was helpless. A weapon. She had the spray in her purse—but her purse was in the car. She desperately wanted to poke her head out and *look*.

Suddenly she heard the engine rev, and she worked up the courage to creep toward the far side of her car and peek. The SUV was swinging in a sharp U-turn and accelerating. Disappearing from her sight.

A dry sob escaped her before she could muffle it with her hand. What if there'd been *two* people in that SUV, and one of them had slipped out to hunt her?

No, that didn't make any sense. It had to be Blake, didn't it? Only…he'd never had a gun that she knew of. They'd talked about things like that. He'd been a big believer in tighter gun control.

That's when she heard the engine again. *Oh, God, oh, God, he's coming back.* She pulled herself to a crouching position and prepared to dash for the trees. But the vehicle she saw wasn't silver; it was black, and it was way bigger than the SUV she'd recognized as a crossover.

This one was slowing as if to stop, too, but instead it turned in and she saw the familiar insignia and front grill. Chevy Suburban.

Noah. Could it be?

Cait dropped to her knees, then to her butt. She leaned against the bumper, afraid she'd topple over without its support.

The engine was turned off; a door opened and then slammed.

"Cait?" he bellowed. "Cait!"

"I'm here," she called, then realized how whispery and tremulous her voice was. "I'm here," she repeated louder.

In seconds, he rounded her car, the fear on his roughcast face enough to turn her to jelly.

"Oh, damn." He crouched in front of her. "You're hurt."

She shook her head and tried to smile, although her eyes were filling with tears. "No. Just, um…" She fingered tattered tights. "I think my suit is toast."

He swore and fell to his knees, wrapping his arms around her as if he had to feel her against him to know she was all right. Cait seized on to him with more strength than she'd known she had. Nothing had ever sounded better than the slam of his heart beneath her ear.

NOAH DIDN'T THINK he'd ever been as scared in his life as when he had seen the bullet hole through the rear window of Cait's little Mazda—and then realized that the glass was missing altogether on the driver's-side window. There was the door, just standing open, and no sign of her. It had looked like a classic abduction scene. All he could think was, *That bastard has her.* His knees had about buckled when he'd heard her voice.

Noah and Cait held each other for a long time, him kneeling in the dirt, his cheek against her hair. He'd been scared badly enough that it was a while before he started noticing that her breasts were pressed against his belly and that her hair smelled really good.

It was probably just as well that her grip loosened about then and she finally eased back. He kept his hands on her upper arms.

"What happened?" he demanded.

She sniffed and swiped at her cheeks and then her nose. For someone with her air of class, the gesture was unexpectedly childish. If terror hadn't still been electrifying his body, it might have made him smile.

"Somebody shot at me."

"I figured that out."

She frowned at him. "How?"

"There's a bullet hole through the back window of your car." He lifted his head. "Out through the front."

She followed his gaze and blanched. "Oh. I guess I should call 911."

"You haven't?" He swore and reached for his phone at his belt.

"I didn't exactly have time." She looked and sounded affronted.

Noah held up a finger. Once he had the promise of units on the way, he glanced around. Here the two of them were, out in the open. "Is he gone?"

"Yes. I think he must have seen you coming."

"Shit," he growled. "An SUV went flying by."

"Silver?"

"That was it. Oh, hell. I didn't pay any attention except to think he was driving too fast."

"He?"

Noah shook his head. "No idea. I made an assumption."

She told him what happened, not all in sequence, but he could see why.

"Your tire was shot out," he realized, and she bit her lip and nodded.

"I didn't know. I heard a sort of pop, but I thought I just had a flat, like maybe I'd hit a rock and the tire had split open or something. Do they do that anymore?" she asked as if it mattered. She didn't wait for an answer. "I wasn't going very fast because I'd already turned in here, but the drop is really steep." She gulped. "It was hard to keep the car on the road."

That tightened the tangle in his chest some more. "We'd better call your brother," he said.

"Yes." She sank back until she was leaning against the bumper again. "My phone."

They discovered she was almost sitting on it. Noah rose to his feet while she dialed. She'd worn that sunny yellow suit today, the one that had inspired such an idiotic and uncharacteristic flight of fancy in him, and she was right—it was ruined. The sight of her sitting there in the dirt, her palms skinned and her face filthy and her mascara smudged, looking defeated as he'd never seen her, filled him with an unfamiliar fury he had no way to vent. He listened with half an ear to the brief conversation, his gaze moving over the car, noting the crumbled glass beneath the open door.

If he hadn't decided to follow her out there...

She'd be dead.

The knowledge slammed into him, a kick to the chest that felt as if *he'd* been shot.

Not a single other vehicle had passed since he had pulled in. Her assailant—*why not name him, Blake Ralston*—would have had all the time in the world to finish her off.

When she started to struggle to her feet, he reached down to help her. She wasn't wearing heels, he saw; she had changed to athletic shoes before she'd headed out on this expedition. The rusty red dirt coated the gray-and-white leather and mesh.

"It's lucky you weren't wearing heels," he said hoarsely.

She looked at her feet as if she hadn't noticed,

but then she shook her head. "It wouldn't have mattered. I was already out of the car when—um, when I think I saw the gun. I just…fell. And then I crawled."

Churning with emotions he had no ability to decipher, Noah couldn't help himself. He yanked her back into his arms, with no consideration for her fragile state. If she noticed, she didn't protest. She leaned into him as if she belonged right there, resting against him. Was that a very distant siren? He didn't care.

"Cait," he said hoarsely.

She looked up, her eyes dark, and the power of all that rage, helplessness and tenderness overcame him.

He kissed her.

Not as gently as he should have. He nipped at her lips, rocked his until she opened her mouth and let him in. And then his tongue drove in, as if, God help him, he was claiming her.

She didn't sag in his arms; she hugged him hard and responded with a ferocity to equal his. The kiss got deep and slick and hot. One of his hands closed over her ass and lifted her. She helped by rising on tiptoe and trying to climb him. He'd have laid her back on the hood of that car and hiked her skirt if…

His long-lost sense of self-preservation awoke with a jolt. The siren was screaming now. A blue-and-white police unit screeched to a stop at the head of the access road. His large SUV blocked some of the responding officers' view, thank the Lord, but he needed to unpeel her body from his *now.*

No matter how fiercely his body protested the loss.

He untangled his fingers from her short hair. "Cait," he said in not much better than a growl.

She stared at him without comprehension.

"The cops are here."

Her eyes widened. "Oh, my God," she exclaimed in a tone of sheer horror that pissed him off. She tried to leap back, colliding with the bumper of her car. He grabbed her arm. Staggering, she righted herself with his help, then retreated again so that several feet separated them. "Colin?" she asked.

"Uh…" He looked past her. "I don't think so. Not yet." Yeah, that wouldn't have been so good.

Not five minutes later, her brother's 4Runner barreled to a stop on the verge of the road, and he strode down to join them, his gaze pinned on his sister.

Who now stood a safe distance from Noah, hugging herself in the way she did when she was upset and feeling vulnerable. Although Noah suspected she wouldn't like knowing how much she was giving away. She had recited her story again, in better order this time, and was now trying to answer questions.

The two young officers turned, their expressions

pathetically grateful when they saw the new arrival. "Captain."

He spared them a fleeting glance, nodded, then let his gaze pass coldly over Noah before returning his attention to Cait.

"You're all right."

She bit her lip and nodded. "A few scrapes and bruises. The worst damage is to my wardrobe."

Something dark rose in his eyes that Noah recognized and felt. Colin stood in front of her, his hands lifting and then falling back to his sides as if he believed an embrace would be unwelcome.

But tears welled in her eyes and she stepped forward, just for an instant leaning her forehead against his shoulder. His arms closed around her, and Noah had to turn away, not sure what he felt but not liking it.

This tumult couldn't be jealousy. Why would it be? This was her brother. He should be—was—glad that she was letting herself need him.

Noah had already held her. Stupidly, suicidally close. If he had half a brain, this was a good time for him to say, *I'll leave you in your brother's hands,* and depart.

Anguish coalesced in his chest. No way in hell was he going anywhere without her. Even if the actual intention had formed, he wouldn't have been able to act on it when he saw her straighten and turn her head quickly until her gaze latched on to his, as if she needed to know he was there. Noah had no idea what his face showed her, but she relaxed as if it was what she was looking for.

I am in deep shit, he thought, and he couldn't seem to do a damn thing to get himself out of it.

Her brother joined the grilling, but Cait kept shaking her head. She didn't even know how she'd seen the weapon. She wasn't positive she *had.* Something in her subconscious had triggered the leap of panic; that's all she knew. But she was sure she hadn't seen her assailant's face. Or even enough of the set of his shoulders or his hand or silhouette to recognize her ex-boyfriend.

"I don't know," she said doubtfully, and about the third time she repeated the same thing Noah began to get a bad feeling about it.

She'd been with this guy for a couple of years. Noah wasn't clear on how long she'd actually lived with him, but long enough. Someone she'd been that intimate with, she would know on a different level than she would anyone else. The very fact that she was having trouble fitting him into the frame where they all thought he belonged triggered alarms.

Why would anyone else have come after her?

She was a woman alone out there. An attempted rape or robbery might have made sense. But this guy—or conceivably even woman, he supposed—hadn't even stepped out of the vehicle. It had essentially been an assassination attempt by someone who didn't want to take a chance of being recognized if he failed.

No, damn it! Who else could it be but Ralston? *He* made sense.

Noah scrubbed a hand over his face, struggling for the self-control that rarely failed him.

"Let me drive you home," he heard her brother say.

At that, Noah stepped forward. "Why don't you let me do that. You'll want to stay while your people investigate."

McAllister's internal battle was obvious, but finally he gave a short, unhappy nod. "That might be better. Cait—"

"No, that's fine." She summoned a smile for him. "Thank you for coming running." Her voice wavered. "You always have when I needed you."

Her brother's face softened. With one arm, he caught her close again for a quick hug. "You're my sister," he murmured.

She nodded, bumping his chin.

When the two of them separated, Noah asked if there was anything she needed out of the car. Colin gave permission for her to take that huge bag she carried around, a cross between a purse and a briefcase, Noah guessed. She grabbed her yellow high heels, too, from the floor behind the seats.

"You will find the bullets?" Noah asked Colin, who gave him a sardonic look.

"You think I have no idea what I'm doing? And I wondered why you blocked my hiring."

Damn. Noah checked to be sure neither of the two young officers had heard the exchange.

"That's not what I meant."

Colin turned away without a word and strode over to talk to one of the two young officers. Noah realized Cait had heard the exchange and was looking after her brother anxiously.

Making Noah the bad guy.

To hell with it. Without asking for permission, he lifted the bag away from her and slung it over his own shoulder, then took hold of her elbow to support her as they hiked up the incline to his Suburban. It stood unlocked. After opening the passenger door, he put his hands around her waist and lifted as she scrambled up. Normally she'd probably have kicked him for the unwanted help, but today she gave him a shaky smile of thanks that made him wonder if he'd misinterpreted that last expression.

God.

He was the one shaken to his foundation. *If I hadn't followed her.* It ran on a loop. *She'd be dead.*

She'd told a couple of people of her intention to drive out there, but the afternoon had been far enough advanced no one expected her back at the office. Living alone as she was insisting on doing, there wouldn't have been anyone to miss her when she didn't show up. What little passing traffic there was out there, what were the odds anyone would have glanced down and wondered about the small car seemingly abandoned on the dirt road? Reality: she wouldn't have been missed until midmorning tomorrow at the soonest.

If one of those first shots had hit her, he couldn't help thinking, her body might have been lying in plain sight. Then a passing motorist *would* have noticed.

That image made him so sick, angry and frustrated, he ground his teeth together and took a minute to get a grip before he opened his door, deposited her bag behind the seat and got in. Even then, he couldn't look at her.

She squeezed her hands together on her lap and didn't say anything as he backed out, raising a cloud of red dust. During the short drive to town, Cait mostly had her head turned so she could look out the side window.

He went straight to her town house even though he hoped she'd see sense now and move back in with her brother. He parked in front and opened his door.

"You don't have to come in," she began.

She thought he'd drop her off at the curb and drive away. *Nice.*

Once again, he grabbed her bag and circled to her side. She'd already opened the door but was bending to pick up the heels from the floor. The ones that went with the ruined suit. The reminder darkened his already roiling mood.

Still, his hands were gentle as he helped her down. When he saw a wince, he said, "You're going to have bruises."

She made a face, her eyes not quite meeting his. "I guess so. My knees don't feel so good. And my hands sting."

Noah frowned. "Maybe we should have gone by the E.R."

"Don't be silly. I need a hot shower and a couple of ice packs. Or maybe I'll go straight for the wine."

He was probably supposed to laugh. His sense of humor was MIA.

He kept his hand cupped under her elbow as they made their slow way to the front door. After rooting in the gigantic bag, which he swore weighed twenty-five pounds, she produced keys and unlocked the door.

He stepped in first and was met with silence. And furniture. By God, the moving truck had come and gone. She now had a simple entertainment center with flat-screen TV and modest stereo system, a coffee table and a big upholstered rocker with a flowery print in her favorite yellows and pinks. Dining room table and chairs.

"I'll walk through," he said.

She bit her lip and nodded.

The tour didn't take long. Nothing had been smashed or slashed. Upstairs the smaller room now had a desk with a printer, presumably for her laptop, a pair of tall bookcases and a pile of unpacked boxes. Two cherrywood dressers had been added to the bedroom along with a free-standing full-length mirror. He even glanced in the bathroom, although he was sorry right away. He felt about a woman's clutter the way a man from another century might have about the sight of a woman letting down her hair. It was too personal.

Sexual.

He backed out quickly and returned downstairs to find she had waited barely inside the door. She was once again wringing her hands together. She took in his face and then looked away. She hadn't wanted to meet his eyes since that kiss, Noah belatedly realized.

He had blown it.

"All clear," he reported. "I even glanced outside in back. Not so much as a note."

"Oh, okay. Time for that shower, then." She pinned on a smile. "Thank you. I mean it."

He nodded. "I'll stay at least until you're out of the shower." Kill him though it might, hearing the water run and knowing she was standing under it naked. Tipping her head back, maybe, eyes closed, letting that water stream over her breasts and belly and down her thighs.

He could see that he'd alarmed her. Because of the offer, or because he'd given away thoughts that were dangerously carnal?

"Oh, you don't need—"

"I do," he said grimly. "With the shower running, you wouldn't hear someone kicking in your door."

Her face got pinched. Finally she gave a small nod. "All right. Thank you. If you want to grab a beer or anything—"

"Go." That probably sounded grim, too. He wanted to grab her again, go sit on the sofa with her on his lap and just hold her.

Or maybe more.

Cait nodded again, backing away until she bumped into the wall beside the stairs. Then she fled, leaving those sexy high heels sitting on a dainty table to the right of the front door.

Noah waited until he heard her bedroom door shut. Then he groaned, turned and flattened his hands on the wall.

He did not understand why he was giving in to this inexplicable need to take care of Cait McAllister. Who *had* family. Who didn't need him, even though sometimes she looked at him as if she did.

Time to back off, he told himself. Before it was too late.

CHAPTER EIGHT

"A REFILL?" LIKE a polite waitress, Nell lifted the coffee carafe.

"Thank you, no." Even the toasted bagel Cait had eaten for breakfast wasn't sitting well in her stomach. This freezing civility with her sister-in-law was all she needed. Cait would have been mad, except she was to blame. Of course.

What choice had she had but to move back in with Colin?

The plan was for her to move temporarily into the apartment above his garage, but last night she'd slept in the guest room again.

He appeared now through the kitchen, still adjusting the knot of his tie. Nell's face softened when she saw him, and his smile for her was tender and something more that filled Cait with...oh, not envy, she *wanted* him to be happy, but a sense of her own loneliness, she supposed.

He kissed his wife, then glanced at Cait, expression guarded as it always was these days. "You about ready to go?"

Her poor car, fenders barely smoothed out, now

needed three windows replaced. "I'm sorry you're stuck driving me," she said.

Her brother's jaw squared. "I don't mind."

Of course. She forced a smile. "Give me a second. Nell, thanks for breakfast."

"You're welcome."

She heard low voices while she hurried to the guest room to slip on her jacket and shoes. She had that shame-filled feeling they were talking about her, but she knew how self-centered that was.

She tried to hurry but was moving stiffly this morning. Her knees sported big purple bruises and her legs didn't want to swing with their usual ease. Her palms were scraped, and she had ruined her fingernails scrabbling in the dirt. She'd chosen trousers rather than a skirt, but there wasn't much she could do to hide her hands beyond discreetly tucking them out of sight as much as possible.

"Have a good day," Nell said as Colin and Cait went out the door. He wore a sappy smile until he saw Cait looking at him; then he wiped it out of existence.

And *that* made her feel crummy.

He backed out of the garage before she got into his SUV. At the end of the driveway, Colin had to wait for a couple of oncoming cars.

"I lived alone for a lot of years," he said suddenly.

"What?" She turned her head.

He frowned. "Having somebody kiss me goodbye and be happy to see me when I get home, that means something."

She got a lump in her throat. "I understand. You're...lucky. Nell's great."

She felt his scrutiny, but now she couldn't look at him. He nodded. They drove a distance in silence before Cait spoke.

"I can tell Nell really loves you. She, um, gave me hell for hurting you."

Her brother slanted a glance at her. "Did she?"

"She didn't tell you?"

"No."

"I was having lunch at the Subway right by the Safeway store. Evidently, she saw my car. She marched in, reamed me and marched out." Now Cait was smiling.

Colin chuckled but then returned to brooding silence. Not until he pulled into an unload zone in front of city hall did he say, "Cait..."

She unfastened the seat belt and leaned over to kiss his angular cheek. "No. This is my fault. I hope—" her breath hitched "—that I can earn your trust again. Nell's, too." She fumbled for the door handle and got it opened. "Thanks for the lift. I'll call you later."

She got out without looking to see how he responded. He was driving away before she entered the building.

As Cait stepped off the elevator on her floor, she saw Noah standing in the hall, carrying on a conversation with someone from the city clerk's office, which happened to be right across from Planning. A couple of inches over six feet and even broader in the shoulders than her brother, Noah stood out amid the morning bustle. But she knew her instant awareness of him had nothing to do with his size. There was the kiss, which seemed to be haunting her. But even aside from that, it was just him; those laser-sharp blue eyes, rumpled dark hair, the quick way he had of turning his head to home in on her. Yes, even the sense that he looked wrong in the handsome charcoal suit, white shirt and red tie.

She wondered suddenly if he'd ruined his suit pants yesterday when he'd knelt in the dirt to hold her.

Even as he seemed to make a couple of points, nod and listen, he watched her approach. And, gee, what a surprise, he managed to wind up that discussion at precisely the moment she came abreast of him.

"Cait."

"Good morning, Noah." She turned into the outer office, said hello to several people and resigned herself to the fact that he was right behind her when she went into her own office. "Did you want something?" she asked politely as she lowered her messenger bag to the floor behind the desk and pulled out her chair.

He shoved his hands in his pants pockets. "How are you?"

Terrified, what did he think? But she was astonished at how many other answers she could have given him.

She was childishly resentful because the independence she was trying so hard to claim was being stolen from her. Miserable because maybe things going wrong with Blake *had* been her fault. Look how she'd screwed up her relationship with Colin. And scared in a different way because she wanted Noah to put his arms around her again. She wanted to lean on him. She wanted to go home with him instead of her brother. She wanted him to kiss her again.

"Surviving," she said. "A little stiff today."

His eyes narrowed slightly, if anything intensifying the keen way he assessed her. "You stayed at your brother's last night."

"Yes." She planted her fists on her hips. "You thought I was dumb enough to say no?"

"*Dumb* isn't the word I would have used."

"What is?" She still sounded almost polite. "Suicidal?"

"*Bullheaded* crossed my mind."

A sound escaped her lips she didn't think she'd ever heard before. Had she *growled?*

Noah's eyebrows climbed. "What? You're the woman who insisted on staying alone in her house after a maniac spray-painted messages all over the outside!" His voice had climbed, too.

Get a grip.

"You've uplifted my morning enough, thank you. If you're not here to discuss city business, can we end this conversation?"

"Yeah. We can do that." Now he was gruff, his face impassive. "Don't go out by yourself. That's an order."

"And here I'd planned a hike in the woods all by myself on my lunch hour."

His last look at her smoldered.

Left alone, she sank into her chair. Oh, God, why was she antagonizing the man who came to her rescue every time she needed him?

Because that *scares me.*

When had she turned into this pathetic creature who stumbled from one domineering man to another?

Fortunately, her day didn't require any field trips. She concentrated on educating herself, studying tax records for a better understanding of how particular neighborhoods compared, how mixed-use the new development had been. Scrutinizing the building permits that had been issued in the past year, she found herself acquiring new sympathy for Michael Kalitovic's point of view. No house she would call even remotely affordable was being built. Supposedly, central Oregon was appealing to new retirees who could take advantage of the natural beauty and abundant recreational opportunities while living more affordably than they could in the Portland area, say. If so, they wouldn't be buying in Angel

Butte. Most of the developments were aimed at people with real money or were intended to be vacation homes—again, for the wealthy who might spend only a few weeks or months there a year, for the skiing or fishing. Cait imagined Angel Butte as a giant ghost town for much of the year, with hundreds of huge empty houses while the people who clerked at Walmart and Safeway, cleaned the rooms at the increasing number of resorts, waitressed at Chandler's Brew Pub, all had to commute from... who knew, La Pine or farther.

Of course she was getting carried away and knew it. The already existing homes in the older parts of town tended to be modest. Heaven knew the three-bedroom, one-bath rambler she and Colin had grown up in was.

She had so far been very careful not to turn down that street even when she was in the neighborhood. She'd have to ask Colin if he ever drove by out of curiosity.

Cait grimaced. Okay, maybe not such a good idea. Raising the subject of those tumultuous years wouldn't exactly help smooth their existing relationship.

She ordered lunch in, relieved when Noah didn't appear, although she hadn't really expected him to. He'd looked pretty mad when he'd left that morning. Besides, there had to already be talk about the two of them. He'd spent more time with her than was wise. Plus, once yesterday's police reports became common knowledge, city hall workers might speculate as to why he had followed her out to Bond Road.

Come to think of it, she hadn't thought to ask why he had.

Did it matter? He'd been there when she'd needed him. He had been exactly what she needed.

Yes, I am officially pathetic, she decided.

At four-thirty, she dutifully placed a call to Colin and learned her poor car had now been towed to an auto body shop. It would be ready as soon as tomorrow afternoon. Aside from the windows, the only damage had been to the wheel, bent after the tire blew. She and Colin agreed on a time for him to pick her up.

Cait was aware of a sickening wash of fear when she realized it didn't really matter whether she had her car back or not. She wouldn't dare drive unless Colin was right behind her in his SUV.

But sooner or later, they'd find Blake. How good could he be at hiding? He was a water systems engineer, for Pete's sake, a regular guy, except for his weird obsession for her. Once he was arrested, she'd have her life back. She could declare her independence again.

But, remembering the terrifying moments of crawling behind her car, imagining the gunman walking down the hill toward her, knowing there was nowhere she could run to, Cait had a feeling real confidence was going to be slow returning.

NOAH TRIED NOT to look at Cait when he didn't have to. He hated seeing the strain on her face, those lines of tension growing more visible as days passed.

Finding the goddamn bullets had turned out to be the proverbial hunt through the haystack. Cait remembered four being fired. One had ripped through her left rear tire. One went straight through her car, leaving those two ugly holes. A third dissolved the glass in the driver's-side door. The fourth had either also gone through that window or missed entirely. Colin had people out combing the woods with, by day four, no success.

Blake Ralston had called the firm he worked for to extend his vacation. If he was staying at any hotel or resort in the surrounding three counties, it wasn't under his own name. He hadn't used a credit or debit card—but he hadn't needed to, the detective heading the hunt for him had determined. He'd taken three thousand dollars out of a savings account the day before he'd begun his "vacation."

During one of Noah's brief encounters with Cait, he had asked where she was staying. Still in her brother's guest room, she'd said. Colin hadn't been comfortable with her moving alone into the garage apartment. He'd rather have her closer.

She was fine, she said, but it didn't take any great insight to see that she wasn't.

Noah kept his distance anyway. If he didn't, he'd find himself somewhere he'd never intended to go.

Cait McAllister, astonishingly strong, stubborn, scared, fragile and lonely all at the same time, was even more dangerous to him than he'd understood when he'd hired her. He already felt too much.

It would go away, he told himself when he saw her down the hall or across a conference room table. It had to.

He'd been getting a hell of a lot done on his house. Visiting his restaurants, harassing managers or poring over business financials after a day spent doing the same over city income and output didn't work as an outlet for his raging physical restlessness. Steaming wallpaper off walls worked; stripping varnish from woodwork was better. Ripping out a wall was best of all. But none of it helped him sleep.

Noah was not amused to realize he was as obsessed with Cait as that son of a bitch Blake Ralston was. So what did that make him?

He knew her brother had escorted her to the one evening meeting she hadn't been able to skip out of that week. She had set it a while ago, calling for public input on a projected rezoning of a slice of the annexed territory. If she'd asked, Noah would have gone with her instead. His presence wouldn't have excited comment. But even knowing she had to attend, he hadn't offered.

Friday night, he decided to walk over to Chandler's and grab a bite before he went home. He shared the elevator down to the lobby with half a dozen other people, all of whom seemed to be in a good mood because they'd be off until Monday. Him? His gut was balled in a knot because for the next two days he wouldn't catch even a glimpse of his director of community development.

Except he did. He stopped dead after exiting the elevator, because there she was by the glass doors, hovering just inside, looking out.

Waiting for her brother, he realized. Either she'd been ordered not to go outside until Colin pulled up or she was afraid.

Noah's feet were moving before his brain caught up. He stopped right beside her. "Call your brother. Tell him I'm taking you out to dinner and I'll bring you home later."

She stared up at him with those beautiful eyes that seemed perpetually darkened these days.

"He should be here any minute."

"Call him anyway."

After a moment, she gave a small nod and drew her phone from her bag. She kept looking at him as she talked to her brother.

"Colin, I'm joining Noah for dinner. He says he'll bring me home." She listened for a minute, then said, "That really isn't any of your business. I'll see you later."

"Let's walk," he said. "You must be feeling housebound."

Her laugh was shaky but real. "That's one way of putting it."

He pushed open the door and laid a hand on her back as he escorted her out. God, she felt good. The muscles moving beneath his fingers were lithe and supple. He kept his hand there as he turned her to head east on the sidewalk.

"How'd the community input meeting go?" he asked easily.

Talking business relaxed her. It carried them for the two-block walk to Chandler's.

Cait glanced at him when he opened the door for her. "Do you ever eat anywhere else?"

"Sometimes." Rarely. Mostly when he was scoping out new places. "I can trust my own employees not to gossip about me."

"That makes sense."

"I cook for myself most of the time."

A shapely brunette who must be a new hire showed them, at his nod, to a very private booth tucked in a corner rather than a window seat. She obviously knew who he was. Noah sat so he could see the restaurant, but no one walking in was likely to notice Cait. They ordered, steak and fries for him, spicy chicken wrap for her. He was a little surprised when she asked for a glass of wine.

They were there early enough, the restaurant hadn't yet filled up. He was glad of the quiet. They'd be long gone by the time the band set up.

"Tell me how you really are."

She gave a short laugh. "Oh, fabulous. Can't you tell? I thrive on tension. Having a guard everywhere I go? One of the perks of surviving a murder attempt."

"I'm serious."

Her smile vanished. "You really want to know? It sucks. Everything sucks. I can't do my job adequately. I can't live in my own home. Nell's mad at me. Colin's mad at me. So we're all excruciatingly polite, and I can't even yell at them because it's my fault they're mad at me. I ruined my favorite suit, my car is starting to feel at home in auto body shops—wow, glad one of us can feel at home somewhere—oh, and I can't sleep for staring at the window thinking how quickly someone could break it. I could be dead by the time Colin got his bedside drawer open."

Jesus. Okay. He'd asked.

"Someone?" was what he said.

"Blake. Is that what you want me to say?"

He hoped she didn't notice how he was clenching his teeth. "You sound like you're hoping it's someone else."

"Why would I be hoping that?" Cait stared at him like he was crazy. "Oh, my God! Do you know how freaky it would be to have *two different people* after me?"

"Uh…yeah. I guess it would be," he admitted. He hadn't thought of it that way. "It seemed to me you might be determined to think Ralston couldn't possibly want to hurt you."

She was still staring, but he had absolutely no

idea what she was thinking beyond feeling sure he wouldn't like it. It had to be thirty seconds before she looked away. "Okay, you've got me," she said. "I do believe Blake would hurt me if he gets mad enough. I'm scared of him, all right? But that's not the same thing as him buying a gun and trying to kill me from a distance like that. It doesn't feel right."

It didn't feel right to Noah, either. It was one of many things that had been eating at him.

But when he didn't respond quickly enough, anger sparked in her eyes. "What is it? You think I'm still nursing fond feelings for him?"

Noah shrugged, watching her. "Happens."

"Well, it's not happening here." She was still mad. "I feel nothing but this kind of horror that he can be totally fixated on making my life miserable. Or, God, ending it. And do you know the worst part? It's trying to figure out how I could have been so blind."

"Hey," he objected. She'd said that before, and he hadn't liked it then, either. He reached for her hand even though the waitress was bearing down on their table with salads. "This is not your fault. Don't go there. How could you ever have anticipated this kind of crazy?"

She bent her head so their eyes weren't meeting again. Because she didn't buy what he was saying? Or because there was something *she* hadn't said? His eyes narrowed, but he let go of her hand, nodded a brusque thanks to the waitress and reached for his napkin.

Cait did the same. "I'm sorry," she said after a minute. "I must be wonderful company. You and Colin have been great, and I keep feeling resentful because I need you. That doesn't say much about me."

"I'd resent it if I needed anyone else, too," he said. The words were barely out when he was hit by a staggering thought. *I do need her.* And part of that witch's brew in his belly was resentment, because he didn't *want* to need anyone. All week long, he'd battled against the magnetic force pulling him toward her so powerfully, sometimes he almost needed to grab a door frame and hold on to keep himself from being sucked down the hall to wherever she was. And, yeah, that made him angry. He tried to blame her. He kept telling himself he wasn't obligated to her. Protecting her was her brother's business, not his.

Except he did want to protect her. He wasn't sure he could live with himself if he didn't. And he wanted to make love with her more than he'd ever wanted anything in his life. And *that* infuriated him, too.

Obsessed.

Who could he blame but her?

She lifted her chin and looked at him with astonishment for what he'd said. "I didn't think anyone would understand."

His tongue felt thick. "I do. You came here to start a new life. Maybe to forge some kind of new relationship with your brother. But even that's been screwed up, because your old life followed you."

Her eyes kept searching his, her expression so open, radiating such pain, it was like she'd taken a meat cleaver to his chest. But what she said took him by surprise.

"Do you have sisters or brothers?"

Noah shook his head. "No siblings. I think after my mother remarried, they tried. Although I could be wrong."

"It's lonely, isn't it?"

He opened his mouth to say, probably rudely, *What do* you *know?* but realized she did. She'd had a brother and lost him. At the same time as she'd lost her father.

Who most people would say was no loss, but most people would say that about Noah's father, too. And they'd be right, but somehow that didn't help.

"Yeah." He had to clear his throat. "It was." *Is.* Even if that's the way he wanted it.

Cait nodded, as if they'd said everything important, and reached for her fork. "It was nice of you to ask me to dinner tonight. You're right. I was going stir-crazy."

In self-defense, he started to eat, too.

He asked about her dissertation, and he wasn't surprised when she admitted she'd managed only a few weekend hours on it.

"Of course, there's no real deadline, and a little break from it might actually be good," she said. "I can see it with a more objective eye. I'm not letting myself worry about it until I'm more settled into the job."

She didn't say, *And until I don't have to worry about somebody trying to kill me.*

Eventually he got her talking about her brother and this new sister-in-law, and he told her what he remembered about Nell Smith aka Maddie Dubeau's reappearance in Angel Butte.

"It was the biggest news we've had since I moved to town," he said wryly. "Got bigger, too, once there were a couple attempts on her life, and your brother's investigation opened such a can of worms."

"The drug trafficking."

He shook his head. "We already knew that was a problem in the area. Our police department has been part of the joint task force for a long time. What we didn't know was that we had corruption in our own department." He still had trouble believing it. "Our own goddamn police chief. And I always thought this town might as well be Mayberry."

"Apple pie, Little League baseball, kids able to play after school with no one having to worry about pedophiles or drunk drivers, moms putting wholesome dinners on the table, dads walking in the door at five-thirty to kiss their wives and talk about their days?"

He looked at her ruefully. "You always knew better, didn't you?"

"My life here was not that idyllic." Her twisted smile made him ache. "The idyllic parts were all because of Colin. I guess I took him for granted."

"You're supposed to be able to take the people you love for granted." He heard himself and was stunned. Did he believe that?

Maybe. What he couldn't do was relate it to himself.

"I suppose so," she said softly.

After that, conversation became easier. He did tell her a little bit about his mother and stepfather, the childhood that hadn't been abusive and sounded okay from the outside, about his teenage ambition to make it to the NFL before a knee injury had put paid to it, him considering going to New York with an aim to be a Broadway star.

"A villain, of course," she teased him.

"Naturally." He smiled without regret at what had both been typically youthful dreams. "Went to the U of O and majored in business. I worked in a sporting goods store the last couple of years of high school, Boulder River Sports Company. Do you know it? Really smart guy started it. He's only a few years older than I am. By the time I was a junior in college, I realized I wanted to be him."

"Does he have political ambitions, too?" She took a big bite of her wrap.

Noah chuckled. "Wouldn't surprise me. It's damn

tempting to try to reshape your environment to suit. He may get there. Although with stores all over the West now, he'd have to run for national office."

Cait tilted her head. "*You* might have to run for state office."

He was already shaking his head. "Don't think so. The mayor gig was an alternative to opening a fourth restaurant. Next time, I'll go with expanding."

He admitted, when she asked, that he hadn't figured out a prospective site, which was one reason he hadn't opened any new locations in the past several years. "Maybe up to The Dalles or Hood River, down to Klamath Falls." He shrugged. "There'd be a lot of driving either way. Not sure that appeals to me."

"Do you have to expand?"

"I get restless."

Noah couldn't remember the last time he'd talked to anyone like this. He had friends, but men didn't talk about Mom and Dad or what their childhoods had been like. Plans for a business, sure, but not the underlying unease. Cait was a good listener. He'd told her more about himself tonight than she had told him, although that was probably fair given how much he already knew about her childhood and problems.

For dessert, they shared a chocolate ganache tart with orange flavoring and cream. Sharing a dessert with someone else was another thing he didn't make a habit of doing. He hadn't much of a sweet tooth, for one thing. There was the unspoken intimacy, too, of their forks sometimes bumping, of knowing as they reached the middle they'd be mingling his and hers.

He hardly tasted the tart. Watching her slip each bite in her mouth and make a low humming sound and seeing her eyelids flutter, that had him so damn aroused, it was all he could think about. After each bite, her tongue would sweep over her lips as if she was savoring the last hint of flavor.

Damn. Noah took a hasty swallow of his coffee and choked on it.

"Are you all right?" Cait asked.

"Didn't know it was still so hot," he said when he could.

"Do you want any more?"

"More?" He looked without comprehension at the dessert, then shook his head. "It's all yours."

"Hah!" She scooted the plate closer. "You can't take it back."

Despite his acute state of arousal, Noah grinned at her greedy pleasure. Partly staged, no doubt, but not altogether. He watched as she finished the last few bites, scraped her fork over the china and studied the plate as if she was seriously thinking about licking it.

"That was so good." She finally sighed.

He laughed. "We aim to please."

For a moment her smile was merry and trouble-free, causing a hitch in his breathing. Happy, she was astonishingly beautiful.

She works for me. She's vulnerable.

Good arguments, but...

She would demand more than Noah wanted to give.

Cait sighed. "I suppose you'd better return me to captivity."

"Would you like to see my place?" he asked, voice husky. *Oh, damn.* Had he just said what he thought he had?

She was staring at him.

He could give her a quick tour of remodeling projects, offer her another cup of coffee. Keep it... collegial.

If only his self-restraint wasn't at such a foolishly low ebb.

Her cheeks had turned pink, her eyes shy. "I'd like that," she said, and triumph roared through him like a high-summer forest fire.

CHAPTER NINE

SHE SHOULD HAVE said "Oh, thanks, but not tonight." Or even just "No."

He'd probably thought she was hinting with that stuff about him returning her to captivity. It *sounded* like a hint. *God, was I?*

Cait truly didn't know.

She had never been as attracted to a man as she was to Noah Chandler, which freaked her out on so many levels, she couldn't identify them all. And didn't need to. The timing alone was so abysmally awful, why go further? She was—what?—seven months out of an abusive relationship. She'd vowed celibacy-slash-independence for the foreseeable future. She *worked* for this man.

Who was not at all her type. Yes, indeed, count the levels, from the longshoreman build to the almost-but-not-quite-homely face. The ruthlessness, the impatience, the automatic assumption of authority.

And she couldn't forget the fact that Colin despised him. Cait shuddered at what her brother would think if Noah brought her home late, looking rumpled, cheeks abraded by that dark stubble on his jaw, lips puffy from his kisses, body limp from complete satisfaction.

Her panic was cousin to the electric shock she'd gotten as a kid when she'd stuck a hairpin decorated with colored glass "jewels" into an electric socket. The cause didn't demonstrate any more intelligence.

I can still say, "You know, this probably isn't a very good idea."

He'd taken several turns and she realized the houses on her right were riverfront. She leaned forward. *Oh, boy.* She did want to see his house, even if she made her excuses before anything happened.

"Here we are." His voice was a quiet rumble in the dark vehicle. The turn signal was on, though they were alone on the street.

She could see enough from streetlights and porch lights to guess this was one of the town's older and most elegant houses. Which really wasn't saying that much; there'd been no big money in Angel Butte until tourism had changed the entire nature of the region. But she liked this part of town way better than she did the developments with outsize log homes she just knew would be decorated with peeled ponderosa pine furniture, lamps fashioned from elk horns and a deer head or two on the walls. Oh, and there were the faux Swiss chalets that were only four or five thousand square feet. Cait had always preferred old. Even knowing they, too, were way too big to actually live in, she had coveted the old mansions on Federal Way in Seattle and up toward Volunteer Park.

Noah killed the engine in the driveway in front of a detached garage and opened his door. Eager despite her voice of common sense, Cait hopped out to join him.

"Did you buy the house right away when you moved here?"

He gave a low, rusty chuckle. "I was twenty-four. I had, oh, about five thousand dollars in the bank, saved to open my own business. No, home-owning was low on my list of priorities then."

"You thought your dad was here," she remembered. "Did you expect to be able to stay with him?"

It seemed to her that he went still for a moment before he put the key in the lock. "No. I was curious, not expecting the great father–son reunion." He sounded curt, even harsh. *Back off.*

Chastened, Cait didn't say anything else until they were inside and he'd turned on lights.

Then she forgot she had irritated him. "Oh, Noah," she breathed, walking into the living room to her right.

Hardwood—maybe hardwood, but definitely not oak—floors gleamed. Molding had been stripped and stained the same warm color. The fireplace had an amazing mantel, also wood and elaborately carved like one of those Victorian-era buffets.

Lions' heads finished each corner. She could only imagine the work it had taken to strip the carving of old varnish. The plastered walls were painted a rich shade of cream. With night behind them, small-paned windows reflected a sparkling view of the interior.

"It's magnificent!"

He glanced around, looking a little self-conscious, Cait thought.

"This is the first room I finished. Dining room was next. Had to work my way up to the kitchen."

"You really are doing it all yourself?"

"Yeah, I guess you could call it a hobby." Now he sounded mildly bemused, as if he didn't understand himself.

"Had you worked construction?"

"No." As if testing for rough spots, he ran his fingers over the broad molding that framed the wide entry. "I educated myself along the way. The wiring, thank God, had been redone. Plumbing was a bitch."

"Of course plumbing has to be feminine," she said sweetly.

He flashed one of those wicked grins that threatened her already shaky knees. "Naturally." It turned into a grimace. "When I run water upstairs, I still hear some strange gurgles," he said, chagrined. "She's probably laughing at me."

Like Cait did. She clapped her hand to her mouth, but the giggles died anyway when she saw the way he was looking at her. His eyes had heated, and his mouth...well, she didn't know, only that it was all she could do not to lift her hand and touch his lips.

"The kitchen." Her voice squeaked.

He nodded and turned away. She trailed him past the staircase with refinished balustrade and steps. The dining room on the opposite side of the entry looked much like the living room, except a built-in buffet filled much of one wall. That wood, too, had been stripped and lovingly refinished to a fine gloss.

Cait felt as if she'd wandered into a house of mirrors. Noah had said he was remodeling a house, but she hadn't really envisioned it. The work this had taken had to be monumental. And the house itself was so...traditional. If she'd had to guess on meeting him, she would have seen him in a place like Colin's: beautiful but modern, simple. Noah seemed like a man who'd demand the best but not be that interested in his surroundings. Instead, he was creating this gorgeous home with his own labor. And love. It had to be.

He wasn't quite who she'd thought he was. Pieces didn't fit.

"I ended up painting the kitchen cabinets," he said, stepping aside so she could pass him. "Maybe I should have hired a cabinetmaker to build new ones, but, uh..." His big shoulders moved in a shrug. "I was trying to stick to the original."

She could see his problem. Additional cabinets

seemed to have been added as the years passed and housewives were dissatisfied with the lack of storage and counter space. He'd unified what must have looked like a mishmash with a soft gray-blue paint that contrasted with the same creamy white wall color, a tiled backsplash and warm wood floors.

"It's perfect," she declared, feeling this weird discomfort inside because, well, if she ever had a home she wanted it to be exactly like this. She stayed with her back to him, pretending to keep looking around, so he wouldn't see the yearning she suspected her face would betray.

Beyond the kitchen proper was a more informal dining space she guessed had begun life as a glassed-in porch. In daylight hours, it would look right out at the river.

"Do you want to see the upstairs?" he asked, voice a notch huskier.

Cait's stomach tightened.

No. Thanks, but I should be getting going.

She managed an almost casual smile and turned to face him. "Is that the 'before'?"

"Something like that." His eyes were dark and unreadable. His very stillness sent a shock of awareness through her body.

"Then…sure." Oh, heaven help her—*her* voice was husky, too.

He turned and led the way, but at the foot of the

stairs he gestured for her to go first. Cait climbed, pricklingly conscious of him behind her.

At the top she glanced into the first open door and saw…"Before," she murmured.

"Yeah." He spoke from so close behind her, she swore she could feel his breath on her nape. "Haven't touched this room yet."

Wallpaper with some sort of paisley print had aged to olive-green and mustard-yellow. The wood floor was scuffed and scarred.

Across the hall was what had once been a child's bedroom. Now yellowed wallpaper decorated with rocking horses hung in tatters. She paused in that doorway, feeling sad.

"Every damn room in the house was papered," Noah said behind her. "Halls, bathrooms, even some ceilings. Someone went way overboard on the wallpaper."

As disgruntled as he sounded, she couldn't help a giggle. "It can be pretty, you know," she said, turning.

He was smiling, but his eyes were still darker than usual. "In moderation."

"In a child's room," she heard herself say. "Are you going to keep this one as a nursery?"

A muscle jumped on one side of his jaw. "Do I look like father material?"

"You could be."

He grunted and looked past her into the room, as if seeing it anew. "This house has four bedrooms plus the library downstairs. Five bedrooms before I just tore out a wall."

It was a family house. He must have known that when he bought it. And yet his expression suggested he wasn't happy with the reminder.

"You don't...want a family?" she asked tentatively.

"I can't see myself." But he was frowning, his face tight.

After hesitating another moment, she slipped past him. She was getting perilously near to his bedroom, but she was past resisting temptation.

The bathroom had a huge cast-iron claw-footed tub circled by a shower curtain on a stainless-steel rail suspended from the ten-foot ceiling. This room he'd finished, down to the white pedestal sink and a floor-to-ceiling cabinet in the corner. A sturdy antique chair sat beside the tub, a couple of clean, folded towels on the seat. His toothbrush and toothpaste were in a china cup on the rim of the sink. She suspected the beveled glass mirror hid a medicine cabinet.

More perfect, except that he had left the rooms so plain.

"No art," she observed.

A shift of air told her he'd shrugged. "Maybe someday. Or maybe I'll get bored once I'm done and decide to turn the house and start over with another one."

That brought her around. "You can't!"

One side of his mouth curled up. "Why not?"

"Because… For heaven's sake! You must have put years of hard work into it. And it's perfect."

His smile disappeared as he searched her face. "I'm glad you think so," he said in the voice that undermined her defenses.

They did nothing but look at each other for a minute. Her skin felt…stretched. She had a very bad feeling her nipples had tightened. And, even though she wouldn't let her gaze lower, she knew he had an erection. Still, he didn't touch her.

Instead, he backed out into the hall again and gestured her ahead.

One more bedroom, this one also featuring faded, undistinguished wallpaper and worn floor. The smell of sawdust was growing sharp in her nostrils. There were two doors remaining on her left. One leaned against the wall, leaving the doorway itself open. It had been yet another bedroom, of course; she tried to distract herself from Noah by trying to imagine life here with a family large enough to require five bedrooms and yet having only *one bathroom* upstairs. A family a hundred years ago might have had kids doubled up in some of those bedrooms, too, it occurred to her. The morning rush must have been a battleground. She hadn't seen the downstairs bathroom, but guessed it was no more than a powder room.

She stepped in and saw from the ceiling and

floor where the wall had been demolished. A heap of dusty plasterboard and old studs still needed to be hauled out, too.

Beyond, of course, was where Noah slept. An antique dresser now held a fine layer of white dust. An old sheet protected a dark comforter on the king-size bed that dominated a room really too small for a bed that big.

"So what's the plan?" she asked, voice a little too high.

He had followed her, footsteps silent.

"Second bathroom, walk-in closet. I thought about ripping out yet another wall to make this bedroom bigger, but..." He shrugged.

He didn't want a family, but he did want a family home. Did he recognize his own dichotomy? Gathering lines on his forehead made her wonder.

But then those vivid blue eyes speared hers. "Cait," he said gruffly. Just that. *Cait.*

She trembled. This was the last thing in the world she ought to do. No men, remember? Didn't work out so well last time. Remember *that?* And, oh, yes, this man was her boss, which meant she was endangering her new life only because she was overcome with lust.

She prayed this hunger to touch him, rub up against him, feel his hands and lips on her, was only lust.

"I..." She squeaked and stopped.

He swore and stepped forward, close enough to touch but didn't. "You know I want you."

Cait bobbed her head. Hard to miss, no pun intended.

"You can say no."

She nodded again.

Frustration crossed his face. "I need to hear you acknowledge out loud that you know there will be no repercussions on the job if you say no. Or yes. Either way, this is separate." He huffed out a breath. "Maybe you don't know me well enough to be sure—"

"I do." He'd come to her rescue over and over, no hesitation. He'd repeated over and over again, "You are not to blame." He had to be the single most confident man she had ever met. He would never lower himself to pressuring a reluctant woman for sex. For heaven's sake, women probably offered themselves to him on a daily basis! "I know this only has to do with us," she said almost steadily.

Now, at last, he slid his hand around the back of her head. He moved forward enough to edge a foot between hers. Cait made a helpless sound as he groaned and bent his head.

His kiss was hot and urgent, blurring her thoughts. His tongue drove into her mouth and she met it with hers, the texture and insistence making her want to climb inside him. She kissed him back, trying to say *yes, yes, yes* without words. That big hand still wrapped the back of her head, angling it to please him, but the other one had made its way beneath her silk shell, roving up and down her back.

At first she'd only grabbed him and held on, but now she wanted her hands on his bare skin, too. She wrenched his white shirt from his dress slacks and found his hard belly. There wasn't room between them, though. In pure frustration, she withdrew her hand and began to fumble with the buttons.

At some point Noah noticed and backed off, enough to let her finish. She pushed his shirt off his shoulders, but it stuck at his wrists. He laughed and took care of the cuffs himself. She was overwhelmed by all that muscle. He was the most physically compelling man she'd ever seen, with those huge, powerful shoulders, arms that could lift her little Mazda, washboard abdomen and V of curling brown hair that arrowed toward the thin black belt at his waist. Busy staring, she hadn't noticed that he was divesting her of her top and then her bra until he cupped her breasts, gently squeezing and rotating his hands so that his calloused palms created friction that brought a cry from her throat.

"You're beautiful," he said hoarsely. "So beautiful."

"You're—"

His laugh vibrated in his chest. "Don't say beautiful. I'll know you're lying through your teeth."

A bubble of amusement rose in her, part of the floating sensation that made her feel as if her feet weren't on the floor. "Magnificent," she murmured, exploring. Her hands were greedy for his textures, for the play of those amazing muscles beneath the taut, hair-roughened skin, the hammer of his heartbeat. And then she couldn't stand it anymore and tugged his head down so that she could kiss him again.

His flavor was intoxicating, as musky as the scent of aroused male. The kiss became frantic, as if he were consuming her and she was trying to do the same to him. Not until she felt pressure against the back of her legs did Cait realize he'd walked her to his bed. Now he reached past her, yanked off the sheet, scooped her up and sat her down.

She tried to pull him with her, but he squatted instead and removed her shoes, carefully, one at a time. He made an indescribable sound when he discovered her stockings were thigh-highs; she couldn't look away from his face as he peeled them down, then engulfed her feet in his hands, kneading, finally moving up to her ankles, her calves. The skin behind her knees was so sensitive she jumped when his fingertips found it. He lifted his gaze to hers and didn't look away as his hands slid up her thighs, higher, higher, until she was trying to cant her hips to meet the touch she knew was to come. The blue of his eyes burned now, and the skin was stretched tight across those blunt cheekbones. His mouth was softer than she had ever seen, a little swollen from that last, fierce kiss, and, oh,

God, she wanted that mouth on hers, on her throat, her shoulders, her breasts, her belly.

He squeezed her hips, hooked her panties and drew them down. She cramped with desperate longing. All she wore now was a very short skirt that didn't hide anything from him if he looked. But he didn't. Still his gaze pinned hers, and *she* couldn't look away.

"Unfasten my belt," he said in a guttural voice.

Tearing her gaze from him, she felt a physical wrench. Her hands shook as she slid the leather from the buckle, parting it. With no prompting, she worked at the button at his waist and then the zipper. Cait heard herself panting as she lowered it over that thick bulge, exposing gray knit boxers. Before she could slide her hands inside them, he rose to his feet, kicked off his shoes and shed pants, boxers and socks in one move. As swiftly as he did it, she reached around to her back, lowered her own zipper and skimmed the skirt over her hips.

She had one instant of thinking how truly magnificent he was before he came down on top of her. They kissed and rolled and touched; eventually his mouth found her breasts and he suckled hard—no preliminaries. By that time all she wanted was him inside her. Oh, heavens, she was whimpering! Legs wrapped around his hips, Cait lifted herself until the blunt head of his penis nudged.

Noah swore, rolling away. "Cait. Just a minute."

She was on birth control, but she had always,

without exception, made it a rule that the man had to wear a condom, too. A couple of times Blake had refused. She couldn't call what he did rape, but it was closer than she wanted to remember.

Don't. Don't let him in your head.

Noah fumbled inside the drawer of the bedside stand, still swearing, but finally came up with a condom. Another time she might enjoy putting it on him, but she didn't think she could right now. She lay quivering, wanting to climb on top of him.

Then he was back, gripping her thighs, parting and lifting them even as he thrust inside her. And, oh, it almost hurt for a moment. He was a bigger man than any of her boyfriends, in every sense, but then she made a strangled sound of satisfaction. He'd been watching her face until then, but now he closed those blue eyes and began to move. Cait moved, too, riding him, struggling for the most intense pressure point, and then she imploded. Was that her crying out in such astonishment? It had to be. As the flash flood of pleasure subsided, she whispered his name, held him tight and reveled in the shudder and buck of his big body.

PANIC HAD NOAH in an icy grip, and he'd never been more ashamed. He'd *known,* damn it, he'd known what a terrible idea this was, and he'd done it anyway. Staring at the ceiling, all he could think was that his brain had gotten hijacked the minute he'd seen her gazing wistfully out at the street waiting for her brother. Two minutes longer in his office, and Colin would already have arrived, saving Noah from this monumentally huge screwup.

What was he supposed to do now? Say, *Wow, babe, that was fun but we shouldn't have done it?* Especially when the coils of panic tightened because what had just happened had been one hell of a lot more than "fun." It was the best sex of his life, and he didn't want to think about what that meant. He desperately wanted to be alone, but he not only had to get her moving without saying anything he'd regret later; he also had to drive her home and potentially face her brother's hostile stare.

"Oh, my God," she mumbled. He could just make out the words. Her face was squashed against his biceps.

Aware her stillness was no longer post-orgasm lassitude but rather her brain gearing up, he gave her a gentle squeeze.

"I hope that was worshipful," he said, trying for light but failing.

"More freaked." Cait lifted her head and blinked a couple of times as if remembering how.

Annoyed, Noah scowled. "I thought it was damn good."

"I work for you." She scooted away, one arm held protectively in front of her breasts. Which left him with a nice view of everything else. His body stirred.

"I thought we cleared that."

"Do you think Earl would agree? Or George Miller?"

"They're not here." His own panic had been completely supplanted by irritation and a different kind of panic. Was she saying this was a one-off she already deeply regretted?

She slid off the bed and scuttled around to the foot, grabbing clothes and holding them in front of her as a more successful shield. "I just…I knew this wasn't smart."

"Maybe not," he admitted, swinging his own feet to the floor. "But we both knew it was coming, didn't we?"

She opened her mouth, then closed it. Points for honesty.

"We're attracted to each other," he said in a milder tone. "We're adults, both single. What we do out of the public eye is no one's business."

That was good, he congratulated himself. He'd been attracted to a lot of women in his lifetime. This wasn't any different. Or not so different, at least. Why shouldn't they have an affair? It would wear out sooner or later; they always did. But, by God, he still wanted her. He'd have reached for her right now if she wasn't making her dismay so plain.

"That's what you want?" she said after a moment, cautiously. "To hook up when no one knows?"

His teeth ground together. "What's that supposed to mean? I took you out to dinner, didn't I? I didn't tell you to duck while I was driving out of the city parking garage. I'm talking about a reasonably private relationship, that's all."

She swallowed, closed her eyes, then bobbed her head. "I'm sorry. I'm being… I don't know what I'm being. I just, um, I love my job, and I swore off men and now look at me."

He was. At her gorgeous long legs and the peep of honey-brown curls her too-skimpy armful of clothing didn't hide, the white swell of breast, her delicate collarbone and perfect curve of lips.

And, hell, he had a hard-on, and he hadn't even gotten the damn condom off.

"I'm not your ex," he said.

Cait gave another of those funny little nods. "I know." She summoned a small apologetic smile. "I wouldn't be here if I thought you were like him."

He scrubbed a hand over his head, probably making his hair stand on end, then stood. "I've got to get rid of this condom."

"Yes, you do." There was a little bit of a sparkle in her eyes, but some pink in her cheeks, too.

He kissed her cheek on the way by. He hated condoms, disposing of them being the number one reason. There was no dignity in his retreat.

Noah wouldn't have been surprised to find her already dressed when he got back to the bedroom. Despite his arousal, he should be relieved if she was, but once he'd beaten back the alarm, he couldn't seem to find it again. Why couldn't they make time for another round before he restored her to her brother's bristling care?

She wore her panties and was reaching behind herself to fasten her bra when he returned, but that was as far as she'd gotten.

Hearing his footstep, she turned. "You must think I'm totally neurotic."

"No." Noah didn't dare tell her what he did think about her. "You're under a lot of stress right now. And I guess you can tell I had some of the same hesitations you did." *Hesitations. Good euphemism for fears.* "I broke one of my cardinal rules tonight. I don't have relationships—" read: sex "—with women who work for me."

There was vulnerability in those soft gray eyes. "You're sure you wouldn't rather end this here? I promise not to make a nuisance of myself."

He shook his head and reached for her hand, drawing her to him. "No. I still want you, Cait. It's been killing me, catching glimpses of you down the hall." He nuzzled her, bumping her nose, touching his lips to the wing of her cheekbone and up to the temple. "Hard to miss you in all those Easter-egg colors."

He could feel the curve of her smile.

"I like pretty colors."

"Tell me you wouldn't wallpaper every room in your house if you could." *Damn,* he thought on an icy wash of alarm. He'd come so close to saying, *In* this *house.* And he'd seen it, a flash between one blink and the next, her wearing old jeans and a T-shirt that stretched over a swollen belly, in that bedroom at the head of the stairs, laughing at him over her shoulder as she stood on a stepladder smoothing a sheet of wallpaper into place, water dripping from the big squishy sponge in her hand. Wallpaper with fluffy yellow ducklings on it.

He had never in his life pictured a woman doing anything like that, and especially not to *his* house. A woman who was pregnant with *his* child.

Yellow ducklings?

She chose that moment to wrap her fingers around his stubbornly erect penis and stroke it. "You must like pretty colors."

God, he did—when she was wearing them. Like the panties she had on right now, the soft purple of lilacs in bloom. Although he liked her even better wearing nothing at all.

He could forget the moment of insanity involving ducklings and—*God forbid!*—pregnancy.

His cock would never forgive him if he didn't.

"Yeah," he said hoarsely and unfastened her bra. "You won't be needing this."

CHAPTER TEN

COLIN FOLLOWED CAIT into the house four days later, suit coat slung over one shoulder, the ends of his tie dangling.

"This is Nell's late night, isn't it?" she asked.

His grunts were as speaking as Noah's. This was an unhappy one. "Yeah, unfortunately. You and I should have grabbed dinner on the way home."

"I'll cook tonight," she offered. "How about something simple? Quesadillas?"

"I'm beat," he admitted. "If you mean it…"

"Of course I do." She smiled at him. Their relationship *was* getting easier.

"Cait." He stopped her with a hand on her arm. "We'll find the son of a bitch."

She nodded. He had told her as soon as he'd picked her up downtown that a county sheriff's deputy had found Blake's camp, tucked on the bank of Bear Creek outside city limits. Neither Blake nor his car had been there, but the tent matched Cait's description, and when the deputy unzipped the small blue tent, he'd seen a white cardboard banker's box filled with file folders. The lid, carelessly tossed aside on top of the sleeping bag, had "Ralston" scrawled on it in black marker.

Really? Blake had brought *work* with him to fill the hours when he wasn't terrorizing her? Now, that infuriated her, maybe because it said, *This man isn't really crazy.*

"I know," she said, patting Colin's shoulder.

Black bean and cheese quesadillas were Cait's go-to dinner when she wanted food on the table in twenty minutes or less. Colin cooperated by putting a salad together while she cooked. Of course, she had to triple the number of quesadillas she made, since her brother's appetite was considerably heartier than hers.

After they had finished eating she was restoring the top to the sour cream and he was leaning back in his chair, sighing in repletion, when his phone rang. Unfortunately, he kept it with him everywhere but the bathroom, as far as she could tell.

He groaned, looked at the number and answered, listening for a minute before he said, "A *what?*"

Interest sharpened, Cait unashamedly eavesdropped but couldn't get anything from his side of the conversation except that he was stunned. "Of course we have to," he said at one point. "I'll be there," he finally growled, ending the call and pushing back from the table.

"As you probably gathered, I've got to go in. Unbelievably enough, we've had a bomb threat."

"In Angel Butte?"

His laugh was unamused. "Better yet. The library."

"You're kidding."

"I wish." He disappeared toward the bedroom, but his voice carried to her. "They have a program going on tonight in the meeting room. Historical society talking about the late nineteenth-and early twentieth-century range wars and vigilantism. To encourage attendance, the children's librarian is holding a preschool story time to include crafts."

"Oh, my God. You mean, the library is packed?"

"Yeah." Badge and gun back at his belt, he was shrugging into the suit coat again as he came back down the hall. "They're going to start evacuating."

"At least Nell doesn't work there."

Her brother's eyes met hers. "Yeah. I'll count my blessings."

She followed him to the front door, where he paused. "Damn it, I don't like leaving you by yourself."

She could see him debating whether she might not be safer with him at the site of a bomb threat. "I'll be fine," she assured him before he got too enthused about that idea.

"Lock," he ordered.

She rolled her eyes but crossed her heart. "Promise."

With his long stride, he crossed the yard and disappeared through the side door into the garage in only seconds. Cait stayed where she was for a moment. Somebody had actually threatened to bomb the library during a preschool story time. *Unbelievable.*

A thud brought her head around in time for her to see a blur of movement. Somebody had leaped over the railing and onto the porch. Her pulse sprang into overdrive, and she opened her mouth to scream.

Blake's hand slapped over her mouth before she could squeak out a sound. He shoved her backward into the house and kicked the door shut behind him. Colin would be backing out of the garage and assume she'd obediently gone back in. He wouldn't hear a scream now even if she could get free.

On a surge of fear, she thought of Noah, as intent as her brother on saving her. Noah, who wouldn't understand how she could ever have forgiven Blake for hitting her and let him do it again.

Noah, she thought with anguish.

"Did you get my messages?" Blake asked, his mouth close to her ear.

Her mind cleared. *He* was responsible for the bomb threat, she understood suddenly. For scaring the crap out of all those people just so he could get her alone. Cait hadn't known it was possible to be so angry she literally saw red.

He was grinning at her, cocky, pleased with his tactics. He even removed his hand from her mouth.

She slammed her knee upward into his balls.

When he screamed and crumpled, Cait backed up just far enough for her leg to reach full extension; then she kicked him in the face on his way down. There was a distinct and satisfying crunch, and blood spurted from his nose.

Curled into a fetal position on the floor, he was making awful sounds. She stared down at him in contempt and that same, bloodred rage.

"I am sick to death of you! Do you hear me?" When he didn't answer, she prodded him, not so gently, with the pointed toe of the shoes she hadn't yet taken off.

He gurgled some kind of acknowledgment.

"I'm calling my brother," she said in a voice so hard it couldn't be hers. "When you get out of jail—*if* you ever get out of jail—I never want to see you again. Is that clear?"

He lifted a wild stare to her. "Jail? What are you talking about?"

"Attempted murder? You…you *creep*."

Creep? That was the best she could do? She wanted to kick him again, but he looked so pathetic.

"I wouldn't hurt you," he wailed.

"Really? You're such a good shot you missed on purpose?"

Shock froze his expression and all she could think was, *Oh, no.*

"What are you talking about?" He pressed his hand to his nose in an attempt to stem the flow of blood. "I hate guns! You know that."

It wasn't him. The thought brought her world to a momentary stop. She felt as if she were hanging over space. *It wasn't him.*

Someone *else* wanted her dead.

Still clutching his genitals, he rolled and started to struggle to his feet. That brought Cait back to the moment. She planted her foot on him and pushed him over.

"Do not move," she ordered. How quick could she grab her phone? Maybe not quick enough. "Did you call in the bomb threat?"

"I just wanted to get you alone," he mumbled. "And you...you *hurt* me."

"Now you know what it feels like." Her vision was still strange, sharpened and almost but not quite distorted at the edges. "Is there a bomb?"

"No! I wouldn't do that."

"But you made the call."

He made a blubbery noise of acquiescence, blood and snot pooling beneath his face. *Ick,* she thought dispassionately; he was making a mess on the shiny wood floor.

She turned and walked away, going into her bedroom for her phone, left in her messenger bag. She had it in her hand when she heard the click of the front door closing. Cait went back to the living room and looked out to see him scuttling across the yard, bent over.

She almost stepped out on the porch to remind

him that she'd better never see him again, but really, why bother?

The sense of release made her light-headed until a sick rolling in her stomach wiped out any triumph.

Someone else is trying to kill me.

Blake, she thought, had been all about threats and impulse and temper. Whoever had pulled the trigger out on Bond Road that day had been entirely cool—and therefore far more dangerous.

She scrolled for Colin's last message and touched Send.

"Cait?" he answered. There were urgent male voices in the background.

"There's no bomb," she told him.

SHE'D TAKEN CARE of him? What did that mean?

Noah drove with his grip so tight on the steering wheel, his knuckles ached.

He had barely arrived at the library, already in the midst of an orderly evacuation made disturbing by the frightened faces and the children with their piercing voices saying things like, "Mommy? You said we could check out books. Why can't we stay? Why are the policemen here?"

He'd gotten out of his SUV and was staring, thinking, *My town is going to hell in a handbasket, and I don't even know why.* And then he saw McAllister, who had also obviously just arrived. As he got out of his SUV, he was talking on his phone; then he put it away and spoke intensely to his officers. From halfway across the parking lot, he spotted Noah. Leaving off whatever he was saying, he strode toward Noah. The people he'd been talking to all gaped at his back, as if he'd walked away midspeech.

"Chandler," he said, "Cait just called. She says there's no bomb. It was that son of a bitch Ralston. He wanted to get her alone."

Fear crested and broke in Noah like some killer wave. His whole body went rigid. "He's got her?"

"She says she took care of him. She sounded... calm."

"Calm."

"Told me to do what I had to do, not to worry."

Somehow he kept from repeating dumbly, *Not to worry?* "Where is she?" he managed instead.

"Still at the house." His jaw tightened. "She says."

He pulled his car keys from his pocket. "I'll go."

"I can send a unit."

"If he's hurt her, I'll kill him."

No caution to remember the law. Instead, "You'll call me?" her brother asked.

Noah nodded and was gone.

A five-minute drive took two. Plus side, he didn't have to worry about getting a ticket; he knew where every cop in town was. The tires squealed on pavement when he turned into McAllister's driveway.

Hearing that, he made himself lift his foot from the pedal so he didn't skid on the gravel.

No other vehicle was in sight. Lights were on in the house. He leaped out and ran for the porch, taking the stairs two at a time. Then he hammered on the door.

"Cait!" he bellowed.

When she opened the door, he almost fell in.

"Noah?"

Despite her bemused expression, he snatched her into his arms. He could hear his own heartbeat, and his lungs were working like old-fashioned bellows. He swore, viciously, nonstop. All he could think was, *She's all right. Not hurt.* Nothing like he'd imagined had happened.

Her arms had locked around him, and he realized she was soothing him by stroking his back. Finally he was able to groan and loosen his hold on her.

"Where is he?"

Her lip curled. "He took off."

His heartbeat was starting to slow. "What happened?"

"Do you want a cup of coffee?"

"I want," he said from between clenched teeth, "for you to tell me *what happened.*"

She blinked. "Blake used the phone call to the library as a diversion. He came, and I kicked his ass." She sounded so satisfied, Noah's relief turned into a choked laugh.

"Okay. Now I'll take the coffee."

Watching her sashay into the kitchen, her butt swinging, he shook his head and took out his phone.

It rang once.

"She's fine," he told Colin. "Ralston is gone. She says she kicked his ass."

Silence.

"I haven't gotten the details yet, but she's unscathed and she sounds pretty pleased with herself."

Her brother uttered an obscenity. "Ask her if she knows where his car was."

Noah relayed question and then answer. "No. Says he scuttled away—her words—into the woods to the north."

"People that own it are never there. He could have parked in their driveway." Voices were talking to him, and Colin had apparently muffled the phone. After a minute he came back. "Tell her I'll be home as soon as I can."

"Okay." Noah was the bemused one now, going into the kitchen, where Cait leaned against the counter edge.

"What'd he say?"

He told her.

"What a mess. I suppose they'll have to search the library anyway."

"Probably." He shook his head. "I assume someone will be waiting for Ralston at his campsite."

"Which he doesn't know has been found." Her eyes sharpened on him. "How did *you* know it was found?"

All Noah did was cock an eyebrow.

Cait made a face at him. "I can't believe my brother is reporting to you. You know he wouldn't if he knew."

"That I'm doing his sister?"

"Doing?" She sounded outraged.

"I can think of cruder ways to put it." He grinned at her. He felt euphoric. She was all right! Not hurt! *Damn.* "You know, your brother is smart enough to suspect."

"He thinks he's hardly taken his eyes off me."

"He knows we've spent a couple of evenings together."

She was silent for a moment. "He might have a suspicion."

"Suspicious is his middle name."

Not denying it, Cait sighed and turned to get mugs out of the cupboard.

Noah didn't want coffee and conversation; he wanted *her.* "Where's Nell?" he asked.

"Work." She saw his expression and backed away. "No way! Nell will be home in less than an hour, and who knows about Colin?"

"Come home with me for the night." Voice gravelly, he caught her by the upper arms, squeezing gently.

"Oh, God." Cait leaned into him, resting her forehead against his shoulder. "I can't. You know I can't."

"You're an adult," he said with sudden frustration. "Big girls can have sleepovers."

She straightened, and he saw her resolve. "Colin would flip. He's going to want to hear every detail. And...I want to know when they've arrested Blake."

A part of him knew she was right. The timing stank. But reason didn't quell his desperate need for her. Ridiculous, when he hadn't even known she was in danger until it was over. This wasn't like last time, when he'd seen her car with the door standing open and the bullet holes and believed for a world-altering moment that she was dead.

"Let me hold you for a minute," he whispered, and she melted against him, her arms wrapping him, too.

He was still aroused, but it helped, just feeling her, full body contact, the rise and fall of breath, the tickle of her hair. He consoled himself with the thought that at least she'd be able to go back to her town house now. Not that they wanted their relationship to be public knowledge, but at least it wouldn't be so teenage with her having to sneak away from her stern guardian's eye. He could park unobtrusively in the alley....

"No."

He pulled back a little. "What?"

"You said at least I can go home tomorrow." She lifted a face to him that was drawn, even haunted. "I can't."

His muscles went into lockdown. "Why not?"

"Noah, it wasn't Blake. He had no idea what I was talking about."

"You asked him about the shooting."

Her head bobbed.

"You believe him."

"I wish I didn't," she said miserably.

Noah swore and pulled her close again. He rubbed his cheek against her hair. "I'll stay until Colin gets home."

He almost missed the tiny sniffle. But not the whispered, "Thank you."

COLIN PERSONALLY GRILLED that bastard two ways from Sunday and became reluctantly convinced that Cait was right—he was telling the truth. He'd been stalking Cait, but he hadn't tried to gun her down in cold blood.

The bomb threat had been the most stupid-ass thing he could have done. Unfortunately, the most they could do was charge him with first-degree disorderly conduct, a misdemeanor that with luck would earn him a year in jail. For terrorizing Cait, Colin wanted to throw away the key.

But the flood of fear he felt had nothing to do with Blake Ralston. Colin left the interview room and Cait's former boyfriend slumped behind the table, eyes vacant as he groped toward a realization of how badly he'd screwed up his life.

Colin had known Noah was standing on the other

side of the one-way glass, but he hadn't tried to deny him the right to hear what Ralston had to say. He didn't like thinking Cait was getting involved with Chandler—but he wouldn't have stopped it if he could. Not now. Chandler would do anything to protect her, and that made two of them instead of only one.

He was surprised to find that the mayor wasn't alone. Lieutenant Jane Vahalik had joined him.

"Captain," Vahalik said, some urgency underlying her tone.

God help them, what now? He raised his eyebrows.

She glanced at Noah, then back at Colin, her hesitation obvious. He gave a brief nod of permission that had Noah's eyes narrowing.

"You know the rounds that killed Hegland were nine millimeter."

He tensed.

"Ballistics report says the same gun was used in the attack on your sister."

"What?" burst out of Noah. Colin was frozen silent.

"I didn't say it made sense," Jane said. "But given the way Hegland was killed, it's not good news."

Gut churning, Colin remembered Cait's description of the SUV sitting on the road, the silence. If her subconscious hadn't kicked in, she'd be dead. Maybe sun had glinted off the barrel as it was raised. Maybe something else. The enemy was faceless, deliberate. Colin couldn't believe they'd ever kidded themselves that Ralston was the gunman.

His eyes met Noah's, and he saw an echo of his fear.

"I'll need to interview her again," Vahalik said. "Is she in her office this afternoon? Do you know?"

"She's there," Noah said, voice sounding raw.

"In the meantime, do you know if she's been involved in anything to do with the airport?"

Noah shook his head. "I'm almost positive she hasn't."

Colin squeezed the back of his neck. "She knew Hegland."

Now they both stared at him. "How?" Jane asked.

"He was…a friend of our mother's. Cait ran into him briefly her first week in town. They chatted for about one minute. She mentioned it to me. As far as I know, she hadn't seen him or heard from him again."

Noah watched him. How he knew there was more to the story, Colin had no idea, but at least he kept his mouth shut.

There wasn't a good reason to keep their mother's transgressions secret, but he wanted to think about this before he told anyone. Talk to Cait about it. He couldn't imagine what an illicit affair that had been broken off damn near twenty years ago could possibly have to do with murder now. It made no sense.

"We need to find out where she was when Hegland was killed. She might have seen something without knowing she did."

"She was living with me."

"But surely not home every evening."

He shook his head numbly. "No. Damn. She'll be able to tell you when she looks at her calendar."

"I'll head over there now, then." She glanced through the glass at Blake Ralston, who stared down at the tabletop as if the fake wood grain held the answers to his own craziness. "Idiot," she muttered, and left.

Noah waited until the door closed behind her. "You going to tell me what this is about?"

Colin could play dumb. "What? Ralston?"

"Hegland."

He shook his head. "Ask Cait. It's—" Family? His mother was a stranger to him. "Private," he settled on. "And can't have anything to do with someone trying to kill her now. For God's sake, she was ten years old the last time she saw the man!"

"I will ask." Noah, too, glanced again at Ralston. "Speaking of, *you* didn't ask what he's so goddamn sorry for."

"You have no idea how much I wanted to." Then he gave a sort of laugh. "What am I saying? Of course you do. But you know I have to stay out of it if we go after him for stalking. Cait's my sister. I can talk to him about making a false threat. Beyond that, I'd have to step back."

Noah surprised him by nodding his acceptance. "Anyway, I wasn't sure Cait would ever forgive me," he admitted. "She's feeling vulnerable enough right now—"

"Feeling? She *is* vulnerable," Noah grumbled.

Colin continued doggedly. "She's entitled to some privacy."

A moment of silence as the other man conducted an inner battle. He rubbed a hand over his jaw in what Colin had learned was a characteristic gesture, as if he thought he could physically wipe expression from his face. "You're right," he said abruptly. "Okay. I'm going back to city hall. I'll look in on Cait."

"Thank you." Two words that almost stuck in his throat but had to be said.

A smile flickered on that ugly face, and Mayor Chandler departed, leaving Colin looking through the glass at Mr. I Really Am Sorry Now.

CAIT HAD MET Lieutenant Vahalik in passing. She was surprised to have her appear in her office.

Jane Vahalik didn't meet Cait's perception of how a woman in law enforcement ought to look, which she knew perfectly well was stereotypical. Colin had said that the lieutenant was thirty-four and unmarried. She was shorter than Cait, maybe five foot five or six, and curvaceous. She must wear at least a C-cup bra, which had to be a major inconvenience, both given the physical requirements of her job and the perception of the men she worked with and the ones she arrested. She was one of those women who could be described as quietly pretty—hazel eyes, curly reddish-brown hair, round, gentle face. Subtle makeup or none, Cait couldn't tell.

And I'm trying to distract myself, she realized, fighting the fear that she didn't want to know why the lieutenant was there, in her office.

"Blake didn't…get away or something, did he?" she asked.

"Mr. Ralston?" She looked surprised. "We're not usually that careless. No, Captain McAllister just finished interviewing him."

"Did he learn anything?"

"You'll have to ask him. I only saw the tail end."

Cait nodded. "Please. Have a seat. What can I do for you?"

She listened in shock as the lieutenant explained to her how they could tell bullets had been fired by the same gun, and how Jerry Hegland's killer was also the individual who had attempted to murder her.

"But…why?" she managed to beg.

"That's what we have to figure out. The captain said you'd run into Mr. Hegland when you first arrived in Angel Butte."

She gave her head a dazed shake. "Yes. It was… really nothing. Nell and I had lunch together. We were leaving and I literally bumped into him. I recognized him—he recognized me. We exchanged a few words, but he was supposed to meet someone, and that was that."

Jane Vahalik's expression had gotten more intent. "Did you see who was he meeting?"

It had been so long since that day, Cait could only shake her head. "I didn't even look. I was too taken aback to see Jerry."

"Why do you say 'taken aback'?"

"Frankly, I wouldn't have expected to recognize anyone," she explained. "You know I haven't been back in Angel Butte at all, don't you? Colin and I got together wherever I lived. Kids don't pay that much attention to adults, and after twenty years? Maybe a teacher. Even my friends from back then would have changed so much."

The lieutenant leaned forward. "Then why is it that you recognized Mr. Hegland right away?"

Cait hesitated. "I don't know how comfortable Colin would be with me telling you this."

"Whatever the connection is between you and Mr. Hegland, we have to find it," the other woman said gently.

"Yes, but this—" Oh, what difference did it make? If her mother lived there in town and had a reputation to protect, it might be different, but as it was, her secret wasn't that important, not to anyone. *Not even me,* she realized in surprise. Sixteen-year-old Cait had cared a whole lot, but now? Maybe after her own relationship with Blake, she'd gained some perspective. Who was she to sit in judgment of Mom?

"My mother had an affair with him," she said flatly—one second before the light rap of knuckles on her not-quite-latched door was followed by Noah stepping into the room. From his expression, she could tell he'd heard.

"Sorry to interrupt," he said, not bothering to sound as if he meant it.

The lieutenant wiped her face clean, the way Colin did so easily. To hide irritation? What could she say, given that Noah was essentially her boss, too?

"There's no reason you can't hear this, Noah," Cait said. "I truly can't imagine it has anything to do with what's happening now."

Jane glanced at her open notebook. "At ten years old, you understood that your mother was sleeping with a man not your father?"

"Of course not." *Brisk,* Cait told herself. *Make it clear to both of them that this is ancient history, that's all.* "I knew he was Mommy's friend. She took me with her sometimes to see him. He bought us burgers and fries. We took a picnic to a lake, that kind of thing. Only…maybe half a dozen times."

"And yet you remembered him." The lieutenant sounded skeptical.

Noah, leaning against the wall just inside the door, was watching Cait, but she didn't look at him.

"I doubt I would have, except when I was sixteen I found a packet of notes from him and a picture that my mother had kept. It was obvious from the notes that their relationship was sexual. I'd say my mother came crashing down from her pedestal, except, well, I was a teenager."

Jane cracked a smile. "And Mom had long since tumbled."

"Exactly. Even so, at the time, it was a big deal. That's why he was stuck in my head."

"Did he seem…dismayed that you recognized him?"

Cait thought back. "No. Surprised, maybe. Otherwise, the meeting was really underwhelming."

"And you haven't seen him again?"

She shook her head. "Nor heard from him. I half expected him to call, if only to ask about Mom, but their thing really was a long time ago."

Jane drilled on it some more, but she finally gave up. The meeting was so inconsequential, it couldn't possibly be relevant unless the fact that Cait and he had run into each other at all seemed significant to someone.

Cait took out her calendar, and they established that Jerry had been murdered the night she had had dinner with Beverly Buhl, Michael Kalitovic and Noah. Noah confirmed that he had followed Cait to her brother's house after the dinner, and he was able to tell Jane precisely what time he'd left Cait. Jane didn't question whether she had actually gone into the house, but close enough that Noah made a point of telling her Colin had come out on the porch to meet his sister. Which all seemed pointless to Cait; Colin had told her enough details, she knew Jerry's murder had happened much later—probably sometime between 11:00 p.m. and 1:00 a.m. If she'd wanted to kill him, she could have sneaked out of the house after Colin and Nell were asleep.

Colin could have done the same.

Appearing disappointed, Lieutenant Vahalik finally left.

Noah reached over and pulled the door completely shut behind her. "How are you?"

"Do you know how often you ask me that?"

"You live a wild life."

She scrunched up her nose at him. "I'm fine. Glad to be rid of Blake. Really freaked to find out someone else hates me."

He opened his mouth, closed it.

"What?" she asked.

"Just thinking this other person doesn't necessarily hate you. He—I say that for convenience and because not many women carry a nine millimeter—may conceivably never even have met you."

"Oh, that's a comfort."

His blue eyes were too perceptive. "How about dinner tonight? I can cook."

"Is it the sleepover you want?" She heard how sharp she sounded.

Something ghosted across Noah's face. She'd have given a lot to identify it.

"We can have a nice evening without you having to face down your brother."

In other words, no. He didn't want the commitment of having a woman—or, more specifically, *her*—actually spend the night. Last night had been different. He'd let his alarm get to him. But now his natural caution and disinterest in real commitment had kicked in.

Part of Cait wanted to tell him she had other plans. But, of course, he'd know better. He *was* her social life. Plus, call her weak, but she wanted to spend the evening with him. She wanted to make love with him, in that big bed amid the construction mess.

So after a minute, she nodded. "I'll let Colin know."

"Good." He didn't move for a long minute, his gaze on her face. Then he took the couple of steps necessary to kiss her lightly before saying, "Later," in a husky voice and leaving.

CHAPTER ELEVEN

THEY BARELY MADE it upstairs to his bed.

Once Noah, still sitting at the table after dinner, had pulled Cait down on his lap and gotten his hands under the petal-pink blazer, then beneath the thin, silky top, he'd been done for. The way she moaned and arched when he sucked her breast right through her bra, he doubted she'd have objected if he had unzipped and put her into place right there.

But then he'd lifted his head for a minute and seen lights across the river and realized that, there in front of the windows, they could be visible to a neighbor who happened to be out in his backyard admiring the stars or doing God knows what else.

Or to a man who had been following her, watching for his opportunity. The reminder that someone wanted to kill her and could conceivably be out there in the darkness this minute, watching, worked like cold water dumped over his head. It restored him to a measure of sanity, enough to enable him to lift her off him and hustle her toward the stairs.

Cait clutched her bra to her breasts—he guessed he must have unfastened it—and didn't object to the speedy pace he set. Beside the bed, she shed her clothes at the same time as he did. Looking at that long, slim body, nipples still tight, he was hit with another realization—he hadn't had any condoms with him downstairs. The idea of *using* a condom hadn't so much as crossed his mind. And that was a mistake he had never once made, not even when he was a perpetually horny sixteen-year-old.

Worse yet, just for a second he imagined that body swelling with pregnancy, and he hardened to the point of pain.

He did get the damn condom on.

They made love almost savagely. He could no longer think, could only try to get deeper, take her harder. She bit him on the shoulder as she came, and that sent him over the edge. Deaf, dumb and blind, all he could do was feel, the pleasure white-hot and the next thing to pain. He sagged on top of her, unable to so much as roll over. If Cait minded, he couldn't tell. Her arms held him tight.

God. He was probably crushing her. He couldn't remember when he'd last felt her breathe. It took a supreme act of will, but Noah finally managed to heave himself off that beautiful body and then gather her against him. She complied, laying a hand on the center of his chest and tucking her head beneath his chin. She wriggled until she was comfortable, then sighed.

Noah tried to lift his head to see her. He didn't

make it more than an inch off the pillow. Couldn't have seen her face anyway.

"Was that a happy sound or a miserable one?" he asked hoarsely.

"Umm…" She didn't sound any more together than he felt. "Contented."

"Good." Although he'd have preferred *ecstatic*. *Contented* sounded…bland. Nothing about what they had just done was bland, not in his book.

They lay in silence for a long time, him aware of her scent, her breath stirring his skin, of the fact that otherwise she wasn't moving at all. He didn't think she was sinking toward sleep, though. He thought she was as aware as he was.

"I suppose I should get dressed," she said eventually, and he knew he'd been right.

"What's your hurry?"

A jerk signified a shrug.

The strength of his annoyance took him by surprise. "I like having you here," he murmured.

"But not for the night."

Yeah, he wanted her all night. Every night. And that was the part that scared the shit out of him.

"I didn't say that."

"Yes, you did." She began to carefully separate herself from him. "It doesn't matter anyway. I just don't want Colin to have to wait up for me. He does, you know."

He rolled his head to see the digital clock. 8:43. "It's not late."

Sitting up now, she had her back to him. A long, slim back, the vertebrae delicate. Despite her height, all of her was delicate, a fact he forgot sometimes given the strength of her personality.

"It was a nice evening. Turns out you can cook," she teased.

He folded an arm to prop his head higher. The annoyance had ratcheted into something more indefinable and worrisome. Trying to keep any hint of whatever that was out of his voice, he said, "What did you think, I eat nothing that doesn't come from the freezer case?"

She twisted to see him. "You said you'd never cooked at Chandler's."

"I'm not creative. I'm capable," he said shortly.

"You're mad at me."

"No, I'm not." Yes, he was.

"Because I suggested going home."

"It's men who have the reputation for getting what they want and immediately having the itch to cut out."

Her eyes, wide, curious but also guarded, searched his for a moment that had his skin prickling. "I didn't mean it that way," she said.

"It doesn't matter." He sat up and put his feet on the floor. "You want to go home—you can go home." Not looking at her, he found his clothes on the floor mixed with hers. He tossed her stuff toward her while getting dressed himself.

After a minute, she did the same.

"It was a nice evening," she repeated after a minute, in a small voice. "I mean that."

He felt like a jackass. He rolled his shoulders, closed his eyes for a minute, then sat on the bed next to her. "Yes, it was. I'm sorry. I don't know what's wrong with me."

"You send mixed messages, you know."

He half smiled. "So do you."

"That's because—" Alarm on her face, she stopped.

She'd been on the verge of real honesty, he gathered. As in, saying something like, *That's because I have mixed feelings.*

As did he.

I'm afraid I'm in love with you. And I don't want to be.

Feeling like this could change everything.

He looped an arm around her, relieved when she leaned into him and pressed her cheek to his chest. "It's okay," he said quietly. "We have plenty of time. The threat to you has us both edgy. It can't help spilling over."

She didn't say anything. Then her head bobbed. "You're right. In fact, earlier I was thinking—" Once again she stopped, but not as abruptly this time, more as if not sure how to say whatever this was.

"Thinking?"

"It probably isn't important at all, but I said

something to Jerry." She tipped her head back to see him. "You know, Hegland?"

"I knew who you meant." He was getting a very bad feeling. "We're dressed. Let's go downstairs and have a cup of coffee or tea if you'd rather, and a slice of the key lime pie I bought at the bakery today. You can tell me what you said and why it's worrying you."

She nodded, forgetting her hurry to get back to her brother's.

She wanted tea, so he put the kettle on while she cut and dished up the pie. He cleared the table quickly, piling their dirty dinner dishes on the counter. Then they sat down and looked at each other.

"It was something I remembered. I didn't even know I did. It just…popped out from nowhere."

It. She was circling the point, and he couldn't help wondering why.

"Start at the beginning," he suggested. "You said, 'Jerry, how are you?'"

Cait wrinkled her nose. "Actually, I think I said, 'You?'"

Noah chuckled. "Then you said, 'How are you?'"

"No-o." She drew out the word. "I said, 'Jerry, right?' and he said he was surprised I recognized him. I think I introduced Nell. I don't know if I told you I was having lunch with her," she added as an aside. She frowned. "In fact, this was right after you called to offer me the job. She and I were just finishing lunch."

He nodded, reining in his chronic impatience.

"Anyway, looking at him, I had this sudden memory. He'd bought a house only a couple of blocks from ours. Not to live in—it was going to be a rental. He showed it to Mom one time when I was with them. Totally bored, of course," she added. "But later I went past it a lot. I liked to get out of the house, so I'd ride my bike. Mornings, sometimes." She gave him a quick glance. "You know my dad owned a tavern?"

Noah nodded.

"If he had to get up early for some reason, he was always really mad. Because he'd been up late, and I suppose he was hungover, too. All I knew was that I didn't like being around him. So if I could sneak out without him noticing, I did."

Noah remembered her describing her home life as unhappy. Was slipping out of the house an alternative to having to hide in her bedroom to avoid her father's fists? Had Dad yelled when he was mad, or expressed that anger physically on the nearest family member? If she'd spent a lot of time trying to pass unnoticed, how had she ended up the confident woman she was?

Picturing her as a big-eyed, skinny, quiet kid, Noah had to wrench his attention back to her when she continued her story.

"So one morning I'd sneaked out really early. I

was biking by the rental when I heard voices from the backyard. It was fenced, but next to it was a weedy vacant lot, so I sneaked in and found a crack between slats big enough I could see what they were doing. I was just curious. It was something to do." Faint creases appeared on her forehead. The teakettle was whistling and she hadn't noticed. Dread gripping him, Noah didn't move, either.

"For a while I couldn't figure it out, because there was string and boards laid out in a square, and inside those Jerry and another man seemed to be filling in a deep hole in the ground. I mean, there was this gigantic pile of dirt, and they were both sweating, and they seemed to be squabbling. You know, snapping at each other."

Her head finally turned. "Oh! The water."

The hell with the water. But he pushed back from the table. "I'll get it."

She waited while he poured and carried the two mugs back to the table, where their pie still sat untouched. He set one mug in front of her and carried the other to his side of the table.

Cait spooned sugar into hers and stirred for a moment, head bent. Then she looked at him again, and he saw her worry.

"I finally decided they were leveling the ground. Which they were. Because eventually a cement truck arrived and I got to watch a patio being poured. It was totally fascinating. At least, *I* thought so. After the truck left, Jerry and the other man smoothed the concrete and then finally they left. I saw Jerry's pickup driving away, but I was sort of hunkered down behind a shrub and I could tell they didn't see me. I liked to hide, so I guess I was going on instinct." She looked down into her tea. "This was a Saturday or a Sunday—I don't remember. I think I went home for breakfast, and I don't know what else, but eventually I gave in to temptation and I went back, let myself in through the gate and picked this place on the corner and pressed my hands into that wet concrete."

"You left handprints," he said slowly.

"Yes."

"Which they would have found later."

Cait nodded, her gaze never leaving his.

"But they'd have had no idea *who* left them."

This time she shook her head.

"And what is it you said, Cait? When you ran into Jerry?"

"I said, 'I'll bet you remember me best for the handprints I left in your concrete.' Or something like that."

"Goddamn, Cait."

"It was the hole, wasn't it?" she said miserably.

"The handprints must have scared the shit out of them. Maybe a kid had come on the wet concrete long after it was poured, but more likely this kid at least saw the truck pouring it. What must have really made them sweat was wondering how early the kid started watching. How much did he or she actually see?"

"It wasn't more than, I don't know, two or three weeks later that Mom took me away from Angel Butte."

"And Jerry and his buddy probably spent months worrying. But eventually, when nothing happened, they'd have quit worrying."

"Until I opened my mouth," she whispered.

He held out a hand. "Come here."

She came. This time, making love wasn't on his mind. Holding her tight, keeping her safe, was.

"You know you need to tell Lieutenant Vahalik, don't you?"

She shook her head. "Colin. I need to tell Colin first."

NOAH DROVE HER home, parked and came in with her as though his doing so was a given. Cait knew she ought to protest. Did he think she was incapable of telling Colin the story herself? Did he believe she'd leave parts out if he wasn't there to keep her honest? Or was he only taking charge, the way he always did?

But she didn't mind as much as she should. She doubted he was in love with her or anything like that, but he cared, and right now, she needed to know someone did.

Oh, who was she kidding? She wanted to know that *Noah* cared.

She wanted him to love her.

Stupid, when it was so impossible for so many reasons.

Colin, of course, had met them on the porch. He looked more curious than irritated when Noah mounted the steps beside her. She hadn't really noticed until now, but...was it possible they were becoming reconciled to each other?

"Chandler," her brother said, nodding.

"McAllister." Noah laid a hand on her back. "Cait's remembered something."

Nell brought them coffee, asked if they'd prefer she not be there, then sat down cuddled up to Colin once Cait said, "Of course you can stay."

Colin listened in increasingly grim silence as Cait told him a slightly condensed version of the story. She didn't have to explain why she'd slipped out of the house early in the morning to ride her bike aimlessly around the neighborhood, for example. He knew.

He didn't say a single word until she was done. Then he gusted out a breath. "Well, damn."

She laughed a little. She was probably semi-hysterical. "Sorry," she said after seeing the others' expressions. "That's pretty much exactly what Noah said."

Her brother made a sound, half hum and half growl, that she'd come to know meant he was thinking. "Actually, this is good. We needed an explanation, and now we have one. Once we dig up the ground there, we might have some answers."

Without even looking at him, Cait felt Noah's tension.

"That doesn't help Cait," he said. "We don't know who the second man is. But Cait *saw* him. Even if it's what we think it might be, she's the only person in the world who can put him there, burying a goddamn body."

"Can you find the house after so long?" Nell asked.

"All we'd have to do is call up property records," Cait told her. "But I'm pretty sure I can. I rode my bike *a lot*. I swear, I can still picture every bump for ten blocks around where the sidewalk was buckling over a tree root."

"First thing in the morning," her brother said decisively. His gaze rested on Noah. "You planning to come with us?"

"Yes." That was all. *Yes*. Noah didn't even look at her.

Hadn't it occurred to him that he was seriously endangering the plan of keeping their relationship clandestine? A plan, it occurred to her, designed to protect *her* job, not his. So maybe he didn't care that much.

He and Colin were discussing when to meet. Not where—they'd already decided that. They would start in front of her childhood home. The one she'd had no desire to visit for old times' sake.

Nell gave her a sudden, sympathetic grin that neither of the men noticed. Cait rolled her eyes in return.

"All right." Noah pushed himself to his feet, apparently satisfied. "I'll see you in the morning." His back to Colin, he smiled at Cait. "It's good you remembered."

"*I* should have remembered," her sister-in-law said.

Colin kissed her cheek. "Yeah, you should have." But he didn't sound at all critical. His Nell walked on water as far as he was concerned.

Cait went to the door with Noah, but he didn't let her step outside. "Sleep tight," he said in a low voice, but there were no good-night kisses for her.

She locked the door behind him and turned to meet her brother's eyes.

"You're getting yourself in trouble there," he said. "You do know that, don't you?"

"What makes you say that?" she asked, with fair dignity, if she did say so.

He shook his head. "I'm not blind."

She was an adult. She did *not* have to answer to her brother. "We're being discreet."

"You barely got rid of one son of a bitch, and you're taking on another?"

"Don't you dare compare Noah to Blake," Cait said hotly.

He blinked in surprise at her furious reaction. "I

didn't mean to. But he can be ruthless. Don't kid yourself he's not."

"He's come to my rescue every time I called."

Her brother relented. "He has. I'll give him that. But long-term…" He shook his head.

"Maybe I'm not looking for long-term." Why even say that when she was? *She was.*

His expression froze. Oh, he didn't like that. But after a moment Colin gave a stiff nod. Cait suspected Nell had squeezed his hand or elbowed him or something.

"I'm going to bed," she announced and went, leaving a crashing silence behind her.

COLIN DIDN'T SEEM any more inclined to talk this morning than she did. Seeing the house where they'd both grown up was unlikely to cause him any heartburn—he'd lived in it for several years after she was gone, after all, and had been the one to have to clean it out and sell it after their father had died. Plus, in all the years since, he was bound to have driven past it now and again.

Her tension grew as the route became increasingly familiar.

She'd been friends with the girl who lived there, on the corner, but couldn't remember her name. Cait had even had sort of a crush on the girl's older brother. *Kurt,* she thought suddenly. *Kurt and… Sarah.* She wondered what had happened to them, and whether she'd recognize either of them if they came face-to-face.

Oh—and there was the spot she'd fallen off her bike and broken her arm. That was an awful summer. She hadn't been able to swim, or ride her bike, or do hardly anything for ages.

They were only a couple of blocks away.

"Did you think about keeping the house?" she asked, her voice tight. "I mean, living here?"

"Hell, no!"

Startled at Colin's vehemence, she realized that his knuckles showed white. Maybe she had been wrong. His memories might be even worse than hers.

"When I left for college, I swore I'd never set foot in the place again," he said after a minute. "Of course, I had to when the time came to put it on the market." He paused. "I wouldn't have kept it no matter what. You were entitled to half of the only estate he had to leave us."

She nodded. "I almost told you I didn't want it."

He laughed. "I gave serious thought to burning the house down and being done with it."

That made her mouth curve. "There were enough zeroes on the check, greed overcame me. It paid a lot of tuition."

"I'm glad." He smiled at her, warmth in those gray eyes. "It gave me a down payment. Something good came from his legacy." He steered his SUV to the curb and set the emergency brake. "Here we are."

Oh, boy.

Reluctantly, she turned her head, felt a momentary lurch in her chest followed by...relief.

She'd have recognized the house, of course she would have, but it had changed so much, too. Painted a sunny yellow with pale rust-and-white trim, the small rambler looked cheerful. Neither of their parents had been gardeners, but someone who lived there now was. A white-painted arch at the side of the house was covered with a rose that wasn't yet in bloom and a blue-flowered clematis. A broad border brimming with perennials separated the small lawn from the sidewalk. A pink girl's bike with handlebar ribbons lay on its side in the driveway.

Cait stared.

Colin hadn't moved. "I also swore I'd never mow another lawn."

"But you would if Nell wanted one, wouldn't you?"

He gave a gruff laugh. "You've got me there. I might even enjoy it."

Tears prickled in the backs of her eyes even as she found herself smiling as she gazed out the side window at a house that looked happy. What better illustration that life does move on?

"So," her brother said, all business again. "Do we walk from here, or do we drive?"

ALEC RAYNOR DIDN'T invite Colin to sit down. After summoning him midmorning with a terse phone call, he kept him standing there like a disobedient kid in the principal's office. All he did was sit behind that desk and survey Colin with scathing dark eyes.

"Tell me about this warrant."

Shit. Colin didn't even know how he'd heard. By nine-thirty that morning, Cait had led them all straight to the house. A search of records showed that Hegland had sold it ten years ago. Jane had gone for a warrant allowing them to look under the concrete patio in the backyard. Just before the phone call from Raynor, Colin had learned the warrant had come through.

"Are you aware that the gun used to fire the shots that killed Jerry Hegland was also used to attempt to kill my sister?" Colin asked.

"I was. Although not from you." The bite wasn't meant to be subtle.

It took a discernible moment for Colin to unclench his jaw. "We've been searching for a connection between Cait and Hegland. We've found one."

"We."

"Last I knew, Investigations is under my authority."

"Under your authority is one thing. But this is your sister. It didn't occur to you that it might be smart to keep some distance?"

"What if this was *your* sister?"

"I don't have one."

"Anyone you love."

A nerve jumped in his cheek. The next moment, his eyebrows peaked. "You're asking if I understand why you don't feel like you can sit back and wait for someone else to figure out who is trying to kill your sister."

"Yes."

"I do understand. Will *you* understand when the D.A. declines to file charges because the investigator was biased?"

He'd have given any underling the same lecture. Fury still burned in his chest and rose like acid in his throat. Swallowing it, he couldn't say a word without risking the wrong ones coming out.

"Your sister knew this Jerry Hegland."

Colin gave a tight nod.

"What about you?"

"Not at all when we were kids. More recently… I don't recall meeting him although it's possible I have."

"Were you aware that your sister knew this man?"

Another *shit*.

"She told me a couple of weeks ago."

A man with a gift for stillness, Raynor finally leaned forward, those dark eyes locked on Colin's. "Did she tell you that Hegland had an affair with your mother?"

"Yes."

"And it never crossed your mind that you are too goddamn personally involved to play *any role at all* in this investigation?"

"Lieutenant Vahalik is leading it," he said woodenly.

"Uh-huh. And did you share with the lieutenant what you knew about Mr. Hegland?"

"I believed it had no relevance."

"Until you found out it did."

"When my sister realized the relevance, she immediately shared the history with Lieutenant Vahalik."

"*She* did."

"Neither of us was hiding anything. There's something *you* have to understand. This isn't Los Angeles. Angel Butte is…not a small town anymore, but it was. I know a good part of the population. I went to school with some of them. I know whose father was a drunk, whose mother burned her with cigarette butts. I didn't like my father's cronies, but when they're victim or perpetrator, I treat them the same as I do anyone else. When something I know becomes relevant, I act on it. Otherwise, I keep confidences. My mother's relationship with this man took place twenty years ago. My family is entitled to some privacy, just like every other family in this town is."

Raynor's eyes had narrowed. For a long time, he didn't say anything. Finally he made a rough sound in his throat.

"You're right. Up until you were wrong."

Colin stood stiffly. At last he bent his head in an acknowledging nod.

"Sit," Raynor snapped.

He closed his eyes, thought about telling the son of a bitch where to go and how long he should roast there, then counted to ten. At which point he was able to unbend enough to take a seat.

"Our detectives aren't as experienced as I'd like," he said, hating that he had to explain himself. "You've looked at the personnel records. People with experience got frustrated and left the department. They weren't getting the pay or support they should have been."

"I'm aware of the issues," Raynor conceded. "I admit I wondered why you chose Vahalik to head Investigations."

"Only a couple of detectives have more experience than she does. Neither of them are as smart, or have people skills to match hers. She's good."

"All right."

He had one last thing to say. "I've tried to stay on the right side of a line while protecting my sister to the best of my ability."

Raynor sat back in his chair, his face showing some wear it hadn't a few minutes before. "I'll say this again. I sympathize, but you have to back off." He held up a hand. "I'm not telling you not to play bodyguard. But you can't talk to witnesses or suspects. You've got to quit pulling Vahalik's strings. You say she's good. Trust her."

Colin had seldom detested anything like he did being censured by the man who sat behind *his* desk, but he had no choice but to take it. What most shamed him was the knowledge he deserved every word. And more. He'd had no business being the one to interview Blake Ralston, even if he had stuck to the present crime.

"Are we done?" he asked.

"Yeah." There was a subtle shift in Raynor's expression. "This doesn't mean you can't go watch the excavation. I admit, I'm curious. I may stop by myself."

Colin pushed himself out of his chair. "Bored so soon?" he asked sardonically.

The new police chief was good at veiling his expression. "It's…not what I'm used to."

They had yet to manage anything really friendly. They weren't going to start now. Colin nodded and left without another word.

CHAPTER TWELVE

THE BACKYARD of the small tract house was a popular place to be, Noah discovered. He understood why. God knew he didn't have any business there, and he couldn't stay away. His initial surprise at seeing Alec Raynor among the spectators faded; he found he even approved. A hands-on administrator himself, he wouldn't have wanted a police chief content to sit on his ass behind the desk any more than he'd appreciated former chief Bystrom's habit of spending half his working days riding a chairlift at Mount Bachelor or thigh-deep in the Deschutes River casting a line, depending on the season.

It was telling, however, that Cait's brother stood on the opposite side of the excavation from Raynor. No fellowship growing there. Which didn't matter to Noah, only that they worked together when they had to. If not, one or both would be gone.

Instinct told him he wouldn't have to interfere, though. Colin had put off announcing his candidacy for county sheriff, probably because of his sister's troubles, but he'd be running. If he lost, Noah guessed he'd find a job somewhere else. He wasn't a personality content to be subordinate to a man not much older than him and possibly less qualified for the job of police chief.

Both men glanced at him, neither looking thrilled to see him, then turned immediately back to the growing hole. To one side of it was the dirt that had been shoveled out; a few feet away, broken concrete had been heaped after it had been jackhammered into pieces.

Jane Vahalik and another plainclothes officer were present, too, as well as a couple of people Noah assumed were crime scene technicians. A young, distressed-looking woman hovering by the sliding door might be the home owner.

Noah nodded at Raynor but circled the yard until he reached Colin's side.

"We're going to feel foolish if there's nothing here," he said in a low voice, only belatedly realizing that by saying "we," he was aligning himself with McAllister.

"We have to look." Colin shook his head. "Who are we kidding? We'll feel more than foolish. We'll discover we still don't have a clue."

Noah grunted agreement. "Were Cait's handprints still visible?"

Colin jerked his head toward the pile. "Take a look. We set that chunk aside."

Noah saw now that one piece of concrete, approximately two feet by two feet, lay separate from the pile. Stepping closer, he stared down at it. There they were—two small handprints, neatly set in place, fingers splayed. Cait's.

His heart lurched, and it was a long time until he could make himself look away.

"You going to take it with you?" he asked.

"Yeah." Colin rotated his shoulders as if to relieve stiffness. "It's part of her life."

"Good." Noah was more relieved than he wanted to be.

After their brief exchange, no one talked except the two guys taking turns in the hole. They had apparently started with shovels but were now working with what appeared to be gardening trowels. Impatient as he was, Noah understood. If there were bones, the medical examiner would want them as intact as possible.

The day was hot. Noah slapped at mosquitoes and flies. Traffic passed out on the street. A lawn mower growled a few houses away. The unmistakable rumble of a school bus came and went, followed by the shouts of kids. The home owner eventually went inside and returned with a pitcher of lemonade and plastic cups for everyone. Phones rang and were mostly ignored, although Raynor stepped away for one intense conversation, as did Vahalik twenty minutes or half an hour later.

Noah began to get restless and think about everything piling up in his absence, but he didn't even consider leaving although he couldn't have said why. Interestingly, Raynor never moved beyond downing a glass of lemonade and nodding his thanks to the young woman.

The guy in the hole said suddenly, "Here we go."

Everyone present pointed as if they were a pack of hunting dogs that had just caught the scent.

There was a lot of discussion among the crime scene people, and the trowels were discarded in favor of brushes and some other tools Noah couldn't make out. A small woman kneeling beside the hole seemed to be in charge. She finally swiveled to look at Lieutenant Vahalik and Colin.

"We've definitely got a skeleton," she said, her voice charged with satisfaction. "It'll take us another few hours to get him out."

Colin stepped forward. "Him?"

"Bones aren't my thing, but I'm betting male. Look at the size of the humerus."

Noah joined the cluster around what they now knew was a grave. The soil lacked the reddish tint that was common in the area, the result of relatively recent volcanic activity. The curve of skull was visible, emerging from the soil, as was the arch of ribs and the bones of one arm. From the position, it appeared it had lain across his chest or belly when the dirt came down on top of him.

Colin, who had squatted behind the woman he called Linda, glanced over his shoulder and met

Noah's eyes. The silent moment of communication didn't call for words.

Noah had seen enough. Cait would be waiting to hear.

CAIT THOUGHT SHE might go crazy. Forbidden from leaving city hall during the day, therefore unable to personally inspect sites, visit ongoing projects or meet with anyone outside her office, she could do about half the job. Otherwise, she was supervised by one of the two men in her life, both alpha males who assumed she'd jump when told to jump and who looked vaguely surprised when she expressed even the slightest bit of frustration. She wondered if they had any idea how much they had in common.

Kindness was one of the qualities they shared, fairness reminded her. Noah had stopped by her office yesterday afternoon to let her know what had been uncovered beneath the patio. He didn't linger, but must have known how tensely she was waiting to hear the news.

Midmorning today, Jane Vahalik knocked and came in. "I'm sure you know the remains are now with the medical examiner," she began.

Cait nodded. "Has he learned anything yet?"

"So far, all we've been told is that the bones definitely belonged to a male, a big guy, likely in his forties."

"How will you be able to identify him?"

"If he was reported missing, that won't be a problem given dental records. Otherwise, it will be a bigger challenge."

A little surprised the lieutenant was being so open with her, Cait decided to push it. "Do you know what killed him?"

Jane eyed her for a minute and then seemed to make a decision. "Likely gunshots. We found two bullets below him. The body decomposed and, uh…"

She couldn't help the shudder. "I get the picture."

"May I sit down?"

Cait half rose. "Of course you can! I'm sorry."

Jane pulled a chair closer to Cait's desk and settled in. "Let's talk about what you saw the day the patio was poured."

"I told Colin—"

"Tell me." Her tone was pleasant but implacable.

Resigned, Cait repeated the story, ending with the handprints.

"All right, let's go back. Obviously, you recognized Mr. Hegland immediately."

"I heard his voice, so I already knew it was him."

"Tell me what he was wearing, if you can recall."

Cait opened her mouth to ask what possible difference that made, but she realized the lieutenant was trying to get her to *see* the scene—including the other man.

She closed her eyes and tried to become that girl, crouched behind the fence with one eye to the crack, not even sure why she cared what the two men were up to.

I might not have, if they hadn't been so angry. Or was it tense?

She remembered being a little chilly because it was such early morning. At first she'd just knelt, but finally she'd sat cross-legged on the shaggy grass even though her butt got damp through the denim of her jeans. Funny, she could look down and see her jeans, one of the ratty pairs she wore on weekends. Mom got mad if she wore her school clothes any other time. These had a big rip that allowed her bony knee to poke out.

"That's good," Jane murmured, and Cait realized she'd been talking out loud.

"Jerry wore khaki trousers and a sweatshirt that he took off not long after I started watching. He kept swiping at his forehead with his forearm. I remember big patches of sweat under his arms and even between his shoulder blades. His hair was kind of wet and poking up. He was really filthy." She giggled, and it was a little girl's giggle. "They used lots of really bad words. Dad did, too, but Mom always tried to shush him when I was around. Except…" When he was drunk. Then Mom, afraid of him, didn't even try.

"What was his voice like, this other man?"

"Just…a regular voice." She frowned. "The weird thing about him was that he hadn't dressed for that kind of work. I think he might have had on good slacks and a white shirt and dress shoes. He took off the white shirt, too. He had on an undershirt, you know, just white. *It* was filthy, too, by the time I got there." She felt dreamy, only idly curious the way a ten-year-old could be. Why had those two men dug such a humongous hole? And how come they were filling it now? Maybe there'd been, like, a pipe leaking or something. She really wanted to know what the boards were for, built like a frame only lying flat on the ground.

"His hair…" She had to hesitate. "I think it was brown. Kind of a medium brown. But he was awfully sweaty, too, so it might have been dark blond. He was…not as big as Jerry. Maybe as tall, but not as wide. More lean. And he wasn't tan like Jerry, so he must not have spent much time outside. His arms were really pale. Like my dad was when he took his shirt off. A lot of the time he had his back to me. I only remember him facing me directly once—" She stiffened, in an echo of her momentary fear that day. "I kind of squirmed and knocked my bike over. It didn't make a lot of noise because it fell on grass, but he swung around and stared. I almost took off."

It chilled her now, knowing what would have happened if he had come looking.

"Can you see his face, Cait?" Jane asked patiently.

"Yes," she breathed. "But…I don't know, there wasn't anything special about it. He was kind of ordinary-looking. The one thing I remember is that Jerry seemed to be afraid of him." Opening her eyes, she thought that over. "*Afraid* isn't the right word. I think the other guy was in charge. Used to being in charge. He expected Jerry to take orders."

"That's interesting," the lieutenant said. "So he was dressed as if he'd expected to go into the office that day, even though it was a weekend."

"Yes."

"As dirty as he'd gotten, he'd have had to go home and change."

Cait nodded. "I remember wondering why, if he was going to help his friend, he hadn't dressed in his working-in-the-yard clothes."

"Because this wasn't planned," Jane said thoughtfully. "Looking back, how do you read what you saw as tension?"

"They were upset." She couldn't be sure how she knew with such certainty, but she did. "Really upset. It came out as urgency and an air of violence, but mostly…" She hesitated. "I think they were probably horrified. Freaked. Maybe they'd never killed a man before."

This shudder made her glance down and see that her arms were crossed and squeezed tight.

"My father was angry a lot," she said after a minute, with some difficulty. "I didn't know many other men very well. I'd never had a male teacher, and my parents weren't churchgoers. I guess I expected men to be angry. I saw what I expected."

"But you'd liked Mr. Hegland, when you and your mother spent time with him."

"He was nice to me," she corrected. "He bought me some treats. I was a kid—of course I liked that. But I was wary of him." Yes, that was how she'd describe her caution that had verged on suspicion.

The same way she'd continued to approach men, she thought with shock.

Too bad she'd relaxed her caution where Blake was concerned.

And—why was she letting herself trust Noah? He sometimes radiated anger and menace that should have her quailing but didn't. Because he'd never turned it on her.

That didn't mean he wouldn't. Blake had hidden his propensity for violence, too. *No,* she thought. The thing with Noah was he didn't. She *knew* what kind of man he was. Which allowed her to—mostly—trust him.

And that makes no sense, she finally concluded.

She realized Jane was studying her, as if speculating on what was going through her head. Cait was embarrassed to realize she'd probably been staring into space for several minutes.

"Would you recognize this man?" Jane asked bluntly.

She found herself shaking her head. "I really doubt it. I have yet to recognize a single other adult I encountered back then. Jerry was a special case, and that was partly because Mom had kept a couple pictures of him. Plus, I guess he was more distinctive-looking. He hadn't changed that much, either. This other guy…" She shrugged. "He could have lost his hair, gained fifty pounds, who knows?"

Jane sighed and closed her notebook. "Well, we have a basic description and we know he was a professional man."

"Of sorts. He could have worked in a store or sold insurance or something like that." Cait grimaced. "What if it was Sunday morning, and he'd planned to attend church?"

"But from what you say, he didn't have the muscles of a working man and didn't have the tan to suggest he got out of an office very often."

"That's true. I'm sorry. I wish I could have been more help."

"Considering you're trying to remember something that happened eighteen years ago—or is it nineteen?—I'd say you have amazing recall."

"It's because I did something daring."

Jane looked intrigued. "Pressing your hands into the concrete."

"Yes. I…wasn't a daring child." At home, she had tried so very hard to go completely unnoticed. She must have been all but a wraith. Suddenly impatient with herself, she said, "Do you have any more questions?"

"No." The lieutenant departed with a reminder to call if she remembered anything else.

She was grateful to have Jane Vahalik coming

to ask her questions and not one of the detectives who worked under her, all men from what Cait understood. She knew perfectly well why she rated a lieutenant and not a mere detective. They must all be eager to please Colin.

Was there any chance she and Jane could be friends when this was all over? Cait would really like to know how a woman not that much older than she was had come to be so confident that she could thrive in a workplace environment brimming with testosterone. Cait couldn't relate it to her own profession, where no one carried a gun.

Of course, it was entirely possible she wouldn't still be in Angel Butte to make friends. She couldn't live at a constant level of fear. Leaving might be best. No matter what, she couldn't imagine how she could balance the job with a relationship with Noah. Or how she could continue to work with him once they no longer *had* a relationship.

She hadn't used her head where he was concerned. *After Noah,* she thought, *I really* will *swear off men.*

Cait already knew he was going to hurt her more than Blake ever had.

EVEN KNOWING IT wasn't helping his cause, Noah scowled at Cait from where he stood in her office doorway. "I'd have sat in with you if you'd called me."

Cait gazed coolly at him. "Lieutenant Vahalik

and I did fine. I didn't need moral support. It's not as if she suspects me of some dire crime."

He glanced over his shoulder, then stepped in and shut the door even though he knew there already had to be gossip circulating about them. "What did she ask you?"

She rolled a pen between her fingers in one of the few nervous gestures he'd seen her make. "She hoped I'd remember the other man."

From that day. As Noah had stood in that backyard earlier, his gaze kept going to the six-foot board fence not twenty feet from the edge of what had been the patio. What if they'd seen her? No, he knew—she'd have died. They could so easily have added her to the open grave. *God.* He was terrified thinking about it, even though the risk to that curious little girl had come and gone so long ago.

"Do you?" Remembered fear roughened his voice.

She shook her head. "Not very well. As I told the lieutenant, the only adult I've recognized since I got here is Jerry. I saw this guy once. I didn't pay that much attention to him."

"You know how important it is."

Suddenly she looked mad. "Is this your idea of a pep talk?"

"Damn it, Cait, your life could depend on recognizing this man if you come face-to-face! How long did you watch them? An hour? More? How can you not remember him?"

"How well do *you* remember things from when you were that young?"

She didn't know that felt like a brutal kick to his kidney.

But, Dad! You said we could go fishing! You promised.

There isn't a single good thing he could have inherited from his father.

Gut roiling, he took a step toward her, until only the desk was a barricade between them. "The ones that count?" His voice was guttural. "A hell of a lot better than you seem to."

Her chair squeaked as she recoiled from him. Noah was stunned to realize he'd bared his teeth. The worst part was seeing the expression on her face, one he knew too well.

"Don't look at me like that."

"Like what?" she shot back.

"Like you're afraid of me."

"My problems aren't yours. You have no right to get mad at me."

Oh, hell. Fighting for control, he turned his back on her for a moment. At last he felt able to face her again. "I'm not mad. I'm afraid for you."

Eyes still dominating her face, she shook her head. "You're angry."

"Cait." He wanted the grit to leave his voice but couldn't seem to make it. "You…reminded me of things I'd rather not remember. That's all. I was angry at other people, not you. Maybe even at myself because there's so little I can do to keep you safe. Being ineffectual doesn't sit well with me."

For a long, quivering moment, she kept staring. "I don't believe you," she said. Only the faintest tremor betrayed her tension. "It was me. *You* would have remembered. *You* could probably pick the guy out of a lineup. Well, I'm sorry I can't, but that's the way it is."

Her phone vibrated on the desk, and her gaze dropped to it. "That'll be Colin. He's letting me know he's on his way to pick me up. You'll have to excuse me, Noah."

He couldn't believe how badly he'd screwed up. He'd *known* she was abused as a child. What did he think, she was going to laugh it off when he was an asshole to her?

"Call him." He let her hear his urgency. "Have dinner with me."

She gave a small laugh that broke. "That's just what I want to do."

"Please."

As if she hadn't even heard, Cait yanked her giant bag from beneath the desk and rose. "I need to go." She dropped the phone into it.

He wanted to block the doorway, make her listen. He might have done that if he'd known what to say. What he felt. What he really wanted.

But the truth was, he had no idea. So after a moment, he opened her door and stepped into the outer office, where a couple of other women were collecting handbags and getting ready to leave, too.

"Tomorrow, Cait," he said gruffly and left before she could, the emotions he didn't want to identify so goddamn tangled inside him, they constricted his lungs and maybe even the basic functioning of his heart.

He stayed late, because what did he have to go home to? Instead of Chandler's—*Do you ever eat anywhere else?*—he continued down the block to the Kingfisher Café, where Nell and Cait had dined the day they ran into Jerry Hegland. He didn't remember ever being in there.

He did recognize the woman who stepped out of the kitchen and glanced around shortly after he'd ordered, though. Her hair wasn't the same color it had been when they'd met—had to be a meeting of the Association of Downtown Merchants, he decided. Then the short spiky hair had been hot pink; now it was turquoise. She'd been especially outspoken.

She saw him, raised her eyebrows and wound her way between tables until she reached his. "Mayor."

He summoned a smile. "I'm afraid I don't remember your name."

"Hailey Allen."

"That's right. Pleasure to meet you again."

"What brings you here?"

"Curiosity. Your café seems to be a favorite lunch spot for a lot of city hall workers."

Satisfaction showed on her face. "That's because I make fabulous food."

If the good smells in here were any indication, she did. He grinned. "Have you eaten at Chandler's?"

"I have. I've tried pretty much every restaurant in town, barring the Red Robin and Olive Gardens."

"And?"

"Your food is good, too." She sounded a little grudging. "You could get more creative, but I liked what I had."

"You're young to have your own place."

"You're young to have three. *And* be mayor."

"I like to be in charge."

She flashed a saucy grin. "Ditto."

His soup arrived. The waitress couldn't hide her curiosity. He began to wonder why Hailey still stood there.

"Care to join me?" he asked.

"Lord, no! I don't have time. Just checking you out."

"Why?" he asked, amused. He wasn't getting any sexual vibe from her, and although he liked her, she didn't do anything for him sexually, either.

"Nell McAllister is one of my best friends. We went to high school together."

"And she's talked about me."

Hailey shrugged. "Sure. I'm getting to know Cait, too."

His amusement passed. Gaze and voice both became unapproachable. He was good at that. "Cait who works for me."

"That would be her." She glanced over her shoulder. "Oh, shoot. I've got to go back to work." One eyebrow rose, looking natural in her quirky, not-quite-symmetrical face. "Good talking, Mayor."

"Noah."

She just smiled and whisked herself back to the kitchen. Intrigued, he watched her go, wondering how she stayed plump given her air of unending vitality.

Once he started eating, he had his answer. She was too good a cook. He indulged himself in plotting to lure her to Chandler's—but this was a weeknight, and the tables in *her* restaurant were staying full with a cluster of people waiting to be seated. Something told him she couldn't be lured, not by anything he had to offer, anyway.

He studied faces as he ate, his gaze pausing on men in the right age range. Who had Jerry Hegland been with the day he encountered Cait? Unlikely it had been the man who was trying to kill her. Still, Jerry must have called him or gone to see him right away and said, *You'll never believe this.*

But why had *he* had to die?

Noah turned that over in his mind as he concluded his meal with a Kahlúa-swirl cheesecake that almost made him moan out loud.

Hell. Maybe he could hire Ms. Allen to create a few new dessert items for Chandler's.

He walked back to the garage to reclaim his Suburban and drove home. The house had never felt emptier when he let himself in. His usual pleasure in what he'd accomplished seemed to be missing. He'd wanted Cait there tonight.

He wanted her there every night.

He'd known better than to start anything with her. This was why, damn it. He'd sworn he would never let himself feel like this.

That was almost funny. Let himself? He'd never believed he *could* feel like this.

Noah hadn't moved; still stood at the foot of the stairs, paralyzed because he'd been stupid enough to fall in love for the first time in his life. What other explanation was there for this powerful need to protect her, this blinding anger at anyone who had ever hurt her or even thought about hurting her? This hunger for her body, her laugh, her take on whatever he was thinking about at any given time? What else could it be?

He wished he still had a wall to rip out. It was too late in the evening to work on his bedroom. He had to do some patching, floor, walls and ceiling, before he could start constructing new walls. He needed something mindless and more physical than that.

He could start on that front bedroom, the one Cait had called the nursery. Steam the old wallpaper off or sand the floor. Strip woodwork. His intention had been to finish the small bedrooms all the same way, maybe vary paint color. Now—goddamn it, now he kept seeing those yellow ducklings.

If he was going to turn the house over, it wouldn't hurt to finish a couple of the bedrooms to appeal to kids.

He'd intended to stay in this house, just as he intended to stay in Angel Butte. A man who knew what he wanted, he'd dug in there. He didn't like being confused.

He had to decide what to do about these feelings.

Walking away? Not an option given the danger that stalked Cait.

Yeah? mocked a voice in his head. *Why not? Her brother's a cop. He's more qualified than you are to protect her. She doesn't need you.*

He ignored the voice.

He also ignored the one pointing out that, if he got in a whole lot deeper, he might as well let her start dragging home wallpaper books.

Maybe that wouldn't be so bad.

Jesus, he thought incredulously, *it's already too late.*

CHAPTER THIRTEEN

CAIT POURED DETERGENT into the dishwasher and then straightened. She'd hold off starting it since she could hear Nell still in the shower. Colin was grabbing the dish towel and reaching for a saucepan in the drainer when Cait shut the dishwasher.

"I'm going to call Mom tonight," she said. "She still doesn't know I've moved back here."

Her brother hung up the dish towel, his eyes on her. He was good at giving nothing away. "All right," he said slowly. "Probably past time. Can you ask her some questions about Hegland while you're at it? I doubt she had any idea what he was into, but you never know."

"I wonder." And had all too many times as she lay awake thinking about why someone wanted to kill her. "Remember, in one of the notes Mom had kept, he said something about how she was wrong, whatever she thought, and why wouldn't she call him. What if she heard or saw something that made her suspect he was into bad stuff? Maybe she *was* thinking about marrying him until then."

"Which would explain why she ran instead of

just asking Dad for a divorce and staying in town."
He frowned. "I always assumed it was because she
was scared of him."

"Me, too."

"Will she tell you if you ask?"

"I don't know," she admitted. "After our huge
blowup, we've never talked about Jerry again."

"Try," he said, and, after a moment, she nodded.

Instead of retreating to her bedroom, she took
her phone to the living room. If Colin overheard
from the kitchen, that was fine with her.

She kicked off her shoes, curled up on one end
of the sofa and punched in her mom's number.

Her mother answered on the third ring. "Cait?
It's been months! Why haven't you returned any
of my calls?"

"It's been maybe two months," she retorted, re-
calling all too well their last conversation. She'd
been hiding so much. Mom did know she'd broken
up with Blake, but not why, of course. She made
light of the fact that she was staying with a friend
rather than renting a place of her own. No mention of her stalker, or that she was hunting desperately for a job so she could get out of Seattle. She
hadn't exactly lied, but she wasn't exactly honest
about her life, either. "And, well, I've kind of been
in transition," she continued.

"In transition?"

Cait had no trouble picturing the expression on
her mother's face.

"I've taken a job in Angel Butte."

The silence was so complete, she wasn't sure her mother was still breathing.

"There was a perfect opening for me. And…I wanted to get to know Colin again. I'm actually staying with him and his wife right now."

"What about your PhD?" Mom asked after a minute. "And…what kind of job?"

She did have good reasons for putting off working on her dissertation, but the mention still made her wince. Cait was embarrassed at how little thought she'd given to it.

"I'm the director of community development. The area is booming economically, and I'll have the chance to really help shape the city to improve livability." She was starting to sound like a press release. "I like the job," she finished more weakly.

"I don't understand." Mom's voice wavered, as if she'd aged twenty years in the past minute. "What would make you go back? You *know* what we escaped."

"And *you* know Dad has been dead a long time." It came out more sharply than she'd intended.

"Your brother—"

"Turned into a good, strong man." She turned her head to see that Colin, while still in the kitchen, was watching her. "Did you know he's planning to run for sheriff of Butte County?"

"I hate the idea of him carrying a gun!" Mom was verging on hysteria.

"He's just the kind of man who should." Of course he would never have gone after Jerry Hegland. Not Colin, a man whose sense of honor was as much a part of him as was his protective nature—and his willingness to do anything for her, the sister who had rebuffed him over and over. In that moment, Cait would have given anything to take back the words she'd spoken so unthinkingly to him.

"You don't know him, Mom."

"I can only pray you're right," she said stiffly.

Mom wasn't going to accept that she could have been wrong about Colin. Maybe she *couldn't,* not and live with herself.

"I am," Cait said. "Listen, I called mostly to let you know where I am, but there's something else." She hesitated. "When I first got here, I ran into Jerry Hegland."

"Jerry?" her mother whispered.

"He hadn't changed that much. It was more of a surprise that he knew me."

"I don't understand. How could he possibly have recognized you?" She sounded stunned.

"Well, it's not like we ran into each other in Seattle where there wouldn't have been any context. Colin's in the news all the time. It would be logical that I'd be in town once in a while." She took a deep breath. "Mom, Jerry is dead. That's what I wanted to tell you. He was murdered a couple of weeks ago."

"Dear God."

"I'm sorry."

"I haven't seen the man in eighteen years." Her mother's voice had risen. "Why you think you even have to *tell* me—"

"I remembered what he wrote in that note, Mom. About how you were wrong in what you were thinking about him. And, well, I can't help wondering if you found out he was involved in something illegal. This wasn't a murder in the middle of a burglary or anything like that. It was more of an execution. Right now, the police have no idea what the motive could have been."

"I don't know anything," her mother said. "And I don't appreciate you suggesting that I might. You completely misunderstood what he meant."

"What *did* he mean?" Cait asked softly.

"What does it matter to you anyway? This is ancient history and none of your business. If all you're going to do is grill me, I'll say good-night right now."

"Mom, why would you keep his secrets?"

"How dare you?" her mother cried and hung up.

After a moment, Cait did the same, carefully placing her phone on the end table. She felt… Oh, she hardly knew. Shaken.

Colin moved into sight, sitting in the recliner facing her. His eyes were kind. "Didn't go so well?"

Cait drew her knees up and wrapped her arms around them. "It was weird." She bit her lip. "Did it bother you? Listening to me talk to her?"

"I didn't like hearing you sound upset. Otherwise..." He shook his head. "I don't relate much to the idea of her being my mother anymore. If I tried, I could stir up a little anger, and that's about all." He smiled. "Thank you for defending me."

"I meant it. I feel dumb that it's taken me this many years to realize how much I let her influence my memories of you. I don't know if she was really scared of you or not. I guess she must have been. What I do know is that she can't let herself conceive that she might have been wrong to leave you behind. So she has to keep bolstering her belief that you were just like Dad."

He nodded. "Human nature."

"Yes." She was silent for a moment, and then met his eyes. "You heard me ask her about Jerry."

He waited.

"She lied. I think she did learn something about him, but I doubt she'll ever admit it."

Her brother was silent for a while, his brows knit as he thought. He finally shrugged. "What if she thought she'd found a great guy? Planned to leave Dad for him? And then it turns out he's a crook. She's O and two. She doesn't want you to know that."

"Or maybe *she* doesn't want to know that."

His gaze never left her. "Maybe she doesn't."

Understanding her mother better than she wanted to, Cait felt sick. Shame had kept her silent, too. Was still keeping her silent.

Oh, God, she thought. *I don't want to be like her.*

She bent, so her forehead bumped her knees and she didn't have to see her brother's face.

"Blake was abusive," she said, her throat thick with tears. "And I let it happen."

The next thing she knew, the sofa cushion beside her depressed and Colin took her in his arms. She swiveled and let him hold her while she cried.

HAVING HEARD NOTHING by midafternoon the next day, Noah called his police chief first, only to be told that Chief Raynor was in a meeting and would have to return his call. Frustrated and irritated even though he knew he was being unreasonable, Noah dialed McAllister's number.

"Mayor," Colin said, sounding resigned.

"What's the holdup?" Noah demanded. "Hasn't the M.E. gotten to the skeleton?"

"Have you talked to Raynor?"

"Why bother? He doesn't know anything you haven't told him."

Cait's brother chuckled. "I doubt he sees it that way."

Noah didn't have the patience to talk about Alec Raynor right now. "Well?"

"Sanchez isn't a bone man. He's asked for a forensic anthropologist from the state. I understand the guy's coming in tomorrow."

"So we know nothing."

"Identifying this guy is unlikely to keep Cait any safer."

Intellectually, Noah knew that. His gut said different. "It's important."

"I agree. And we're trying. Knowing when he died narrows down the missing-person reports we have to review. I'm told he has unusual dental work. That'll help, when we have a name to match him to."

"What do you mean, unusual?"

"Sanchez is thinking now this man was in his thirties to forty. Not as old as we first thought. Confirmation of that is one of the reasons he's bringing in an expert. His teeth look more like an older man's, though. He lost quite a few of them at some point. He had six bridges, all in pieces now, of course. The remaining teeth look as though they were healthy—I'm told there are only a couple of small fillings—so the M.E. is thinking the teeth were knocked out."

A buzzing in his ears was the first symptom. The next moment, Noah felt as if he were floating up by the ceiling, looking down at the man sitting behind the desk in his office, phone to his ear, a stranger he didn't know.

He closed his eyes and pinched the bridge of his nose hard enough to make cartilage creak. The pain pulled him back into his body.

"My father disappeared when I was a teenager. Probably around sixteen," he said in a guttural voice. His throat had thickened to the point where it was hard to speak at all. "Mom got checks from him so erratically, we're not sure when. Angel Butte was his last known address."

There was a moment of silence as Colin did the math. "Nineteen years ago."

"He was in a motorcycle accident when he was in his twenties. The handlebar rammed into his mouth."

"But what could he possibly have had to do with Jerry Hegland?"

"My father started out as a pharmaceutical rep. He got addicted to painkillers and eventually involved in selling illegal drugs." Noah's mother had talked bitterly about her first husband's downfall enough times, but he'd never been sure he believed her. The dad he remembered wasn't like that. But now he made himself keep talking. "He served a year in jail once."

"In Oregon?"

Strange, how numb he felt. "Washington. My mother worked in Portland, but we lived across the river in Vancouver."

"Do you remember what dentist he might have seen?"

"When I was a kid, we went to a Dr. Warren. Can't remember the name of the clinic, but it was in Vancouver. I'm assuming my father saw him, too."

Colin was quiet for a moment. A moment later

he confirmed Noah's guess that he was online. "Dr. Paul Warren?"

"That sounds right."

"If it turns out this is him…I don't know how we can keep it quiet."

"You don't have to keep it quiet. Last time I saw my father I was eight years old. I am not responsible for him or his choices."

"No. Jesus, Noah." Something indefinable had changed in Colin's voice. "I'm sorry."

He cleared his throat. "Can't pick our parents."

"No. I wouldn't pick either of mine."

Noah wasn't going to cut himself open and bleed here and now even though he felt a sense of kinship unfamiliar to him. He had a meeting with the facilities manager scheduled to start in ten minutes. Nothing had really changed. "You'll let me know?" he asked.

"The minute we find out."

He made it through the meeting, and the dozen routine phone calls he had to make thereafter.

The Novocaine wore off at some point, leaving him with a sensation that felt more like pressure than pain. It made it hard to sit. Muscles began to jerk in rebellion. He needed to run, to hammer a punching bag, to do *something*. Finally he shot to his feet, told Ruth he had to talk to someone and took the stairs rather than the elevator down one floor. Nobody in Development and Planning appeared surprised to see him. City Councilman

George Miller was leaning against the counter looking mad, his face and balding pate both red. He straightened, but Noah only shook his head.

"Not now, George."

He rapped lightly on Cait's door, hoping like hell she was there.

"Come in," she called.

He did, and, upon seeing that she was alone, he shut the door behind him, leaning back against it.

Her face was drawn and tired, but she was beautiful anyway. Today's outfit made him think of fresh peaches, blushing with color. She looked at him warily.

"Will you have dinner with me tonight?" he asked.

Those soft gray eyes studied him for an uncomfortable length of time. "Is something wrong?"

Wrong? He examined the concept. Finding out his father had been dead all this time, had been murdered, wouldn't alter Noah's life in any meaningful way. The dead part was no surprise. People didn't usually disappear as thoroughly as Brian Chandler had unless they had died. Even so... The pressure inside his chest was still increasing. Sooner or later it would boil over. It had to.

Yeah, he guessed it was fair to say something was wrong.

"I don't know yet," he said. "Will you spend the evening with me?"

He didn't think he could stand it if she made a jab implying all he wanted was sex.

Sex—well, that might be one way to release this near-unbearable force building inside him, but it wasn't what he wanted most. Right now, he would have given anything to hold her. Take her weight against his and let her bear some of his. With employees, not to mention a city councilman, right on the other side of the door, that wasn't possible here and now, but he thought he could hold on if only he knew she would leave with him at five o'clock.

She smiled at him, though it wavered a little. "I'd love to, Noah. I was going to call you and…and say I'm sorry for reacting the way I did the last time you asked me. Maybe the stress is getting to me."

"I don't see how it can help but be."

"Let me know when you want to go."

He nodded and reached without looking for the door handle. "George is out there," he warned.

Her eyes widened. "George Miller?" She whispered even though it wasn't necessary.

"None other."

"Oh, Lord." She kept her voice hushed. "He's not happy. I'm starting to wonder if Phil wasn't the only one who had a little arrangement with someone in the department. George is acting shocked to be asked to complete more steps in an application, as if he'd never had to hire water or septic or traffic engineers before and considers them a waste of money. His latest project is…well, maybe not ill-conceived, but not carefully conceived, either. I know Earl rubs you the wrong way, but at least he dots his *i*'s and crosses his *t*'s."

One side of his mouth lifted in the first glimmer of humor he'd felt all day. No, in longer than that. Since he'd scared Cait with his display of temper.

"Then I'll never complain about Earl again," he swore.

She laughed. "Do you have your fingers crossed behind your back? Grumble all you want. I just thought you ought to know he has his virtues."

"Understood." He braced himself and opened the door. Carrying the image of Cait's laughing face, he was able to nod at the councilman who was a perpetual thorn in his side. His "What can I do for you, George?" almost sounded as if he wanted to be helpful.

Fifteen minutes later, he managed to extract himself.

Once again, he went for the stairs, mostly to avoid anyone he didn't absolutely have to talk to. He was alone in the stairwell when his phone rang. He took it from his belt and his heart kicked at the name displayed.

"Yeah?" he said hoarsely.

Noah came by for her at five-thirty. She was shocked at the sight of his face. Lines she'd never noticed before seemed etched into his forehead.

The ones between his nose and mouth had deep-ened. His mouth was compressed into a hard line.

She rose to her feet without a second thought. "Noah?"

"You mind Chandler's again?" he asked as if tonight was any other night. "I'm not much in the mood for cooking."

"Of course not," she said. "But if you'd rather, I wouldn't mind making dinner."

He hesitated, then grimaced. "I don't remember the last time I grocery shopped and I can't say I want to do it right now."

They walked again, and she reveled in the chance to be out on a warm evening even as she watched faces and passing vehicles and kept sneak-ing looks to see who was coming up behind them. Cait was learning that, as afraid as she'd become of Blake, that was nothing compared to the ever-present memory of the silver SUV, the window rolled down, the shadow of movement. *Pop.* The sound of glass crumbling. Her own harsh breath-ing and dry, stifled sobs. The grit under her knees and hands.

Even in her office at city hall and her bedroom at Colin's, she didn't feel completely safe. Each knock on the door had her freezing; in bed she kept think-ing she heard a scuffing sound outside or a tap on the window glass.

She noticed that Noah stayed on the curbside as they walked, and that he didn't let anybody get close to her. He'd pull her to his side and use his big body to block passersby. Like hers, his gaze roved nonstop. His expression was flat and hard. Neither of them talked until they were tucked away in the familiar booth at Chandler's in the back. She'd begun to wonder if it was saved for him, like his parking spot at city hall.

She looked across the table at him. "Now something is wrong."

"Let's order."

Searching his face, she nodded.

Even she knew the menu well enough now not to need to look at it, so they were able to make their choices quickly. While they waited for their drinks, she asked how it had gone with George Miller.

"I walked him to the elevator, nodded a lot and said, 'I'll be sure to look into that, George' half a dozen times."

Cait smiled even though she was too anxious to feel real amusement. "All lies."

"Every word."

The waitress smilingly delivered drinks. The moment she walked away, Cait reached across the table for his hand. It turned and gripped hers hard.

"Will you tell me?" she asked.

"The man you saw buried? He was my father, Cait."

Her mouth dropped open. "What?" she finally managed.

"You heard me." Blue eyes that could be so sharp

and clear were opaque. Only the strength of his grip betrayed his turmoil.

"But…how do you know?" That might not be the most important question, but she had to start somewhere.

He told her about the damage his father had suffered in a motorcycle accident, and the medical examiner's puzzlement at the extent of the dental work the dead man had had. "The minute I heard that…" His jaws flexed and the first hint of pain showed. "He dealt drugs. My father. Mom divorced him when he was doing a stint in prison. He didn't start like that, but he somehow got addicted to opioids."

"Maybe it was after the accident," Cait suggested tentatively. "If he was in pain for long—"

"I don't know. Mom didn't talk about it much. I guess he went through treatment a few times. He must have tried, for our sake. I never saw his problems, but I wasn't very old, either. I think my mother got so she hated him. He wasn't very reliable, but I loved him anyway. I didn't want to believe all the things she said about him. The last time I heard from him, he'd promised to take me to a baseball game, but he called something like an hour before we were supposed to leave and canceled. He'd make it up, he promised. I said something like, 'Yeah, sure,' and hung up on him. I never talked to him again. A few weeks after that, my mother told me he'd moved. Later I realized he probably had called and she wouldn't let him talk to me. He might have kept calling. I don't know." He ran a hand over his face, as if trying to loosen taut muscles, or maybe to wipe away any expression that would reveal emotions he wasn't willing to display. "I guess I understand why she'd think that was best. A couple of times I heard her and my stepfather talking, so I knew Dad sent money occasionally. Not reliably, of course." What was probably meant to be bitterness sounded more like grief. "He'd quit being reliable years before."

Cait squeezed his hand in a gentle warning. "Our salads are coming."

He nodded and let her go. Except for the harsh lines in his face, he looked much as usual as he thanked the waitress.

"You know all your employees?" Cait asked.

He shook out his napkin. "I used to. These days, I still try, but I don't get up to Bend or Sisters more than every couple of weeks. I have good managers and I watch the bottom line."

She bit her lip. "So you think your father was involved in drug trafficking here in Angel Butte."

"That's a logical assumption," he said flatly. "Probably small-time. According to Mom, he always talked about making enough money to start over somewhere. He wanted me to be proud of him, he said. I guess I'd like to think he wasn't ruthless enough to climb the ladder."

"You know for sure this was him?"

"Your brother called this afternoon. They were able to compare dental records."

"I'm so sorry," she said, wanting to touch him again but sensing he needed to stay aloof, at least while they were in public.

He nodded acknowledgment. "Why don't we eat? I didn't get any lunch."

They found things to talk about; they always did. They steered away from the subject of family, of the current mysteries that preoccupied the police department, even of city government. He told her he was working on one of the front bedrooms.

"Every time I strip molding, the whole house stinks for days," he grumbled.

She almost asked if it was the child's bedroom he was working on, but she refrained. Besides, if a family bought that house, at least a couple of the bedrooms would be for the children.

She mentioned a book she was in the middle of, and it turned out he'd read it and took pleasure in countering every argument the author had made. Arguing actually seemed to relax him, so she let herself enjoy it, too.

Not until they had finished dinner, walked back to city hall and were making the short drive to his house did she ask tentatively about his mother.

"Will you let her know?"

The car's dark interior didn't allow her to read his expression. "I suppose," he said after a minute.

"I don't know that she'll care one way or another, but I could be wrong."

"She remarried? You said you have a stepfather?"

"Yeah, I think I was seven when she got married again. They've stuck it out, so I guess they're happy enough."

"I take it you're not crazy about him."

"No. We never had much of a relationship. He left the parenting to her."

"I see."

He angled a glance at her. "What about your mother? You haven't mentioned a stepfather."

"No. I'm not really sure why she never remarried. She's still an attractive woman. She did date, but I don't remember anyone being around long enough for me to think it was serious."

She heard what Colin had said. *What if she thought she'd found a great guy? Planned to leave Dad for him? And then it turns out he's a crook. She's O and two.* Had Mom lost her ability to trust? Any desire even to try?

Would that happen to her eventually, too?

"I called my mother," Cait said. "I hadn't told her yet I was back in Angel Butte."

He turned into his driveway and braked. "How'd she take it?"

"She was horrified. 'You know what we escaped,' she said."

"But your father is long dead." Noah sounded thoughtful.

"Which leaves me wondering if it was really Dad she was running from. I mentioned seeing Jerry, and I could tell that shocked her, too, and then I capped a fun conversation by telling her he'd been murdered and asking if she'd had any idea back then that he might be into something illegal."

He chuckled and slid his hand around her nape, gently squeezing. "Went for broke, did you?"

Cait found herself smiling ruefully even as she turned her head to rub her cheek against the inside of his wrist. "There's a whole lot I *didn't* tell her. That when I was ten I saw her lover bury a body in the backyard of his rental house. And the biggie, that someone is trying to kill me."

"She's your mother," he said in a deep, tender voice. "You don't think she'd want to know?"

"It would confirm all her worst fears about Angel Butte. She'd want *me* to run."

"Sometimes I think you should, too." He kept up the massage that made her want to groan with pleasure. "But what if he follows you?"

"Like Blake did."

"Yeah. Here you have Colin and, because of him, the whole police department." There was an infinitesimal pause. "And me."

Cait leaned over to nestle her head against his brawny chest. "I am…so glad I have you."

Right this minute, she would rejoice in that and not wish for more.

His hand left her neck to unclick her seat belt. "Let's go in," he said, voice hoarse.

Suddenly, they were both in a hurry.

CHAPTER FOURTEEN

NOAH STARED AT the ceiling. "I didn't mean to do that."

Curled against him, Cait stirred. "You mean make love to me?"

"Yeah. I didn't want you to think—"

"That's the only reason you had me over?"

He sighed, and her head rode the movement of his chest. "Yeah."

"You fed me first."

"Even *I'm* getting tired of Chandler's."

Her laugh made his skin shiver. "About time, there, guy. Maybe we should explore the culinary possibilities of Angel Butte."

"Like Newberry Inn."

Cait rose on one elbow to look down at him. Her nose looked cute scrunched up. "Nell's friend Hailey owns this place—"

"Kingfisher Café. I had lunch there the other day. While I ate, I gave thought to hiring her away, but right now she's too successful to be bought." He smiled. "She came out to look me over."

"Because you're the competition?"

He snorted. "I think she was warning me not to hurt you. Said Nell's her best friend and she's getting to be friends with you, too."

"Well." She blinked in surprise. "That's really sweet."

He cupped her cheek. "She bakes damn good sweets."

"Yes, she does." Cait sat up all the way so she could really see him. "I hate knowing that was your father."

Noah laid his forearm across his face. The habit of self-defense was hard to break. "I hate it, too," he said gruffly.

"Did you...suspect he was dead?" she asked, soft and tentative.

He let out a long breath, made himself lift his arm and curve it around her. "Yeah. Once I was making some money, I went so far as to hire a P.I. He came up with zip. Disappearing so completely—it's not easy to do."

"Nell did it."

"Yeah." He tipped his head in acknowledgment. "And she was only fifteen."

"She said in a way that made it easier. She wasn't really on the radar yet, you know? Didn't have to worry about a job history or references or anything like that. She says, looking back, that the miracle is that no one recognized her given that her face was in all the newspapers every day for a while."

"She's a gutsy woman, your sister-in-law."

A shadow crossed Cait's face, one he didn't understand. "I know she is."

"Your brother must be feeling cursed. What are the odds you and she would both end up in danger?"

She made a face at that. "We'd have both been safer if we'd never come back to this town."

His heart gave a quick, hard squeeze. He discovered how much he disliked the idea of never having met Cait McAllister.

Those soft gray eyes were looking deep into his. "Will you have a funeral?" she asked.

She was determined to talk about his father, when he didn't have a clue what he felt. He'd needed to be with her, but not so he'd have to admit to unwelcome emotions.

Or was he lying to himself?

"And who would I invite?" He shook his head. "Once they're done with his bones, I'll have them buried."

"I'd come."

He tugged her down for a kiss. "Thank you," he murmured against her lips.

"Do you have pictures of him?"

"What you mean is, do I look like him?" That came out harsh enough to have her drawing back, her expression hurt. He held on to her hand so she couldn't scramble off the bed. "Yes. He was a big, ugly son of a bitch, just like me."

Her face softened. "You're the sexiest man I've

ever met, and I can't possibly be the first woman to tell you that."

He smiled, although inside he was a mass of all those emotions he didn't understand. "Maybe."

"He must have appealed to your mother."

Noah heard himself make a sound that had Cait's gaze sharpening.

Your ex must've been an even uglier son of a bitch than he looks in pictures, if the kid is anything to go by.

Why had he let himself be haunted by something so meaningless?

"I heard my mother and stepfather talking about it once. He said I must have taken after my father, as ugly as I was."

"What?" Cait's outrage warmed him.

"My mother admitted it bothered her, how much I looked like my dad. She said—" God, he'd never told anyone this, but still he stumbled on. "That there wasn't a single good thing I could have inherited from Dad."

Pure fury blazed in Cait's eyes. "That's horrible! How could she?"

Her anger relaxed something in him. "She had reason to be bitter."

"So what?" Her chin had never looked so square or pugnacious. He especially loved the effect when she was naked. "She wouldn't have loved him if he hadn't had good qualities. Addiction is…it's a disease! What if he'd had cancer and gotten weak and whiny?"

"Addiction involves choices," Noah felt obligated to point out, however much he appreciated her fiery defense.

"Sure. So do diabetes and lung cancer for a smoker and a lot of other diseases."

He started to laugh. "You're right. No, don't punch me." He grabbed her fist. "Settle down."

Cait made a disgusted sound but subsided. "She's your mother. I should keep my mouth shut."

"I'm glad you didn't." That came out hoarse. *Shit,* he thought. She was punching holes in every defense he had. Suddenly, he felt naked, and not because he was sprawled in bed not wearing any clothes.

She stroked his chest, her hand slender and fine-boned. "You must have loved him."

"I guess I did," Noah said slowly. "At least—" No, he refused to sound pathetic.

But Cait only waited. He looked for pity on her face and saw compassion.

Oh, hell. "I wanted to believe he was worth loving. That he loved me. My mother was decent to me, don't get me wrong, but I was never sure she loved me. I think she was telling Dennis the truth. It did bother her that I took more after Dad than her."

"I can't imagine." Her eyes showed disbelief.

"What if you'd had a kid with Ralston? Now you

know what a crazy he is. What if the kid looked just like him? Wouldn't you find yourself wondering?"

"You're justifying her behavior?"

"Understanding."

She made another of those disdainful sounds. "Kids take after both their parents. Looks are the least important part of what they get from us. Not only would my child be *mine,* but I'd make sure he knew how many great qualities he got from his father."

"Yeah." He touched her lips, feeling them quiver beneath the pads of his fingers. "That's what I'd do, too. If…" He had to clear his throat. "If I ever have kids."

She gave a laugh that sounded more sad than funny. "I don't know what makes me think I'm qualified to carry on like this. Mom…well, she did love me. Does," she corrected herself. "But I never forgot that she left Colin behind and just, I don't know, pretended he didn't exist after that. That couldn't help but make me wonder how much I could depend on her love. You know? And Dad…" Her shoulders moved. "I don't have much in the way of good memories of him. Maybe if you don't learn from your own parents, there's no hope."

Why that should piss him off when he'd made the same argument in relation to himself, Noah couldn't have said. All he knew was that it did.

"That's bull! You're smart and sweet. You make

me laugh. The way you just fired up tells me you'd be every bit as feisty in defense of your kid."

She sat back and contemplated him. "You mean, I shouldn't let my parents' failings stop me from having a full life."

Did she look smug? His eyes narrowed. "Did you just set me up?"

"Maybe." She smiled at him. "All I can say is—ditto."

"Message received." Although nobody would call him sweet. He had a bad feeling that as a parent he'd be as impatient and dictatorial as he was with his staff. And as incapable as he was of making emotional connections, what if he distanced himself from his own kids?

And why in hell was he thinking about this at all?

Because of Cait, of course.

Hiding his perturbation, he lifted his hands to her breasts, which nicely filled his palms. She looked down, watching as he played. He splayed his fingers enough to let her nipples peek out, then rubbed them between those fingers.

"Pretty," he said thickly.

She swallowed. "We were talking."

"Now we're done." He was afraid to think what would come out of his mouth if they kept talking. He didn't like needing her the way he had today. Needing her body, he was okay with that.

There were better things than talking he could do with his mouth.

He reared up and captured one of those pretty breasts in his mouth and sucked until she arched and moaned.

EVERY STEP FORWARD with Noah was followed by two back.

No surprise, he spent the next couple of days dodging her.

Friday night, she retreated to her bedroom when Colin and Nell did. The main living space felt too exposed when she was alone out there. The house had entire walls of windows, many of which didn't even have blinds. At least in the guest bedroom she knew no one could look in.

The room did have a comfortable upholstered chair and reading lamp. Feet drawn up beneath her, she sat with a book on her lap that she hadn't bothered opening. Instead she thought about Noah.

Oh, why had she said so much? Cait mourned her stupidity. Noah might deny taking her home only because he wanted sex, but she knew that's essentially what he'd done.

So, okay, he'd said enough to surprise her, but only because she'd pushed. *And why not be honest?* she thought. The fact that she *had* pushed was a bad sign. Even he must realize she was really asking for more from him. More intimacy. More trust. A real relationship. The kind of sharing a couple allowed themselves to do. And he had never said a single thing to make her think he was interested in being half of a couple.

If he did, he would never have suggested they keep their affair furtive the way he had.

Face it. He wanted sex. Full stop.

Maybe she was more of an optimist than she'd believed, because an argumentative voice in her pointed out that he hadn't been all that sneaky, nothing like she'd expected. People were noticing how often he stopped by her office and that he usually closed the door so they were alone together. And that he took her out to lunch and dinner. Everyone at city hall must have seen them leaving together at one time or another.

Instead of reassuring her, that thought filled her with dread. If the gossip reached the city council, she didn't know what would happen. She could lose her job. Or he could lose his. As her boss, he might be seen as having stepped over a line, made her feel as if she *couldn't* refuse him.

He'd never forgive her if he ended up embroiled in a scandal because of her.

God, that's probably why he was doing the disappearing thing again. Or maybe only because he hated having opened up to her as much as he had.

Or—here was another possibility—because he'd said, *You have me.* He might be making sure she didn't read too much into that.

Whatever it was, she wouldn't beg. Maybe this

would be a good time for them to end their relationship, such as it was.

Sex. That's what it is.

She'd known all along he was the absolute wrong personality for her. Predicting what would happen if they did get serious was all too easy. He'd issue orders and be scathing if she tried to stand up for herself. Noah wouldn't be able to help squelching her, and she wouldn't be able to help submitting, and then she would hate him and herself both while he'd end up feeling nothing but contempt for her.

She heard again the admiration in his voice when he described Nell as gutsy.

And then there's me.

Maybe the time would come when she could have faith in herself again, but right now was too soon. Yes, it had felt good to stand up to Blake. To have him cowering at her feet. She wanted to think she'd never again find excuses for a man who'd hit her. But that was only a small part of the ways she'd allowed Blake to diminish her. Somehow she'd conceded almost all the decisions to him, from how she wore her hair to whether she could go out with friends. Remembering made her shudder.

She hadn't been able to figure out how she could have let anything like that happen to her, not after having seen her mother's example, but since coming back to Angel Butte she had begun to understand that it had worked the other way around.

Oh, she'd learned from her mother's example,

all right—to do exactly what Mommy did. When Daddy bellowed, you kept your head down and never, never argued because that only enraged him further. When he got mad, you shrank into corners. When he threw his fists, you endured and pretended to everyone outside the family that nothing had happened.

Maybe lessons learned when you were so young couldn't be unlearned, she thought bleakly. Maybe with Blake she'd been replicating the only kind of family she'd ever known. What other explanation was there?

Of course, Noah wasn't like Blake. He was bossy and impatient and a lot of other things, but it was hard for her to imagine him ever striking a woman.

I thought the same about Blake.

Yes, but Noah barely even raised his voice. He had too much confidence to need to yell at anyone.

Forehead puckering, Cait laid her book aside.

She hadn't been with Blake all that long when she'd realized he *wasn't* very confident. He'd hated having any of his decisions questioned. Or even his opinion, really. She hadn't noticed that at first because they agreed on a lot of the bigger issues. He couldn't stand to be embarrassed. He'd been in a quiet fury for days after being pulled over by a cop for making a rolling right turn at a red light. The officer made him get out of the car and take a breathalyzer test. Blake was humiliated because passing motorists saw him. Afterward, he'd gone on and on.

The cop had to be blind. Of course he'd stopped. Probably the cop wanted to fill some quota.

And me? she thought sadly. *I murmured sympathy and agreement even though I knew perfectly well that he didn't stop and he deserved that ticket.*

Because she'd wanted peace more than she had wanted honesty or self-respect.

She moved restlessly in the chair. This new start had been really important to her. Instead, first Blake and then this unknown man whose face she hardly remembered had forced her into a state of fear and dependency that was undermining any belief she'd started with that she could be strong.

Instead, she got to spend a lot of time being grateful that she had Colin and Noah and, because of them, so many other people to protect her.

THE NEXT MORNING, Colin wandered into the kitchen, where Cait was pouring herself a cup of coffee. Despite it being Saturday, he was dressed for work, lacking only the suit coat. He'd already clipped his holster and badge to his narrow black belt.

"That's a big gun," she observed, nodding at his waist. "Do you have to hoist your pants to keep it up?"

He laughed. "Funny, Nell asked me the same thing one time. No, I keep my belt tight enough to hold up the weight. The only time it's a problem is when I, uh, have to sit on the toilet. Which isn't often when I'm working, thank God."

She made a face at him. "Thank you for that visual."

"Having your weapon tangled up with your pants around your ankles isn't a good thing. I heard about a cop who died when someone reached under the stall and snatched his handgun."

"Wow. Okay, so it's not only undignified, it's dangerous."

He grinned. "Mostly undignified." His expression sobered. "Cait, I haven't said anything, but this choice ought to be yours. Ralston keeps asking to see you."

She went still. "Why would he want to see me?"

Her brother grimaced. "He wants to tell you how sorry he is."

Cait stared at him. "No."

"Yeah, I'm afraid so."

"He didn't think writing 'I'm sorry' thirty-five times on the side of my house covered it?" Her voice was rising by the end.

"He claims he means it this time."

She snorted. "No. No more."

"Good." He bent his head and kissed her cheek. "I'm off."

"It's Saturday."

"I need to do some catch-up. Nell's home, so you won't be alone. Do me a favor and don't so much as step outside."

"Or stand by a window."

"I'm sorry, Cait." His mouth twisted. "Poor choice of words."

She wanted to be able to laugh, but her sense of humor had gone into deep freeze lately. All she could do was shake her head. "*I'm* the one who should say I'm sorry. I had no business running to Angel Butte because you were here without talking to you about it. You got stuck taking care of me, and that's not fair to you *or* Nell."

Colin's expression was rarely unguarded, but for once he let her see emotions that choked her up. "I spent years telling you I was here if you needed me. I meant every word, Cait."

"And then I was such a shit," she managed, although tears threatened and her nose ran.

"I love you."

She threw herself into his arms and wept for a moment into his crisp white shirt, so grateful for the strength of his arms around her, even as that gratitude made her cringe inside. Finally, snuffling, she retreated. "I got you wet."

Colin chuckled. "I'll dry." He kissed her cheek and departed.

Cait grabbed a paper towel, mopped her eyes and blew her nose vigorously, emerging from behind the paper towel to find her sister-in-law pouring herself a cup of coffee and smiling.

"Just so you know," Nell said, "having you need him is one of the best things that's happened to

Colin. And I know you must be chafing, but don't waste a minute feeling guilty because you sucked him in."

Cait swallowed and nodded. "I came to Angel Butte because Colin always protected me."

"That's who he is." Nell wrinkled her small freckled nose. "I don't suppose he gave us permission to go shopping?"

"I believe his exact words were 'Don't so much as step outside.'" She sighed. "It so happens I'm free to clean house."

"Let's at least bake. I love baking, even if nothing I make tastes like Hailey's food."

The thought was at least slightly cheering. "Chocolate chip cookies?"

Nell gave her a cherubic grin that made her look about twelve years old. "What else?"

COLIN HAD WORKED before with Ronald Floyd, a deputy D.A. for Butte County, the lucky guy who got to prosecute Blake Ralston. Floyd stopped by to talk about another case and only smiled wryly when Colin said, "And you didn't have anything better to do on a sunny Saturday afternoon than come in to work?"

"Says the man behind the desk."

"Seems like we've had a crime spree lately. If they're growing pains, I don't like them."

"I had the same thought," Floyd admitted. Middle-aged and graying, though so far he'd kept his hair, he'd been a prosecutor a lot longer than Colin had been a cop. He was a good one, too, hardworking, dedicated and patient. "The Hegland killing, though. Jesus, Colin! The guy was an airport manager. What, did somebody want to hijack an airplane?"

The department was keeping Hegland's possible link to drug traffickers quiet. There was undoubtedly gossip about the officers who had been fired, but no announcements had been made about the reasons. Until the Feds were ready to move forward, Colin couldn't say anything. The one positive of all the foot-dragging was that nobody in the department could be sure the investigation was ongoing. If the reason for Bystrom's resignation had been widely known back in December when it happened, the rats would have all jumped ship immediately.

"Did you know him?" he asked.

"Hegland?" Floyd looked surprised. "Only in passing. Can't remember the last time I so much as set eyes on him. You?"

"I might have met him, I'm not sure." *And, oh, yeah, he screwed my mother, but who am I to hold that against a dead man?*

"This thing with your sister must have you on edge."

"Ralston?"

"Not what I was thinking about, but at least she won't have to worry about him for a while.

I'm going for the maximum sentencing. I mean, the library?"

Colin shared the sentiment. Threatening to bomb the courthouse or the public safety building? Inconvenient, but sure. Scaring all those moms and little kids was something else. "By the way," he said, "will you be talking to his attorney?"

"Undoubtedly. Why?"

"Tell him Cait says no. She's not interested in any more apologies from him and sure as hell isn't going to indulge him by letting him issue one in person."

"Can't say I blame her. Do you have any idea who took those potshots at her?"

People kept asking Colin that. It really grated that he had to shake his head. "So far, the investigation has stalled." Only a few people knew that her assailant and Hegland's killer were likely one and the same.

"I haven't met your sister yet, but someone pointed her out to me. In fact, I saw her out with the mayor the other night," Floyd said casually.

Colin still didn't know what Cait was thinking, but Noah had begun to grow on him. The last thing either of them needed was to be the butt of gossip. They weren't using their heads, but Colin knew why. He'd seen the way Noah looked at her.

Now he shrugged. "Maybe work-related, but I guess they've gotten to be friends." He hesitated. "Something you might not have heard yet, Ronald.

You know those bones we dug out of a backyard? We've identified the guy. He turned out to be Noah Chandler's father."

"What?" The D.A. stared at him in shock.

"You heard me."

"But...Chandler isn't even from around here."

"Apparently he came to Angel Butte because it was his father's last known address."

Floyd swore a few times. He was still shaking his head when he left.

Growing pains. Colin brooded, leaning back in his leather desk chair. Who was he kidding? Angel Butte never had been the safe small town they had all believed it was, and Butte County wasn't the rural backwater they'd deluded themselves it was, either. Too many of the recent crimes had their roots in the past.

It was time he quit waffling and threw his hat in the ring. He could make as much or more difference as county sheriff as he could have as Angel Butte police chief.

The job, he reminded himself, that Noah Chandler had robbed him of.

And my sister is sleeping with this man.

The sound he made in his throat was not a happy one.

SUNDAY MORNING, BEFORE most people were awake, Noah ran to the top of Angel Butte and back home again. Early as it was, the day was promising to be hot. Draining a bottle of water, he thought about staining the now stripped woodwork in the two front bedrooms and couldn't work up any enthusiasm. Better he wait until he had the floors sanded anyway. Last time he'd done the two jobs ass-backward, he'd had to touch up the stain.

He wondered what Cait was doing this weekend. The look of desperation he'd seen on her face a few times kept tormenting him. She couldn't go for a run or head out for an aerobics class at the health club if she'd joined yet. Her new town house was gathering dust. As far as he knew, the only times she left her brother's house or city hall was when she was with Colin, hidden behind the tinted windows in his SUV.

Or with me.

Would she rather have spent the weekend with him? The thought was insidious. If Colin didn't talk, no one would know she was there. What would she have said if he'd asked her? Noah wondered. It wasn't too late. What would she say if he called and asked her to spend the day with him?

Noah wished he knew whether she'd so much as given him a thought the past few days. If so, there was no reason she couldn't have called him, was there? he asked himself defensively.

And do what? asked an irritating voice in his head. *Invite you to hang out at her brother's house?*

This was a woman who had no privacy and damn few choices these days.

Guilt speared him. He dried himself, got dressed and went downstairs. He could have breakfast first. But his usual bowl of cereal didn't sound very appealing. And maybe it was too early to call Cait, but he doubted she was staying up into the wee hours and sleeping late these days, either.

Even if she was up, he half expected her to let his call go to voice mail. That's what he deserved. But instead she answered, although she didn't sound all that excited.

"Noah."

"Ah…wondered if you have plans today?"

"Nell and I thought we might prepare some dinners for the week."

"Could I talk you into coming to brunch instead? I make damn good waffles."

There was a really long silence. He braced himself.

"You know, this might be a good time for us to do the smart thing and call it quits."

He didn't like the echo of what he'd been telling himself. "No."

"I'd swear Friday I saw you duck into Shirley Suh's office because you saw me coming down the hall," Cait said acidly.

He couldn't stand Shirley, and Cait knew it.

"I don't 'duck,'" he protested, knowing he'd done exactly that.

Silence.

"Hell," he growled, goaded. "I admit, I had some second thoughts."

"And?" Cait McAllister could be as uncompromising as he was.

Noah closed his eyes. This whole conversation was outside his comfort zone. *She* was outside his comfort zone. But he'd seen that he had two choices: take the chance of being hurt beyond his wildest fears or let her go.

Too late.

Every muscle in his body had gone rigid. His SUV had gone off the road and hurtled toward a tree. He had the flicker of knowledge that he might not survive the collision.

"I may be slow," he said, "but I eventually recognized it was the boy in me running scared." He didn't think he *could* finish the thought. Say, *That's the boy who was sure even his own parents didn't really love him. The one who'd decided never to risk putting himself out there again, yearning for something impossible.*

But he didn't have to say any of that, because Cait would understand.

"I'm done with that," he concluded.

Control, focus, ambition had been all-important to him. Two months ago he wouldn't have been able to imagine letting go of them, making himself vulnerable. Knowing what he wanted most was out of his hands might kill him.

"I'm…beginning to realize how much I've listened to the little girl in me, too," she said, softly, haltingly.

The distress in her voice reached right inside his chest and squeezed off the blood flow for a minute.

"I would love to have brunch with you, Noah."

God. His whole body sagged with the intense relief.

If you're going to jump, then do it, he told himself.

"So, how would you feel about packing enough to stay the night?" he asked.

CHAPTER FIFTEEN

THE ALARM SOUNDED as if it needed to gargle.

Not quite awake, Cait puzzled over where she had spent the night. She hated being on the move like this, living out of a suitcase, but she had to be careful not to wear out any of her friends' generosity. Usually she plugged in her own alarm clock, but…

The heavy, muscled arm that lay across her wasn't part of her usual morning, either. She came awake abruptly, remembering. She wasn't in Seattle; she was in Angel Butte. And she had spent the night with Noah, the second that week.

Colin wasn't happy about it, although she had to believe he and Nell would like some time alone together, considering they hadn't been married very long.

The arm tightened, and Noah nuzzled her nape. "Morning," he murmured with a rasp that hadn't yet cleared from his voice.

She tipped her head forward to give him better access. "Good morning." She wriggled a little, enjoying the feel of his erection pressed against her butt. "You know we don't have time for this."

"Sure we do." His big hand gently squeezed her breast, and she shivered. "I gave us an extra half an hour."

"You're kidding."

"Nope. Planned ahead."

She wasn't averse. His hand smoothed over her rib cage and belly and slipped between her thighs. She moaned and let him work his magic. It didn't take long until she wanted more, but when she started to roll to face him, he held her in place and nipped a sensitive spot on the side of her neck.

"I'm liking this." His voice was edged with pleasure. He kept stroking her until her hips were moving involuntarily and he was rocking against her, too. "God, you feel good," he said hoarsely, and then he pushed into her.

Cait's back arched in a great spasm. Lovemaking with Noah had always been hard and urgent. This morning he seemed to be taking his time. Her eyes closed, and she savored the sensations. She gripped his strong forearm even as his fingers still played between her legs. He used his teeth and lips on her neck and the muscles that ran to her shoulder, stinging her with tiny bites, then soothing the skin with a damp lick. He sucked until she knew she'd show the mark, but right this minute she didn't care.

He began moving faster, driving harder, deeper. Finally he groaned and half lifted her onto her knees, rising behind her to thrust in a powerful rhythm that sent her over the edge, her body shuddering in astonishing pleasure. With a long, guttural sound, he pulsed inside her, and as she sagged to the mattress he came down on top of her.

It was a minute before she noticed she couldn't breathe. She squirmed. Noah grumbled in his throat and rolled off her, coming down on his back.

"Hell of a way to start the morning," he said in a voice that was still rusty but obviously satisfied.

Cait struggled to turn over so she could see him. "Are we late?"

His mouth lifted in a smile that fleetingly made him handsome. "Five minutes to spare."

"Did you give me a hickey?"

He lifted his head and inspected her. His lips curved. "Yeah, I guess I did."

"I should give you one in revenge."

He lifted his chin, baring his neck to her. "Have fun."

She gave serious thought to it, but settled for making a face at him. "As nice as today is going to be, I'd look like an idiot wearing a turtleneck, even assuming I had one in my bag." Not that *she'd* be outside in the beautiful June weather. "What will people think?"

His eyebrows rose. "That you're having great sex?"

Cait sighed. She couldn't argue with that. "Dibs on the first shower."

He slapped her butt as she slipped out of bed. "I

might get somewhere on the second bathroom if you weren't keeping me so busy."

Time for a saucy smile and a waggle of her hips as she headed for the hall. "One is enough as long as I get to go first."

Having to climb into the claw-footed tub to shower had made it a challenge for two, one they'd overcome on Monday morning, since Noah hadn't had the forethought to set the alarm for earlier. Unfortunately, they had not only used all the hot water, Cait had slipped and banged her knee painfully, leaving a bruise. On top of that, they'd been late arriving at city hall.

Or maybe *that* was fortunate, she thought now, massaging his shampoo into her hair. She was pretty sure nobody had seen them arrive together.

They weren't going to get away with this for long. Because she had a bag in his Suburban, Noah would have to take her back to Colin's that afternoon. Which meant they were both arriving *and* leaving together.

As she was stepping out of the shower and reaching for a towel, the bathroom door opened. Noah walked in. He was an impressive sight naked, solid and muscular. When her gaze finally made it up to his face, she saw that he had a strange expression.

"I didn't use a condom."

"I'm on the pill," she said slowly, stunned to realize she hadn't given a thought to a precaution she

had never willingly dispensed with before. "Um…
we could quit using condoms."

Noah's stare was unnerving. It was a long time
before he gave a short nod. "All right."

Leaving him to shower, she wondered if she'd
freaked him out again. What had he thought, that
he might have impregnated her? Cait was dismayed
at the funny cramp she felt down low at the idea.
What would it be like to make love with the hope of
getting pregnant? Noah didn't sound as if he'd ever
want children. He'd looked really disturbed when
he'd realized he'd forgotten the condom. Remembering the expression on his face hurt even though
she knew they didn't have that kind of relationship.

As if she had the slightest idea what kind of relationship they *did* have.

He was done with running scared, he'd said,
without elaborating on what he'd been scared *of.*
He had asked her to stay the night, knowing they
were risking their relationship—for want of a better word—becoming public knowledge. That was
the sum total of his commitment thus far.

She'd had an amazing time with him that week.
He had been less guarded, letting her see some
doubts and self-mockery he'd always hidden before. His sense of humor was more evident, too.
And she couldn't doubt his physical hunger for her.

Why was she even thinking like this? *New life,
independence, remember? No men?* Shouldn't that
ring a bell? And, especially, no domineering men?

But, heaven help her, she was beginning to wonder if that description actually fit Noah, at least in the way she'd feared. Yes, of course he was bossy. Definitely impatient. He evaluated evidence and made decisions quickly and had little tolerance for the wait while other people caught up with him. Unlike Blake, he did listen, though, and even changed his mind based on new information. She hadn't been able to help noticing that the people he had hired since winning the election were more capable and stronger-minded than the old-timers. That suggested he actively sought out managers likely to challenge him.

She thought about how much he seemed to enjoy arguing. Not once had he behaved as if she threatened his masculinity or sovereignty when she contradicted him or won an argument with superior firepower.

As she rolled thigh-high stockings up her legs, partly to cover the bathtub bruise that was still mostly purple, she reflected again on how much he had in common with her brother. Neither man would like hearing that, she knew; in fact, she could just imagine Noah's expression if she suggested any such thing. But it was true. And what she'd seen was that Colin had two sides—the police captain who elevated *guarded* to ten-foot-thick stone walls with slits for pouring boiling oil on the enemy, and then Nell's husband and Cait's brother, a man who was patient, gentle and infinitely dependable. A man she'd known she could run to, despite eighteen years of estrangement.

For the first time, she understood how, even in his absence, Colin had shaped her idea of the ideal man. His one check in the debit column was his capacity for violence, so like their father's to her child's eyes. Thus explaining her choice of smart, not-so-physical guys. One of whom brutalized her, while Noah, both smart and unnervingly physical, seemed willing to do anything to keep her safe.

Caught up in her reflections, she didn't even look at Noah when they traded places again. She used gel in her hair and dried it quickly, then applied a minimum of makeup. No need to worry about suntan lotion, either, when the sum total of her outdoor time today would be walking thirty feet to Noah's SUV and then, at the end of the day, an even shorter distance from it to Colin's front door. She didn't have to worry about the sweat factor, either. If this went on much longer, she was not only going to look pasty; she was going to have to start worrying about getting enough vitamin D.

Right. There was the biggest source of anxiety in her life.

She packed her overnight bag and carried it downstairs, leaving it by the front door, then followed the smell of brewing coffee to the kitchen. Noah already had a raisin-cinnamon bagel in the toaster, which she stole when it popped up. He put another in and poured two cups of coffee. He was quieter than usual as they ate, which made her wonder what he was thinking and how much of him she'd see the rest of the week.

It stung that she *had* to wonder.

"Ready?" he asked.

"Sure." She grabbed her messenger bag and let him carry the overnight bag. He locked the door, and they cut across the lawn to the driveway.

"Oh, shit," he said suddenly under his breath.

Cait turned her head. A balding man approached on the sidewalk, towed by a golden retriever on the end of a leash. George Miller, city council member and developer. She didn't even have time to avert her face before stunned recognition dawned on his face.

Noah reached out and gripped her arm. Both of them stopped where they were. Tail swinging happily, the dog tried to get to them but was brought up short by his leash.

"George," Noah said, nodding.

Turning red, he looked from one to the other of them. "Goddamn it! I'd heard the rumors, but I didn't believe them. What in the hell were the two of you thinking?"

OF ALL THE LUCK.

Miller had to be the last council member Noah would have wanted to encounter under these circumstances.

Noah knew his fingers had to be biting into

Cait's arm. She seemed to be struck dumb, not even blinking.

He thought quickly, but there weren't many options. No point in denying she'd spent the night, not when the bag that dangled from his other hand was peach-colored and clearly feminine.

"We're both single adults," he said evenly. "We're not stepping on anyone's toes."

George's eyes narrowed. Chances were he was seeing a gift placed right in his hands. He'd like nothing better than to force Noah's resignation.

"The woman works for you, Chandler." He shook his head in disgust. "You're playing with fire here."

Cait stiffened. "I can assure you there was no coercion involved, George. The city won't be looking at a suit for sexual harassment, if that's what you're afraid of."

George didn't so much as bother glancing at her. Neither did Noah, who appreciated the sentiment but almost shook his head at her naïveté. George wasn't afraid of a lawsuit—he'd like nothing better.

This was politics, plain and simple.

"This is a little more than the two of us sleeping together," Noah said easily. "Cait has agreed to marry me."

"What?" she gasped.

This time George's sharp gaze did slice to her.

Noah tightened his fingers even more. "As it happens, you're the first to know. We haven't even told

Cait's brother yet. We'd appreciate it if you'd keep the news to yourself for a day or two."

The dog squatted and peed on Noah's lawn. George scowled at Cait and Noah.

"What do you plan to do about the job?"

"We wouldn't be the first married couple to work together."

Noah sensed words wanting to burst out of Cait, but for the moment she kept her mouth shut.

"Hmph." The city councilman yanked on his dog's leash. "We'll see about that," he snapped and turned back the way he came.

For a moment, Noah didn't move. Then he steered Cait to the Suburban. As always when she wore her high heels, he stood behind her until she was safely in, tossed her bag in the rear, then went around and got in behind the wheel. He stuck the key in the ignition but didn't turn it. His hand fell to his thigh.

He couldn't decide if he was in shock or not. A man who'd sworn never to marry had just announced his engagement.

"Are you crazy?" she burst out.

He turned his head to look at her. "What did you want me to say?"

"'It's none of your business, George'? Or stop with reminding him that we're two adults?" Her eyes shot sparks. "And, by the way, you couldn't have mentioned that he's a neighbor of yours?"

"He lives two blocks down." Noah clenched and

unclenched his jaw. "Howard Fulton is three blocks the other way. You know at heart this is a small town."

"Oh, God." Her voice had sunk to a whisper and she crossed her arms as if to hold herself together. "I knew this was going to happen. I'll lose my job."

"You won't," he said sharply.

"Oh, come on. You're important—I'm not. I haven't made any mark at all yet."

He shook his head. "You don't get it. If there's trouble, it will be aimed at me. As your boss, I'm the predator and you're the victim."

"Oh, God," she said again and bent forward as if her stomach hurt.

"You had to know we were heading in this direction."

She looked at him with a complete lack of comprehension. "What are you talking about?"

"Marriage."

Cait snorted. "Give me a break. Have you *ever* thought the word in relation to yourself?"

Stung, he gritted his teeth before responding. "I wouldn't have said it to George if I hadn't meant it."

"To salvage your political career?" Her tone was scathing.

Clearly, she *hadn't* been thinking long-term.

Pride made him try to sound matter-of-fact. "If I'd been thinking about my political career, I wouldn't have brought you home with me at all, much less to spend the night."

That silenced her for a moment. It didn't quell the panic in her eyes. "Why didn't you say anything?"

"I was giving us both time." He hesitated. "I'd intended to wait until the scum who tried to kill you has been arrested."

"Because I'm so irrational right now?"

He didn't say anything.

She puffed out air hard enough to lift the feathery strands of hair on her forehead. "I'm sorry. You were trying to help."

Once again, he took refuge in silence.

"We can pretend and…well, break it off after a while."

He gazed straight ahead at his garage. "Is that what you want?"

"I don't know!" she cried in obvious distress. "Were you being chivalrous? Is that what this is about? Now you think you have to go through with it?"

His muscles were rigid, his hands fisted on his thighs. He couldn't believe he'd let himself love this woman and imagine a future. Wasn't this exactly the kind of rejection he'd never wanted to have to endure?

"You can say no," he said woodenly. "I told you at the beginning, nothing personal between us will affect your job or our relationship at work."

"It's just…you've never said anything, and now this. I thought—"

"We were having hot sex, no harm, no foul?"

"No!"

She looked completely miserable, but he couldn't seem to summon any sympathy. He felt too wounded himself.

"Cait, let's let it ride for now," he said wearily. "You're not committed to anything. We'll see what happens, okay?"

Lips compressed, she finally nodded.

He started the engine, released the emergency brake and backed out of the driveway as if nothing had changed. They didn't talk during the ten-minute trip. He parked in the mayor's reserved slot beneath city hall and got out, barely conscious of the dozen or more people locking cars, hurrying across the garage or waiting for the elevator. No point in subterfuge now.

Cait joined him, her face as pinched as it had been after her ex's escapades, and they joined the stream of city employees.

Packed in the elevator with others, both stared at the lighted numbers. They reached her floor first. "I'll call," he said, and she nodded and exited with a couple of other women.

It took Noah longer than it should have to get over being an idiot.

He'd stalked past his assistant with a curt "I don't want to be interrupted," closed his office door behind him and dropped down in his desk chair to brood. As usual, he swiveled the chair so he could look out the window toward the butte and the angel atop it.

Hurt was a knot in his chest and acid in his belly. He hadn't been so devastated since he was a boy coming to terms with how little he mattered to either of his parents. His thoughts swung wildly between this morning's sweet lovemaking and the scene after George had left.

It had to be an hour or more before the cramp of pain let up enough for him to really think.

There *was* a good reason he had planned to take it slowly with Cait. She'd been stalked for months by her creepy ex-boyfriend. Barely free of him, but dealing with the fact that he was going to jail because of his obsession with her, she had become the target of a cold-blooded killer. And, oh, yeah, meantime she'd come home to a town that didn't seem to hold many good memories for her.

Sometimes he thought there was yet more bothering her. Her relationship with her brother had a level of discomfort on both sides that Noah didn't entirely understand. Like him, she'd grown up in a dysfunctional family. Afraid of her father, she had ended up disillusioned with her mother, which left her more alone than a woman should be when someone like Ralston put her in his sights. And that following whatever Ralston had done that he had to be so damn sorry for.

On top of all that, right now she needed both

Noah and her brother to keep her safe. If things blew up between them, Noah had been afraid she'd be reluctant to turn to him.

Keeping her safe mattered more than his wounded feelings, his ambitions, his business. He would do anything for her.

Including marry her? Wasn't that what she had accused him of this morning? Making that stupid announcement out of misguided chivalry rather than love and commitment?

Circling back to his own idiocy and insensitivity was all too easy. He made love to her with blistering desire and enjoyed her company at the dinner and breakfast table. But he distinctly remembered telling her he didn't see himself as a family man. He hadn't so much as hinted at a future. And even this morning, the words *I love you* had stuck in his throat.

How could she not be shocked by his declaration? And why would she think for a minute that he actually wanted her and her alone till death do them part?

No, he still had no idea whether she had any interest in a future with him. The tightening in his belly and chest had him bowing his head, elbows braced on his knees. *God!* What this debacle meant was he'd have to lay himself open again. Invite her to hurt him.

And that was what he'd never wanted. The lesson

was one only Cait could teach him. With a ferocity that stunned him, he had discovered that he wanted a woman to love and to love him, even children. The trust it took to get there was where he faltered.

Which was probably why those three all-important words had stuck in his throat.

Oh, hell, he thought. Waiting was no longer an option. Neither was sulking. He had to talk to her; he had to be honest.

He had to get her alone first, in the middle of city hall, where they were already the subject of too many whispers.

CAIT TURNED DOWN his offer to take her to lunch. She was burningly, painfully aware of appearances. It was like having to get dressed and go to work despite being fiery red and blistering head to toe from having forgotten suntan lotion during a day on the water.

In a way, she thought miserably, that's exactly what she'd done—let herself forget to take any precaution. How could she have plunged from the disaster of her last romantic relationship into this one?

And why did this hurt so much worse?

She felt even more singed every time she remembered Noah's cool declaration.

This is a little more than the two of us sleeping together. Cait has agreed to marry me.

And, yes, she had behaved badly. She *knew* he'd said that to protect her. She should be touched instead of hurt, shouldn't she?

All she could think when he called was *I'm not ready.*

Of course, they had to talk before George spread the word and people started wanting to congratulate her, commiserate with her or demand explanations.

Cait cringed. Colin would definitely fall into the latter category. Oh, Lord—no matter what, she'd have to tell him so he wasn't blindsided. She didn't even want to think about what would happen if he and Noah came face-to-face right now.

I could call Colin and ask him to pick me up after work. She could live for one night without anything in her bag—um, except for her birth control pills, she realized. They were kind of significant right now, given how sexually active she'd been this past week.

Anyway—remember how it felt when Noah seemed to be dodging her? Didn't her resolve to start over include the determination that she'd never be a coward again?

The drive to Colin's would take just about the right length of time for Cait to tell Noah about Blake. She had to get that out of the way, to find out how he'd look at her once she let him see beneath the shell of confident, professional woman to the weakling inside.

SHE WAS READY to go when Noah stopped by her office at five. He was frowning and reserved. The comparison with his laughing, sexy, sated expression that morning after they'd made love was painful.

They walked silently down the hall and joined other people in the elevator. He looked just grim enough to keep anyone else from trying to make conversation.

In the parking garage, he stayed right at her side. Cait felt peculiar. Engines were starting up around them, brakes squealing, even the click of her heels echoing. Ahead, through the gated exit, she could see out to the heavy traffic on the street. It all felt and sounded…distant, as if the two of them were in a bubble. Too bad the atmosphere wasn't quite breathable in there.

Once in the SUV, he glanced to be sure she'd put on her seat belt, then backed out and joined the line of vehicles exiting the garage.

Cait squeezed her hands together. "There's something I have to tell you," she said in a voice that came out a little too high.

He shot her a look. "Did someone say something to you today?"

"What? Oh. No. Nothing like that. It's about me."

Out of the corner of her eye, she saw his fingers flex hard on the steering wheel.

"All right," he said, sounding wary.

"I'd sworn off men when I came to Angel Butte."

And how dumb was that as a beginning? Especially when her swearing off lasted such a millisecond?

They turned out onto the street. Noah waited for her to go on. She was becoming used to his surprising ability to be patient when he wanted to. He was quite capable of relentlessly using silence as a tool.

"Because of Blake, of course. The thing is…" *Get on with it.* "You've probably guessed that my father hit my mother. Me, too, when I got in the way. Colin, when he was younger and smaller. But mostly Mom. Until I found out about Jerry, I was proud of her, that she'd eventually found the courage to leave Dad."

"I understand," Noah said, voice a notch huskier even than usual.

He accelerated when the light ahead turned green. Traffic was beginning to open up as they left downtown behind. She had only a few minutes.

"She didn't think she could support herself and two kids, or she'd have left him way sooner. That's what she told me. And it was true. She and I lived in shelters off and on for a while before she finally found a decent job."

He made a sound in his throat she couldn't interpret.

"I was so filled with hate, I couldn't imagine how she had stayed with Dad. Acted so *normal* in the morning when she was moving stiffly from the night before. I didn't understand how a woman could blame herself when a man hits her." The sharp pain in Cait's knuckles came from the way she was knotting her hands so tightly. She was glad of it, needing to hurt on the outside to go with the hurt that was deep inside. "I swore I would never let anyone treat me that way."

"Cait…"

"Until I did." In her shame, she couldn't look at Noah. "Until I let him brainwash me into believing it was my fault he got mad at me. I quit getting together with friends because he didn't like it. The last time I saw Colin, Blake insisted on going with me. I sat there quiet as a mouse. It wasn't until he hurt me enough to put me in the hospital that I realized what had happened to me."

"May he rot in hell," Noah snarled as he pulled into Colin's driveway.

Aching to escape, she finally turned her head to see his furious face. "I'm talking about *me,* Noah. Not him. Don't you understand? I *let* him do that to me."

The muscle in his jaw flexing, he braked in front of the house and turned searing blue eyes on her. "If you think that, you're still letting him victimize you."

There it was, the contempt she'd feared most. With one hand she unfastened the seat belt even as she opened the door. "Then I guess I'm just cut out to be a victim."

"Goddamn it, Cait, that's not what I meant!"

"Please open the back so I can get my bag."

He came around and unlocked it, giving a hunted glance toward the house. "Cait, come home with me again. Please."

Determined not to cry in front of him, she shook her head. She grabbed the bag and backed away. "I needed to tell you what happened with Blake so you'd know that I'm not who you think I am." Her smile didn't quite come off, but she'd tried. "I hope you're not a man who *wants* a woman who is a wimp. I don't know if I can be anything else, Noah."

He appeared so stunned, she took pity on him and kept backing up until she bumped into the porch steps. Children's laughter and then a screech came from beyond a veil of pines.

"Thank you for the ride," she said politely and fled up the steps.

She was barely inside when he drove away.

The house was completely silent. "Colin?" she called.

No answer.

Too soon for Nell to be home and—oh, no— Colin was speaking to some community group. Eagles or Jaycees or... She didn't remember. Because of her, he was still putting off announcing his candidacy for sheriff, but when his bodyguard duties allowed, he was trying to squeeze in more of these kinds of events to bring name and face recognition.

The worry was sticking with her like a burr.

There were already a couple of other candidates besides the incumbent sheriff. What if her problems dragged on and Colin entered the race too late?

And yet, for all her guilt, right this minute she was ungrateful enough to be swept with relief because she *could* be alone, if only for a few minutes.

Still carrying both bags, she had started down the hall toward the bedroom when she heard the sound of breaking glass.

CHAPTER SIXTEEN

NOAH WASN'T TWO minutes down the road when he abruptly wrenched the wheel to the side and skidded to a stop on the shoulder.

"Shit," he said explosively.

How could he have left her like that, thinking there was any truth at all in the crap about being a wimp. He winced at the memory of her eyes, darkened to charcoal by pain he hadn't done a single thing to ease.

If you think that, you're still letting him victimize you.

"Letting him" had to be the worst thing he could have said, after she'd just finished telling him that she'd "let" that bastard Ralston brainwash her, dominate her, hit her. As if "letting him" wasn't bad enough—he'd tacked *still* onto it.

Noah groaned, hearing her response.

Then I guess I'm just cut out to be a victim.

The irony was, despite what she had to have seen as his cruelty, her chin had had a belligerent cast, her wounded eyes were dry, her pride alive and well.

Couldn't she see that her childhood had set her up to accept abuse? Living in fear of her father, seeing her mother cower? Noah had read between the lines in Cait's few stories about her childhood. To survive, she'd made herself the next thing to invisible. She grew up knowing only two survival tactics: going unnoticed and enduring.

Animals like Blake Ralston seemed to have a gift for homing in on susceptible women. Noah guessed that Cait had had no idea she was until she'd gotten involved with him. She'd made herself into a strong woman in so many ways. Why would she suspect her instinct would be to revert to those childhood lessons?

Noah swore a few more times, then checked the road both ways and swung into a sharp U-turn. He should have marched right in the house with Cait, told her brother and his wife that they needed privacy and straightened her out. Instead, he'd left her thinking…

He didn't like knowing what she was thinking.

CAIT FROZE. IT was all her nighttime fears made real. *The bedroom,* she thought frantically. She could push the dresser over to block the door, give herself time to get out the window.

Heart slamming, she ran in, closed the door and pushed the useless little button to lock it. Her bags dropped with a thud and she began to wrestle the tall dresser across the floor.

The door splintered, and she whirled as the lock gave and a man shoved his way in. The lethal-looking gun in his hand riveted her. And, oh, God, that hand wore a thin latex glove. Only slowly did she lift her gaze to his face.

An ordinary face. Thin, to go with his medium height and lean runner's build. Graying brown hair, brown eyes.

Shaking, she whispered, "I would never have recognized you."

His expression didn't even change. "I couldn't take that chance. You did recognize Jerry."

"Only because I knew him."

He shook his head and stepped away from the door. "We need to go."

"I won't."

"Your choice." He sounded truly indifferent, although beads of sweat dripped down his forehead. "There are kids playing outside next door so I'd rather not kill you here, but I will if you're too much trouble."

She thought frantically. In the self-defense class, they'd taught that a woman should never go with the man. They hadn't mentioned the choice of being alone with him or…alone with him.

And she could see in his flat gaze that he really would do it. At least if she walked out of the house with him, she'd buy herself a few minutes.

Oh, Noah.

She prayed Nell wouldn't come home right now.

This man would think nothing of killing two women instead of one.

Stiffly, feeling a hundred years old, she walked past him. The moment she did, he thrust the barrel of the handgun hard into her back.

"Kitchen," he said.

NOAH BRAKED AS close to the front porch as he could get and leaped out. Children's voices and then a happy shriek came from one direction. The sound of a car door slamming had his head turning momentarily. Had to be at the place on the other side, he realized as he mounted the steps two at a time and leaned on Colin's doorbell.

Nothing. The house remained silent.

Was she huddled in her bedroom ignoring him? Hoping he'd go away? But where the *hell* was her brother?

Noah stepped to the side and cupped his hands to get the best view through the window. There was no movement inside at all.

For the first time, he felt a flicker of alarm. When he'd left her, he'd assumed Colin would be home, or Nell at least. Hesitating only briefly, he bounded down off the porch and circled the house. As he did, he heard the vehicle next door start. Someone was leaving rather than arriving, then.

The back door stood open. What the hell? Why would Cait have gone out— The sight of the shattered window beside it made his blood chill. What

if Colin *had* been home? They could both already
be dead.

Using his shoulder in case there were fingerprints on the door, Noah pushed it wider and
stepped in. He scanned the main living space at
a glance, then raced for the bedroom wing. One
door was splintered into pieces that hung from the
hinges. The terror of that day when he saw that the
windows of Cait's car had been shot out returned
in full force. Redoubled, because now he knew that
he loved her.

His heart pounded in sickening jerks as he
stepped over the threshold, his gaze going straight
to her two bags, abandoned in the middle of the
floor. The dresser stood askew, and he guessed
she'd been trying to block the door but had run
out of time.

He looked in the other bedroom and the two
bathrooms to be sure Cait wasn't there.

911.

No, think. Goddamn it, think.

When he had left only a few minutes ago, he
hadn't gone far down the road. No traffic had
passed heading into town. A few vehicles going
the other way. He'd swear there hadn't been time
for someone to pull into Colin's driveway, park, go
around back and break in, haul Cait out and drive
away. Whoever this guy was, he had to have been
waiting. Prepared to leave if Colin had come home
first or come home with Cait? Had he been wait-

ing every day, concealed in the woods surrounding the house, waiting for the one time Cait was alone?

Oh, hell. Galvanized, Noah remembered the slam of that car door, the vehicle he'd heard starting. He was willing to bet the sound had come from the house to the north. The night of the bomb threat, Colin had mentioned that the owner was rarely there. Noah hadn't seen a car passing the driveway, heading toward town. He might have missed it—but he had to gamble one way or the other, and he doubted Cait's abductor would have wanted to get into heavy end-of-day traffic with her sitting beside him under duress.

Noah wouldn't let himself think about the possibility that she was unconscious or even dead in the trunk of the car.

He ran, leaping into his SUV, gunning the engine the moment it caught. Gravel spurted under his tires. He barely paused at the foot of the driveway, accelerating to the left, away from town. Flooring it as he fumbled for his phone.

Even traveling at a reckless speed for this narrow, two-lane road, he thumbed through contacts until he found her brother's number.

Answer, Goddamn it, answer.

"Noah?" Colin said, his voice already edgy.

"YOU KILLED JERRY," Cait said. He'd made her scramble in on the driver's side and crawl over the console to the passenger seat before getting in himself. This wasn't the silver crossover he had driven the other time; today he drove an almost new dark gray sedan.

She had both her hands flattened on the dashboard, per orders.

"Move your hands and I'll shoot you," he had told her matter-of-factly before starting the car. He drove one-handed; the other held the gun on her.

Now she thought in despair that she might as well have spared her breath.

She tried again. "Weren't you together in…whatever you were doing?"

"You know what we were doing." This time she thought there was a hint of stress in his voice.

"Burying a body." She sounded weirdly calm, considering. She was glad, although she didn't think he cared one way or another whether she was terrified.

He drove, his gaze flicking from the road ahead to the rearview mirror and back again, only sliding toward her occasionally.

"He had a soft spot for you," the man said after a minute or more had elapsed, surprising her. "He didn't want to admit we had to eliminate you."

"Why would you think I'd even seen you that day?"

"Why take chances?" he said again with the faintest of shrugs.

Would he tell her his name if she asked? Did it matter who he was?

In the ensuing silence, she ran over and over again through the steps she'd have to take to escape. Get the seat belt off. Unlock and then open the door. Throw herself out. Which might kill her, but she didn't think so. He was driving at a careful forty-five miles an hour, not one mile above the speed limit. Broken bones were a risk she'd take.

Except—what was to stop him from backing up and getting out just long enough to shoot her? There was so little traffic.

Plus, she had to remove her hands from the dashboard to take even the first step. Unfortunately, he was keeping the gun steady on her.

Her thoughts were pinging like the ball in an old-fashioned pinball machine.

Whap. If this was his car, he probably didn't want to shoot her *in* it.

Except she had no idea who he was, and neither did Colin or anyone else. Why would his car ever be looked at?

Whap. Oh, God—where was he taking her? What if they were almost there, while she tried desperately to decide whether *now* was her only chance?

Pricklingly aware of him, she knew the instant he tightened. His eyes narrowed on the road behind them. The air in the car seemed suddenly charged with electricity.

Cait tried without being obvious to angle herself to see the road through her side-view mirror.

Her heart jumped. A big black pickup or SUV was closing fast on them.

Speeding? Or chasing them?

Colin.

She didn't realize she'd said her brother's name aloud until the man beside her snarled, "Don't get your hopes up. We both know he's got other fish to fry tonight."

He hadn't totally convinced himself, though. He was watching the road behind them more than the road ahead—or her.

Now, she thought, her muscles bunching, but her eyes stole to the gauge and she saw that his speed was climbing. Fifty, fifty-two, fifty-five.

The vehicle behind was filling her side mirror, and hope bounced in her. *Noah?* But how could he have known?

And what could he possibly do if he did catch them?

COMING CLOSER TO praying than he had since he was a credulous kid, Noah kept snatching looks in the rearview mirror. No flashing lights yet.

He still didn't know if Cait was in the car ahead. There were two people, he could see that much. The scum who'd snatched her might conceivably have already turned off, into one of the several dozen driveways or private roads—or Noah might have miscalculated in the beginning, and turned the wrong direction. This could be a couple of innocent people driving home after a day at work or tourists out for a drive or returning to their resort. But he didn't think so.

He couldn't think of a resort out here, and this wasn't a particularly scenic drive. The road eventually intersected one that led to Sunriver and thus to Highway 97, but it wouldn't be a commonly chosen route.

Noah glanced at the speedometer. He was going seventy but not gaining as quickly as he should be. The son of a bitch ahead was speeding up. Noah's pulse rocketed. Oh, yeah, the guy was definitely getting nervous.

Close enough to see the license plate, he hit redial and waited while Colin had the plates run.

"Son of a bitch," said her brother. "Ronald Floyd."

"The assistant D.A.?" Noah knew of him but couldn't bring his face to mind.

"Might be him and his wife on their way somewhere. Or someone stole the car."

"I'm making whoever it is nervous. He's running for it."

"Floyd." Colin still sounded stunned. "Do you have any idea how many drug crimes he's prosecuted? Even worse, how many he's *declined* to prosecute? Damn. We should have been looking beyond the police department."

Right that moment, Noah didn't give a flying you-know-what. All he could think was, *Cait.*

"I'll leave you on speaker," he said, and dropped

the phone on the seat beside him before pressing harder on the gas. Seventy-five. He hoped like hell they didn't meet anyone coming toward them. Except a cop. A cop would be good.

Eighty.

What if, by engaging in a high-speed chase, he endangered Cait?

Could he risk doing nothing but riding the bumper until the cavalry showed up?

"Goddamn it, I need help here," he snapped.

"Try slowing down. See what he does."

He eased up slightly.

A hand thrust out of the driver's-side window of the Camry, which swerved, then steadied while straddling the double yellow line. Wrong side of the car if the guy was trying to get rid of an incriminating item....

Something pinged off the metal of his Suburban. A rock— *No. Shit.*

"He's shooting at me!" he yelled.

FLASHER GOING ON his roof, siren screaming, Colin was already driving faster than was safe. He was gaining on the patrol unit ahead.

"A sheriff's deputy is coming from the other direction, but he's probably ten, fifteen minutes out."

Even through the phone, he heard the *pop* this time.

Noah swore viciously. "If he gets a tire or my radiator, he'll disappear." Then, again, *"Shit!"*

Colin hadn't been so scared since the night Nell had been snatched and he'd had to pursue in a helicopter, praying she'd survive until he got there. If he failed his sister—

Long experience let him shake off the panic. *Use your head. Do your job,* he ordered himself.

"Drop way back, stay in visual."

"Not happening," Noah said with sudden calm. "I've got steam coming out of the hood."

Colin's turn to let loose an expletive. Their options had just shrunk to one.

"Can you force him off the road?"

"As soon as we come out of the trees."

Encouraging a civilian to do something this dangerous went against every cop instinct Colin had. "When you see your chance, do it," he said anyway, clear and cold.

THE WAY THEY'D been swerving, Cait had long since taken her hands from the dashboard. One clutched the armrest, the other her seat belt. She hadn't known it was possible to be so terrified and live through it.

The next shot could go through the windshield and kill Noah. She pictured it, the punch through the glass, the blood blossoming, Noah slumping forward.

She could grab for the steering wheel. Or lunge across the man for the gun. Was she strong enough? What if they crashed?

She wanted the car to crash. But, God, they were going sixty miles an hour now. No, sixty-five. Her terrified gaze returned to the side mirror and she saw the black monster of an SUV closing fast again, filling the entire mirror. What was he *doing?*

The man beside her snarled something and started to stick the gun back out the window. The Suburban bumped the rear, and the car lurched and swerved. Cait couldn't hold back a squeak. The man had to grab for the wheel with both hands.

The swearing was nonstop. After straightening their path, he shoved the handgun beneath his thigh before clamping that hand, too, back on the wheel. Another thump, enough to have the car rocking. She heard a high-pitched moan and realized it came from her throat.

Ahead the dry forestland ended abruptly, re-placed by pasture enclosed in barbwire fencing. There wasn't much of a ditch. Could she get her leg over the console and somehow press on the brake? Or...or even grab the wheel and try to take them off the road?

Thump. The car swerved toward the shoulder, and the wheels momentarily skidded on gravel.

Cait's thoughts were as disjointed and fleeting as a strobe light. One instant she had her mouth open and knew she was screaming. He was fight-ing to get the car back on the road. Oh, God, was that smoke coming out of Noah's Suburban? *Please,*

please, please. She didn't even know what she was begging for.

Then, with a rush, the Suburban started to pass them.

The gun. If Noah forced them off the road, she had to get her hands on it. She would do anything—

It was alongside them. She turned her head and caught one wild glimpse of Noah's face, feral with determination, and then metal screamed and the car jolted so hard, her head snapped back.

The next instant, the car swerved sharply. They were momentarily airborne as they left the road.

NOAH BURNED RUBBER braking. It took him longer than he'd expected to regain enough control to drive off-road himself. The big SUV took a bone-jarring bounce, then grabbed for purchase. The Camry was enveloped in a swirling cloud of red dirt that began to look like a rooster tail. Yeah—son of a bitch, the guy was accelerating, still trying to escape.

Cait, he thought in agony.

Noah pushed it harder. He had better traction. He caught up, started to pass, then swung the wheel hard, connecting with the driver's side. Please, God, let her have a seat belt on. The sedan went into a spin that brought it around to smash into his rear fender.

The Camry came to a shuddering stop.

Noah threw himself out. The dust filled the air

and his lungs. At last he heard sirens. *Keep her alive until they get here.*

The two in the front seat were grappling. Was she trying for the gun?

"Cait!" he roared, and yanked at the driver's-side door. Her captor hadn't been smart enough to lock it. Noah reached in and grabbed, hauling the piece of scum out. He couldn't do a thing to protect himself when the gun swung his way and barked.

The pain that struck was so immense, all he could do was try to hold on, to fall on the asshole and use his weight to give her time to run.

CAIT'S DOOR OPENED and she tumbled out, landing on her hands and knees. *He shot Noah. Oh, God, he shot Noah. He'll shoot me next.* She found she didn't care about herself. If Noah was dead, had died for her—

No, she didn't care what happened to her.

Something was screaming. Maybe it was her. She looked around for anything that could be a weapon, but they were in the middle of a sea of thin grass. Her hand landed on a dry cow patty. She crawled forward, around the front bumper, until she saw the two men.

He was pushing his way out from beneath Noah, who sprawled facedown, unmoving. *Dead. Oh, God, he's dead.* The man reached his knees and pushed himself to his feet. With a terrible look on his face as he stared down at Noah, he lifted the gun. From nowhere, Cait found the energy to explode into motion. At the last second he saw her coming and started to turn, but she was already midair, her foot leading. It connected with his arm and the gun spiraled away.

She was falling backward, with him rearing above her, hands extended like claws, his face contorted with rage. For the space of a few heartbeats, time slowed. She saw him that day, staring hard at the fence behind which she huddled. Now. Then.

She slammed to the ground.

"Put your hands up! *Do it!*" The voice seemed unreal.

The man threw himself toward the gun. Somehow Cait rolled over, thinking she could stop him, but she was too far away.

Even as he lifted it, guns fired—*bang, bang, bang*—and he fell back like a rag doll, the red blossoming just as she'd imagined it on Noah's broad chest.

With a whimper, Cait crawled to Noah's big body, lying so terrifyingly still.

"I CAN'T STAND it." Cait shot to her feet. "Why is it taking so long?"

Colin rose with her. The kindness on his face had her close to blubbering. "It hasn't been that long. I know you're scared, Cait. Just hold on."

She was suddenly trembling, head to foot. Her teeth chattered. Her brother swore and stepped forward, engulfing her in an embrace. She leaned on him, eyes dry, trying to close her mind to what was happening somewhere past those huge double doors she could see across the hall from their small waiting room.

He had to be all right. He had to.

"I love him," she whispered.

"Yeah." Colin's voice was as gentle as his arms around her. "I kind of guessed that."

"He knew what he was doing."

"He knew." Her rock-steady brother harrumphed a few times, and she knew he was nearly as shaken as she was. One last throat clearing. "I think it's safe to say he loves you, too."

Cheek against Colin's strong chest, she breathed in the knowledge, the certain wryness in his voice, and steadied a little. Enough to lean back and smile crookedly at him.

"Have you gotten over despising him?"

The corner of his mouth lifted. "We've been coming to an understanding."

Behind Cait, Nell chuckled. "Haven't you noticed that he trusted Noah to take care of you?"

She had. She'd also noticed how often the two men had worked in concert.

She half turned to include her sister-in-law. "He asked me to marry him." She bit her lip. "Actually, he didn't ask. He told George Miller we were getting married. I thought he said it because that was part of the protect-Cait plan."

Now Nell gave her a little hug. "From what I've heard about Noah Chandler, that's further than he'd go for any other woman in the world. He's not known for being softhearted."

"He should be," Cait heard herself say. "He didn't need to make Angel Butte better for himself. He's already successful. He was thinking about everyone else."

Colin gave another harrumph that might have been skeptical but might not. Nell laughed again.

A lean, dark man filled the doorway to the hall. Alec Raynor, who Cait hadn't met until two hours ago. "Still no word?" he asked.

She shook her head.

She wouldn't have guessed he could be kind, either, but would have been wrong. His eyes rested on her. "Noah's tougher than any of us. He'll pull through."

Her smile wobbled. "Thank you."

He nodded and retreated. Either he was trying to give them privacy or was incapable of doing nothing but sitting, she couldn't decide. So far as she could tell, he'd spent most of the past two hours pacing the hospital's wide corridors. A few times, Colin had left Cait holding Nell's hand and walked with the police chief. She'd seen them pass, talking quietly. Once they came back with soft drinks for her and Nell.

The double doors opened, but for an orderly to push an elderly man in a wheelchair out.

Cait sank back down into the same chair, the one that gave her the best view of those doors. Once again, Nell took her hand, and Cait held on to it, a lifeline.

"What if—"

Nell's grip tightened. "Don't think it."

She could barely squeeze the words out. "He looked really bad."

Nell didn't say anything. Neither did Cait.

Please.

Colin rejoined them and took his seat on her other side. He laid his arm over her shoulders, his fingertips touching Nell's upper arm so that all three of them were linked.

Please.

A nurse came out through the doors, then returned a while later. Someone on a gurney was wheeled in, his face hidden by an oxygen mask. It had to be another half hour before a man in green scrubs pushed his way through, his surgical mask pulled down around his throat. His gaze went right to them.

Cait wasn't sure she could have stood if Colin hadn't hoisted her to her feet.

Or spoken.

Please, God, please.

He nodded. "Captain McAllister. I gather Mayor Chandler has no family here?"

"My sister, Cait, here is the closest. They're engaged," Colin said.

"Ah." He smiled. "He's in recovery and doing well. He's lost his spleen and we had to do a fair amount of repair work in there, but I see no reason not to anticipate a complete recovery."

He went on to detail some of that "repair work." There was something about a "bleed" and a cracked rib. Cait couldn't take it in. A complete recovery. That's what he'd said, wasn't it?

Oh, thank God. Thank you, thank you, thank you.

Her knees were suddenly so weak, she dropped back into the chair. To her shock, a sob ripped through her. She buried her face in her hands and began to weep helplessly.

Nell sat down and held her while Colin and the doctor talked quietly for another minute. Somehow Cait knew that Alec Raynor had stepped in, and probably retreated in alarm, but Colin went after him.

Cait kept crying. Cried like she hadn't in years. No, ever.

He had been willing to die for her but somehow survived.

She cried harder.

CHAPTER SEVENTEEN

NOAH WOKE FEELING like a heavy beam had dropped across his belly. And it had to have glanced off his head on its way down, as foggy as he was. Opening leaden eyelids took enormous effort. He tried to move his lips to form a word.

"You're in recovery after surgery," a woman said from right above him. "You were shot and the surgeon had to remove a bullet."

Shot. He tried to consider that, but his mind drifted.

He came to again. *Shot.* This time he got out a ragged, desperate "Cait."

"What is it? Do you need something?"

"Cait." It took him a moment to work up enough spit to allow his tongue to function. His lips felt cracked. "Want Cait."

"Oh. I'm afraid we can't let family into recovery…"

"…all right?" he managed to say.

"Your fiancée? Is that who you're asking about?"

He finally pried his eyes open to glare fiercely at the plump, kindly woman. "Fiancée."

"I know you must have questions—"

"Alive?"

"Oh!" This time she sounded startled. "Let me find out more about the incident."

He was too scared to doze this time. A second nurse appeared and persuaded him to suck on some ice chips. His tension grew as he waited.

The first nurse reappeared in his range of vision. She was smiling. "Do you mean Cait McAllister?"

"Yes."

"I'm told she's fine. A few bumps and bruises. The man who kidnapped her and shot you was killed by police."

He was able to grapple with the news. Longtime Deputy District Attorney Ronald Floyd had been desperate enough to kill and kill again. Pulling him out of the car, Noah had recognized him.

Time passed. They insisted he couldn't see Cait until they moved him upstairs to a room. The mist gradually cleared from Noah's head, allowing him to think more clearly. Shouldn't he hurt more than he did? He did know vaguely that these days they used painkillers internally before closing the patient. He had confidence he'd hurt eventually.

Sure as hell his Suburban would be totaled. He wondered whether he could persuade the insurance adjustor to consider what happened an accident. That almost amused him. *Yeah, probably not. Ah, well.* Buying a new vehicle was a small price to pay if Cait really had survived unscathed.

He had nodded off again when they finally announced that they were ready to move him to a room. Thankfully, that involved no more than adjusting IV lines and rolling the bed he was in out through a pair of doors and down a hall.

"Noah?"

Was that Cait? His head turned as he searched for her, and suddenly there she was, right next to the bed. Reaching over the rails for his hand. Her eyes were damp and puffy, and shock infused her expression. He guessed that meant he didn't look very good.

"Cait." He was able to grip her hand and almost smile at how chilly it was.

The orderly was saying something cheerful, and Noah suddenly realized he was surrounded. Colin and his wife were there, too, and, of all people, Alec Raynor hovered in the background. He caught a brief glimpse of his PA, Ruth Lang, unless he was seeing things.

After scanning the small crowd, his gaze locked back on Cait's distraught face.

He wanted to tell her he loved her, but his last public announcement hadn't gone so well.

Most of the people jammed themselves into the elevator that carried him up. Once the orderly, joined by a nurse, began to maneuver the bed into a patient room, though, they asked everyone to wait outside until they had him "settled." He hoped that didn't involve shifting him to another bed. That *would* hurt.

The only person he really wanted to see was Cait. He frowned. No, maybe Colin, too. He'd like to find out what happened after he had checked out. Doctor, too. Nobody had yet told him what damage that bullet had done. He could move his feet—he demonstrated to himself, watching them rotate beneath the thin white blanket—so he knew he wasn't paralyzed. But there were other ugly possibilities.

He got to stay in the same bed, but it was an annoying length of time before the nurse seemed satisfied that he *was* settled. She took his blood pressure and temperature, shifted the IV to a different pole, made notes on a whiteboard below the wall-hung television. The one positive was that he seemed to be alone in the room. There wasn't even an empty bed on the other side of the room, just an empty space.

"We don't want you tiring yourself out," the nurse said cheerily. "But I'll let your family in briefly."

To his relief, only Cait and her brother appeared. Colin eased the door shut, cutting off most sound from the hall and giving them some privacy. Cait came straight to the bed and latched on to Noah's hand again, as if resuming a painfully severed connection.

Yes, he thought, that's what it felt like. He never wanted to let her go again.

He looked past her to Colin. "What happened?"

McAllister gave a succinct summation. A pair of sheriff's deputies had reached the scene first, just in time to see Cait kick the weapon out of Ronald Floyd's hand. They had ordered him to put his hands up, and he'd thrown himself at the gun instead. When he'd brought it around toward them, they had both fired. Colin had arrived only moments later.

"I already had an aide car en route, which was a good thing. You bled like the Red Sea."

Maybe that was why he felt so tired.

"It's not a joke!" Cait snapped.

Her brother looked at her in surprise. "Didn't say it was."

Noah managed to smile at her. "Had a lot of blood in me."

Her lips wobbled, and her eyes brimmed with tears.

"Hey," he said huskily. "Alive."

"Yes." Her teeth sank into her lower lip. "I was so scared."

"Me, too."

"Why did you come back?" she asked. "I mean, how did you know I'd been kidnapped?"

"Was an idiot. Didn't like you feeling bad." His eyelids were beginning to feel heavy again. Words weren't coming readily. "Not your fault. None of it."

She bent over the blasted rail and laid her cheek

against his. He felt the dampness of her tears and turned his head, trying to find her mouth. She did the same, and they kissed, a quick, fumbling excuse for a kiss, but she was there, alive, holding his hand.

When she straightened, he asked, "You know what they did to me?" With the hand that had an IV in it, he gestured toward his torso.

Colin was the one to step forward and explain. His spleen was history, Noah learned. Otherwise, there'd been a nick here, a tear there. The surgery had dragged on because he'd continued to bleed even after they thought they'd gotten everything. They'd finally located the mystery bleed, put in a few more stitches. And, oh, yeah, removed a bullet.

"Bet it matches the one that killed Hegland," Noah mumbled, and Colin did chuckle, if very, very drily.

"That's a sucker bet."

He was smiling, too, drinking in the sight of Cait's puffy, splotchy, tear-streaked face, so damn beautiful, when he fell asleep.

CAIT REFUSED TO leave. It took a while to persuade Colin that he and Nell really could go home and leave her at the hospital. She pointed out that Noah would not be enthusiastic about having all three of them standing around like a flock of vultures staring at him.

That made Colin laugh and hug her. "Okay. You're right. But you know he'd be happier if you came with us and got a good night's sleep instead of trying to catch a few z's in a not very comfortable chair."

Her chest constricted. "I'm having trouble believing… I thought he was dead."

Nell smiled at Cait. "You know I was shot, right?"

Cait nodded.

"Colin didn't leave the hospital for at least two days." She tilted her head against his shoulder in a brief, loving contact. "So don't let him tell you he doesn't understand."

After another of his deep, slow chuckles, he hugged Cait. "All right. You win. I'll be back in the morning."

She pulled the chair as close to the bed as she could get it and kept her hand over Noah's even when it was slack in sleep. Every time she dozed, she was jolted awake by a rush of adrenaline. The flash she saw was the blood and Noah toppling, the fury and fear on his face fading into stunned acceptance.

She had believed on such a visceral level that he was dead, she was having trouble convincing herself he wasn't.

A couple of times, he came awake hurting. A nurse slipped in quietly, took his temperature, reminded him how to administer his own pain relief and slipped out, leaving them alone.

The first time he appeared truly awake was

morning. Pale light leaked through the blinds. Activity was increasing out in the hall. Cait heard a far-off rumble and clank she thought might be the arrival of breakfast trays on the tall carts.

Blinking sleep out of her own eyes, she realized he was watching her.

"Good morning," he murmured.

"Good morning." She straightened in the chair and rolled her shoulders to loosen kinks. "I'd kiss you, but I probably have yucky breath."

He laughed, winced, then said, "Don't make me do that. It hurts."

"How do you feel?"

"Crappy," he admitted. "Not surprising considering someone was digging around in me yesterday."

"After you were *shot*."

"Yeah, not one of those things I ever expected to happen."

"I thought he'd killed you." She felt raw. "I thought..." Her voice failed.

"Hey." He reached for her hand, which must have slipped from his when she fell into a deeper sleep. "I'm here. Full recovery, remember?"

"Yes." She made herself breathe. *Full recovery. Nobody really* needs *a spleen.*

"I came back to tell you that business about you 'letting' Ralston hurt you is bull."

"It happened."

"It happened because that's how you were taught to respond." He kept talking, saying things that echoed what she'd begun to realize herself about her parents and the way she'd tried so hard to go unnoticed. Somehow the explanation was more convincing coming from him. She'd been afraid she was trying to justify the unjustifiable.

His very blue eyes held hers. "It's hard to unlearn childhood lessons. I've been a loner because I was so sure..." Finally he hesitated.

"That no one could love you," Cait finished softly.

His eyes searched hers. "Yeah," he said at last, sounding gruff. "I guess that's it."

She studied him, a face that by any standards should be homely and yet...wasn't. Cheekbones that were too broad and blunt, nose that was too large, furrowed forehead, jaw subtly off center—and none of it mattered compared to the intelligence in those blue eyes or the sweetness or humor or rakishness of his smiles.

"You were wrong," she whispered.

A nerve in his cheek pulsed. He stared at her for the longest time. "I love you," he said then in a gravelly voice. "Maybe you won't want to hear it, but you need to know I wasn't being chivalrous." His mouth twitched into a half smile that didn't reach his eyes. "That was your word, wasn't it? You walked into my office that first day and I felt the ground shake. I told myself I shouldn't hire you. If I'd wanted to keep my life the way it was, I shouldn't have."

Hope and joy filled Cait like the water in a reservoir, rising, rising, until it had to spill out somehow.

But she had to ask. "Are you sorry?"

"Never," he said roughly. "Never."

"I fell in love with you so fast." She laughed a little. "And I was off men, remember?"

"Will you come and sit here?" he asked, patting the bed beside him.

She was trembling when she did, bending over to kiss him again. "Who cares if we have morning breath?"

He laughed, then groaned. "Not me." And he finally let go of her hand so he could wrap his around her nape and draw her down again. "Not me."

THREE DAYS LATER, Noah plodded down the hospital corridor clutching his IV pole, his determination to regain his strength so he could get the hell out of there the only thing that kept him going.

Cait had gone by his house and brought him a robe his mother had sent for Christmas one year that he'd never worn and a pair of slippers that he did wear. They wouldn't let him wear his own pajama bottoms, but at least with the robe his ass wasn't bared when he got out of bed.

The positive? Cait was beside him, wearing royal blue jeans that fit her like a second skin and a bright yellow scoop-neck T-shirt as cheerful as that suit of hers that had inspired idiotic flights of fancy in him.

When he got grumpy, she laughed at him.

"I'm like a donkey harnessed to turn one of those wooden wheels to grind corn or something," he complained. "Around and around and around."

"Hopeless," she teased, making her voice slow and dreary. "Knowing you'll spend the rest of your life walking the hospital halls."

"With bare, hairy legs."

"Pooh." She smiled at him. "You have sexy legs, and you know it."

His mood elevated, and he grinned at her. "Now, if *your* legs were bare, it would be another story."

Cait made a face at him. "They keep it too cold in here. Why do they, when patients are in shock or don't feel good or, um, aren't wearing much but a hospital gown?" She crossed her arms and rubbed them, as if chilled.

"Maybe because the average person's thermostat is set higher than yours?" Noah suggested.

She scowled at that but finally conceded, "Maybe."

His mouth tilted up. "I'll concede there's a cold draft coming up from below."

Cait laughed at him. "If you're finding it refreshing, we could buy you a kilt."

"The hell we could." They'd reached the elevators, where they had turned back during his last walk. "I think I can make it all the way down to the windows." He stole a sidelong look at her. This struck him as a good time to move them past the declaration of true love to something more tangible. Hopeful. "I suppose I'll always be turning the heat down and you'll be turning it up," he said casually.

The whites of her eyes showed. "Well...Colin and I argue every day about the air-conditioning in his SUV."

Noah chuckled, pleased that a laugh no longer sent a stab of pain through him. "Then there's those cold feet in bed every night."

Her shyness made him think she'd noticed the way he leaned a little on those two words: *always* and *every*.

Why wasn't *he* panicking?

Maybe because he'd already been there, done that and gotten over it? Even so, he couldn't help marveling at how ready he was, how sure he wanted this woman and this woman alone for the rest of his natural life.

He was more worried about her side of things. He wanted to believe she meant those three little words, *I love you.* But he couldn't help having moments when he wondered if her emotions hadn't been swayed by the euphoria of the rescue, mixed with a heavy dose of guilt and gratitude. Noah especially hated the idea of gratitude.

They reached the tall windows at the end of the corridor. The view looked over the unattractive roof of a wing of the hospital, but included a slice of the butte. He couldn't swear he could see the angel from here, but he liked to think so.

"Do you mind if we sit down for a minute?" he asked.

"Of course not!" Cait rushed to maneuver the damn IV pole and clutch his elbow to help support his weight as he cautiously lowered himself onto the bench upholstered with brown plastic. He couldn't decide if the damage to his gut was what hurt most or the cracked rib.

He hadn't really needed the rest, though, which meant he was making some real progress. God, to get out of there.

Problem was, he didn't want to go home alone. He didn't know how city council members and her brother would see it, but he desperately wanted Cait going home with him.

They sat in silence for a minute. He gave it some time.

"Did you mean it?" she asked finally in a small voice.

He turned his head and saw how big and smoky her eyes were. How anxious.

Noah reached for her hand and relaxed when she met him halfway and held on tight. "Mean what?" he asked.

"The getting married part."

"Yeah." That came out gruff. "I meant it."

"We haven't actually known each other that long."

"Is that how you feel?" he asked carefully. "That

you don't know me well enough to make that kind of commitment?"

"Well...no." She blinked a few times, as if surprised at herself. "I guess I'm thinking more about you. You were so...anticommitment. You have to admit, this is a big turnaround for you."

"Cait, you know there'll be problems if we try to just live together. Or even date for any length of time." From her changing expression, he could tell that wasn't what she wanted to hear. "I'm saying we'll go that route anyway, if you need time."

She stared at him, as if trying to see deeper than anyone ever had. "But...what about *you?*"

"I'm thirty-five years old. You're right. I'd never thought the word *marriage* in connection with myself before. It wasn't long after I kissed you the first time when I started thinking it. You remember when I gave you the grand tour of my house?"

Color heightening in her cheeks, she nodded.

His body stirred at the same memory making her blush. What happened at the end of their tour, when they'd reached his bedroom.

"You said something about decorating one of those front rooms as a nursery. I had a vision. You were pregnant." He smiled faintly. "You were on a ladder putting up wallpaper covered with fluffy yellow ducklings. I thought I had to have lost my mind, because, damn it, I wanted that. All of it."

The intensity in her eyes had softened as he talked. "I want that, too," she said softly, maybe a little tremulous. "I looked at that house made for a family, and at you, and I felt all those things I'd sworn I wouldn't."

He let go of her hand so he could put his arm around her. "So why the hesitation?"

"I just don't want you to feel like you have to do this."

Noah shook his head, his stubbly cheek rubbing against her hair. "Don't be ridiculous. I never do anything I don't want to."

Cait giggled, a watery sound. "That's what Nell said."

"Smart woman."

They sat in contented silence, at least on his part.

It was a minute before he had a disturbing thought. "You're not going to have to choose whether you have your mother or your brother at our wedding, are you?"

Her breath huffed out. "Oh, there's a thought."

"Damn it, you shouldn't have to make that kind of choice."

Cait tilted her head back. "Then I won't make it. I want to get married here, in Angel Butte. If my mother refuses to come...well, that's *her* choice. I do love her, but...did I ever tell you about the last time I talked to her?"

She did then, expressing the disappointment she'd felt, which had become tangled up with the sharp-edged knowledge that her mother had been capable of abandoning one of her two children without any apparent regrets.

His arm tightened around her. "How much of a relationship you want with her is up to you. I'll be polite."

She managed to reach his chin with a kiss. "Thank you."

Neither of them moved. For a man usually too restless to do nothing but sit, he was completely happy to stay right where they were.

"If I'm patient," Cait said thoughtfully, "I ought to be able to get a job with one of the other cities in the area."

Jolted out of the mindless contentment, Noah straightened so he could see her face. "What are you talking about? You *have* a job."

"Yes, but you know George has already started a campaign to get rid of one or both of us."

"And what? You think we should surrender without a fight?"

"No! I'm trying to plan ahead, that's all."

Noah shook his head. "If either of us has to resign, it'll be me."

"What?"

He didn't know if he liked the shock on her face or not. "You heard me."

"But—"

"I'm an elected official, Cait. At most I might run for one more term. I make a damn good living. I *have* a career, and it isn't city government. Urban planning is your career. I repeat, if we lose, I'll go." He watched her mouth open and close a couple of times. "And, no, don't even think about arguing."

"It's just… You'd do that for me?"

She sounded piteous, which pissed him off.

"I love you," he said. "Believe it."

To his astonishment, tears welled in her eyes. With a muffled wail, she threw herself at him, then cried out again and tried to retreat. "Oh, no! I'll hurt you!"

"No." God, it felt good, having both arms around her, breathing in the tang of her hair, being able to close his eyes and see the stunned belief on her face. "Trust me, Cait."

"I do." She snuffled, gulped and repeated more strongly, "I do."

AT HER SUGGESTION, the morning after Noah's surgery, Colin had spread the word at city hall that it would be a few days before the mayor would be ready for visitors. He'd been flooded with cards and flowers. Three-quarters of the bouquets had been distributed to other rooms. His PA, a really nice woman, had timidly appeared but not-so-timidly refused to tell him about any city business going undone, any phone or email messages.

"If I can't deal with it, it will wait," she said firmly. Seeing Cait's expression, she winked.

Noah glowered, but he couldn't move her.

Colin was the second-most frequent visitor. Cait

was amazed he could find the time, since two days ago he had announced his candidacy for sheriff. She suspected that, from there on out, he would be campaigning every waking moment when he wasn't at work, trying to make up for so much lost time spent protecting her. Poor Nell. Although Cait was grateful she hadn't cost her brother too much. He still had almost five months until the election.

Obviously a whole new can of worms had been opened by the discovery that someone in the district attorney's office had been taking bribes either to throw cases or come up with excuses not to prosecute them in the first place. Colin kept Noah apprised of the continuing investigation, reminding her that not only had Noah almost been killed, his father had been the murder victim who'd started all this.

Thinking that felt surreal. All those years ago, as the curious child peeking between fence boards, how would she have imagined what the fallout would be? Or that she would end up in love with the son of the man whose grave was covered by newly poured concrete?

"Yeah," Noah said, when she told him what she was thinking. "It feels like a circle. I'd never have come to Angel Butte if this wasn't Dad's last known address. I'm here because he died here. You're here because of your brother and *he's* here for the same reason I am. Which means he and I have something in common." He grimaced. "Much as I hate to admit it. He's a stubborn son of a gun who wanted to clean up this town and stayed even when a lot of other senior officers in the department left."

Touched by his admission, she stroked his forehead. "Are you sorry you didn't hire him as chief?"

He hesitated, then grinned when he saw her bristle. "Yes and no. Do I think he'd have done a hell of a job? That I could have worked with him? Yeah, I do. But if he wins this election, he can accomplish even more. So I'm thinking it's worked out for the best." He tried to see into the future and shook his head. "If he and Raynor are able to cooperate, they can transform law enforcement in this county."

Her forehead crinkled. "You don't think they can?"

"You know better than I do. Raynor is a closed book to me. And your brother and I still have a ways to go."

She opened her mouth to tell him about the two men walking the hospital corridors, deep in conversation, but didn't have a chance. There was a rap on the half-open door, and the curtain rings rattled as someone started to push them aside.

To her horror, three people walked in. Earl Greig, Beverly Buhl and Kevin Alseth, the unlikeliest trio of city council members she could have come up with.

Cait snatched her hand out of Noah's, which earned her a sardonic glance from him.

She studied them arranging themselves around

the foot of the bed. Earl, suspicious, conservative and pragmatic; Beverly, full of boundless optimism, always ready to leap without knowing where she'd land; and Kevin, far and away the youngest, a newcomer to town, an attorney who was politically liberal. Cait would have guessed that Earl and Kevin didn't speak when they weren't absolutely forced to. Was it chance they had arrived at the same time?

"You've certainly put Angel Butte on the map," Kevin said. His tone was dry.

Cait winced. When she'd shown Noah the copy of *People* magazine with an article about them, he'd been livid. Unfortunately, despite her refusal to answer questions and Colin's wooden statement representing the police department, the reporter had pieced together a reasonably accurate story.

Noah's eyebrows rose. "It was entirely unintentional. Not quite the publicity we want for our city."

"Oh, I don't know." Beverly beamed at them both. "A mystery, a heroic mayor, romance! They even included a picture of the angel with a sidebar about her history. Tourism will boom."

Noah scowled at his visitors. "Shall I park myself on the sidewalk every day so the tourists can snap pictures of me?"

Earl snorted. "Not looking the way you do."

"Actually, you look better than I expected," Kevin remarked.

"I'm told I should be able to go home by Tuesday."

Beverly expressed her delight. Noah suggested he should be back in the office by Thursday or Friday. Cait controlled her instinctive protest.

They all looked at her.

"I know I've missed quite a bit of work, too," she said.

Earl frowned at her. "You had a shock, young lady. Of course you needed to recover."

There was an uncomfortable silence.

"I suppose George has been burning up the phone lines," Noah said irritably.

Cait stared at him in disbelief. He couldn't wait until the battle came to them? Oh, who was she kidding? Of course he couldn't. She'd let herself forget how blunt and aggressive he was.

And—maybe he was even right. Why should they be embarrassed?

Beverly sniffed. "George doesn't have a romantic bone in his body."

"Not that romance is suitable in the workplace." To Cait's dismay, that was Kevin.

Earl studied them with narrowed eyes. "Miller seemed to think you were just shacking up."

Even without touching him, Cait could feel the way Noah's big body tightened.

"We're engaged to be married," he said flatly.

Earl was built like a fireplug, stocky and strong. She couldn't imagine he'd ever been a handsome man. She'd had the occasional, uncharitable thought that his face made her think of a frog's. With his lips thinned, that was even more so.

"You planning to stay on at city hall?" he asked her.

She lifted her chin. "Yes, unless politics makes it impossible."

Earl looked at Noah. "You?"

He stared right back. "I was elected, wasn't I?"

"Well, then," Beverly murmured.

Everyone ignored her.

"Don't see a problem with it," Earl rumbled. "George is just sulking because he isn't getting his way. I can tell you he doesn't speak for any of the rest of us."

"That's true." Kevin smiled. "You might call us a delegation, sent to assure you that you have the council's support."

"You know I'm not always happy with every decision you make," Earl contributed, "but at least you're aboveboard. A businessman." He gave a sharp nod. "And you, Ms. McAllister, have finally lit a fire under some butts. Last thing I want is to see you go."

She couldn't think of anything to say but a pleased "Thank you."

"Thank you all for coming," Noah said. "You'll all be getting invitations to the wedding."

Beverly beamed again. "Oh, what fun!"

"Best be soon," Earl said sourly.

Kevin cleared his throat. Cait thought he was disguising a chuckle.

The three of them departed. Listening as their footsteps receded down the hall, Cait finally let herself look at Noah.

"I hate to sound like Beverly, but...oh, my."

Noah grinned. "What'd I tell you?"

"I thought I'd have a heart attack when you said that about George."

"You know the saying about taking the bull by the horns."

"The bull being Earl?"

"Who else?" He frowned. "Although, squat as he is, I've always thought he looked more like..."

Cait began to giggle, Noah to laugh.

"Damn. Earl Greig approves of me. As my mother used to say, will wonders never cease."

Melting inside, Cait moved from the chair to the bed so she could very carefully lay her head on his broad shoulder. "I hope they never do," she whispered.

His arms closed around her, the one trailing the IV line. "Never," he said in a low, almost harsh voice. "Never."

Cait spread her fingers on his chest, over the thin, faded fabric of the hospital gown, loving the vibration of his heartbeat. "Earl did say one thing I liked," she ventured after a minute.

"How soon can we make it?" Noah asked.

Laughing, Cait lifted her face so that he could

kiss her. In the aftermath, as he nuzzled her, she said, "You do realize our wedding will be a media event? Hmm. Maybe we can sell the right to take photographs for some obscene amount like movie stars do."

"I could say some obscene things about that," Noah suggested.

"Um." She nibbled on his lower lip. "I love you, Mayor."

"Ditto, Ms. McAllister," he said, and tugged her to lie fully beside him so that he could seriously kiss her.

* * * * *

Look for the next
THE MYSTERIES OF ANGEL BUTTE
story by Janice Kay Johnson.
ALL A MAN IS
will be available in March 2014
from Harlequin Superromance.

LARGER-PRINT BOOKS!
GET 2 FREE LARGER-PRINT NOVELS PLUS
2 FREE GIFTS!

HARLEQUIN®

super romance®

More Story...More Romance

LARGER-PRINT BOOKS!
GET 2 FREE LARGER-PRINT NOVELS PLUS
2 FREE GIFTS!

❋HARLEQUIN®

Romance

From the Heart, For the Heart